Now nearly seventeen, Megge and Brighida must endure another brutal loss. And as they perform the rites of transition that precede a burial, Megge accepts a daunting new charge that carries consequences not even her cousin the seer can predict. It brings visions. Dreams. And voices that come to her as she goes about her work.

A silken voice beckons her back to the cliffs of Kernow, which she has seen only in dreams. A commanding voice orders her back. And the menacing voice she's heard since she was a girl is now ever at her ear, bringing a haunting new meaning to her grandmother's words, "You're never alone."

But only when the tales of an old woman, a stranger to Bury Down, echo those voices and conjure those cliffs does Megge embark on a journey that leads her to a secluded cove they call *The Sorrows* and a destiny none of the women of Bury Down could have foreseen.

the LADY *of* THE CLIFFS

The Goddess Trilogy
Published by Rowan Moon

Book One: Megge of Bury Down

Book Two: The Lady of the Cliffs

Book Three: The Sisters of the Sorrows Cove

the LADY *of* THE CLIFFS

The Bury Down Chronicles, Book Two

REBECCA KIGHTLINGER

ROWAN MOON

© 2020

THE LADY OF THE CLIFFS

Cover art and book design by Tamian Wood, www.BeyondDesignBooks.com

Published by ROWAN MOON LLC
Meadville, Pennsylvania
Address inquiries to inquiries@rowanmoonpress.com
Printed in the United States of America
ISBN 978-1-7343168-3-4 (Soft cover)
ISBN: 978-1-7343168-5-8 (EPUB)
ISBN: 978-1-7343168-6-5 (Mobi)
ISBN: 978-1-7343168-7-2 (Audiobook)

Library of Congress Cataloging-in-Publication Data
Names: Kightlinger, Rebecca, 1957 –
Title: The Lady of the Cliffs
Library of Congress Control Number: 2020912613

Subjects:
FIC043000 FICTION | Coming of Age
YAFIC011000 YOUNG ADULT FICTION | Coming of Age
FIC008000 FICTION | Sagas
FIC014020 FICTION | Historical | Medieval
FIC061000 FICTION | Magical Realism

Permissions:
"Samhain" is excerpted from "Samhain," *Spells: New and Selected Poems* by Annie Finch (Wesleyan University Press, 2013). *The Poetry Witch: Little Book of Spells* © 2019 Wesleyan University Press and used with permission.

Map of Cornwall is used with permission from http://fromoldbooks.org/ GroseAntiquities/pages/Grose-map-cornwall/2340x1899-q80.html

For my great-grandmother,
Clara Collins Flaherty

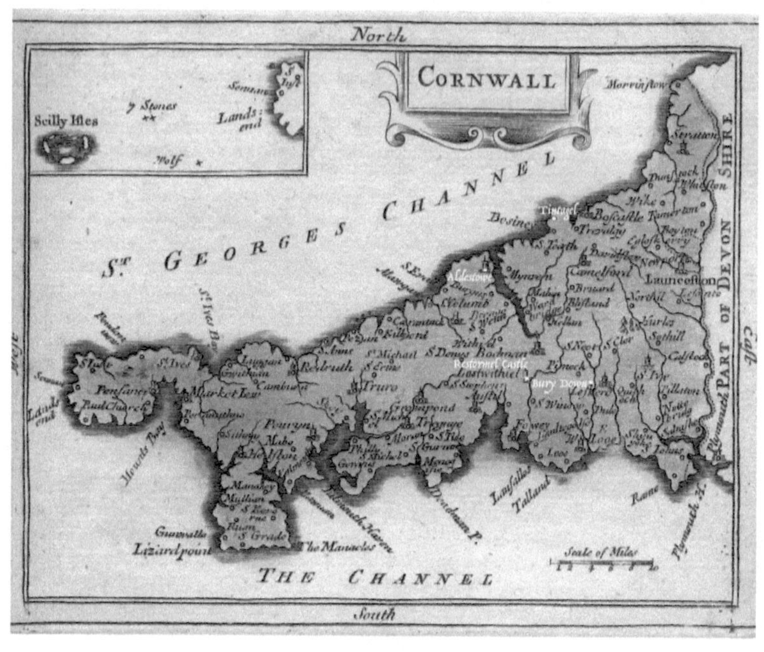

North
CORNWALL
Morrinston
Scilly Isles
7 Stones
Semana
Tyst
Lands end
Wolf
St GEORGES CHANNEL
Seratton
Thorspack
Whalston
Wike
Boscastle Tamerton
Tintagel
Boy tori
Bosiney
Trevilly
Eglosherry
Newt
St Teath
Borolhor
Camelford
Launceston
Aldestowe
Wyneren
Northil Leskate
Matern
Leuguen
Noris
Brasul
St Endy
Colum
Brenna
Bleland
Curles
Carantuck
St Welan
Holton
Sythill
St Dun Kilkent
St Neot
St Cler
Colstock
St Anne
Hethel
St Michail St Denys Bodmen
S. Ive
Shole
St Ives
Lelegan
Redruth St Erme
Rostormel Castle
Pinteck
Tillaton
Pensance
Gwichan
Cambura
Luistwithiel
Letford
Quish
Nutt
PaulChurch
Portigathens
Truro
St Stephen
Bury Down
S. Wivon
Fowey
Land send
Semana
Austel
Duloe
St Iue
Saltal
Market Tew
Siboy
Powyn
Sace
St Much
Grampond
Fowey
E. Looe
St Iohn
Mabo
Tregnye
Moray
Cadlowl
W. Looe
Mounds Bay
Helson
Kelmer
Phylh St Nichol
S. Fide
Looe
Raine
Genan
Gurran
Manacog
Mullion
St Keverne
Manor
Dendennin P.
Lansallas
St Greade
Plymouth Haven
Talland
Plymouth R.
Guensala
Lizard point
Ruan
The Manacles
Scale of Miles
THE CHANNEL
South
Plymouth PART OF DEVON SHIRE
East

Story Locations

Aldestowe (Ăld´-stow)
>Also Aldstow: medieval name for the village of Padstow
>Located southwest of Tintagel, on the estuary of the
>River Camel

Bury Down
>Iron Age hillfort located near Lanreath, Cornwall
>Bury: derived from burh, "a fortified place"
>Down (also don): dun or hill

Lostwithiel (Lost-with´-eel)
>Seat of governance of medieval Cornwall

Restormel Castle (Res-tor´-mel)
>Located in Lostwithiel, Cornwall

River Fowey (Foy)
>Arises on Bodmin Moor, on or near Brown Willy
>(The Hill of Swallows)
>Flows south to the harbor town of Fowey

Tintagel (Tin-tă´-jel)
>Village on Cornwall's north coast. Long associated with the
>legend of King Arthur, it is also the site of a castle constructed
>in the thirteenth century by Richard, Earl of Cornwall.

SAMHAIN

I feel the nights stretching away
thousands long behind the days
till they reach the darkness where
all of me is ancestor.

~ Annie Finch

PART ONE

CHAPTER 1

AUGUST 1285
BURY DOWN, CORNWALL

irst light had yet to make its way through the dense alder canopy when I stepped into the copse to search for Brighida. I wanted to call out, but this little wood, now a place of death, felt sacred, so I whispered her name as I picked my way along its winding path.

"Here, Megge." My cousin's voice came to me from just around the next turn. I found her sitting on the ground shivering in her thin summer tunic. Mud caked her hair, dotted her face, and appeared to have been splashed over her arm, her hand, her nails. The still form of her mother lay on the ground beside her covered by Brighida's cloak. My cousin leaned over and tucked a loose edge of it under her mother's hip.

"Brighida . . ." I dropped my stick and the bundle I carried, took off my cloak, and wrapped it around her.

"What happened here?" I wrapped my arms around her to stop her trembling, then touched her cheek to brush away a speck of mud. I rubbed it between my finger and thumb. That wasn't mud. I touched the hood that covered Claris's face. Black and sticky, it felt as if someone had soaked it in tar.

"Brighida." A chill crawled up my spine. "What happened here?"

She stared into the trees, her eyes dull. "We were on our way home. We had sold all the fleece and were talking about the things we could buy. 'A horse,' Mother had said. 'Perhaps a cart.' And then he—" She looked at me now with the eyes of a child awakening from a nightmare.

"The imposter abbot—" She lifted her arm as if pulling a great cowl over her head. "The blacksmith, Michael Gough. He stepped out from between the trees, put an arm around her neck and jerked it, then dropped her to the ground.

"He said something to me . . ." She seemed to search my eyes for the memory, but then gave up. "I just stood there staring. I, a seer of Bury Down, had seen—could see—nothing."

She still hadn't blinked.

"Brighida?"

"It was dark when it happened. We had stayed in the village too long." She looked with sorrow at her mother. Then, as if seeking comfort, looked back up at me. "Tell me, Megge, did you feel it when her spirit left her? Did you know? Is that how you knew to come for me?"

I shook my head. "I knew only after the Mentors had welcomed her into the ether." *After I had spoken my vow*, I thought but did not say. We would talk of that later. "A vision came to me. Of you . . . here . . . with her."

I reached out to touch bluish fingertips visible at the edge of that sodden cloak.

"Leave her, Megge." She tucked them under the cloak.

"But why? Why can I not see her?"

"Go." Though her voice was firm, her heavy-lidded eyes, pink-rimmed and shot with red, betrayed her fatigue. "I will tend to my mother." She wiped her nose on her sleeve. "You'll help me . . . later . . .

put her to rest in the grove. But for now, I must be the one to care for her. You couldn't possibly understand. But you must go."

"Already I've sent Alf for Martyn and Hugh. They'll be here soon with the cart. Can't I wait with you?"

She shook her head. "You'll be tired, Megge. A vowtaking is a serious matter. You'll not have slept."

"You knew?"

She smiled as gently as her mother might have. "Of course I knew. I was with you in spirit."

"Why, then, will you not let me see her?"

I too am now a woman of Bury Down, I thought, wanting to pull out my hair. *Why can I still not see my cousin's heart or read her thoughts as she can mine?*

"They'll be here soon, Megge. Please. Go back to the cottage. Prepare a place for her in the workroom. That long table—"

"The table is ready."

"Please, Megge." She was weeping now, the sound so strange that I realized I had rarely heard her cry. Not when her legs had been burned and her arm destroyed, nor when Morwen and Aleydis had died, nor even when my mother had been killed. Had she wept alone? Had my own grief kept me from noticing hers?

But I saw it now. And I knew that, at that moment, Brighida was not the seer of Bury Down. She was just a girl who had lost her mother. She was seeing only the horror that had befallen them both, something so awful she had to hide it even from me. But who else could help her now? She had no one left but me.

I leaned forward and touched my fingertips to the hood covering Claris's face. What had that monster done to my beautiful aunt? Rage bubbled in my chest and burned my throat. I swallowed it and spoke quietly, as Claris herself might have done.

"Please, Brighida. Let me help you. Let me help *her*."

Her weeping quieted, and finally she nodded, not turning away as I drew back the hood that covered her mother's face.

Slashed from earlobe to collar bone, the left side of Claris's neck gaped. Blood crusted her hair and pooled around her, staining the ground purple-black.

I threw the hood back over her face and vomited into the bushes, squeezing my eyes shut and trying to purge from my mind that hideous sight.

"He came out of the woods. We never heard him." Brighida looked at her mother's covered form as if seeking confirmation. "It was dark, and I didn't see all he had done, but I believed he would kill me too. Instead, he quickly knelt and put his hand to her neck. He snarled at me, 'Daughter of a whore.' Then he wiped his hands in the grass and got up. He stoppered a small clay vial and slipped it into his pocket.

"I knelt beside my mother. It was only then that I saw the blood. He must have . . . cut her . . . as he broke her neck." She looked away from Claris. "It was so fast, Megge."

"He took her blood?" I asked.

Brighida nodded. "He kept coughing. And his voice was so rough. He said—" Wincing, she looked away. "He called me— oh, Megge, the look he gave me. I thought he was going to slit my throat too. But he said . . . what he said . . . and then he ran into the woods. I heard him ride off on a horse. He was gone."

"What did he say?"

As if she had not heard, she mused aloud, "Why would he, a blacksmith, want her blood?" She looked up as if something had just occurred to her. "Some healers use blood in their remedies. Conjurers use it in their spells. And there are rites. Ancient rites. Ceremonies. Lore. Legend . . . but they've naught to do with us." She rubbed her eyebrow. "But Michael Gough is neither conjurer nor healer." She drew in a hissing breath. "That mother of his dabbled in charms. She hated my mother. Called her a whore. *He* called her a whore."

She was pacing, and I was unable to understand her raving.

"Brighida." I clapped my hands on her shoulders. "You said he called *you* something."

She looked at me as if trying to understand what I was asking.

"You said Michael Gough called you something. What did he call you?"

The chains on Hugh's cart rattled and its wheels groaned in the distance. Brighida slipped out of my grasp and knelt beside her mother, then leaned forward and rested her cheek on Claris's cloaked face.

Stepping carefully so as not to disturb her final intimate moment with her mother by breaking twigs or crunching dry leaves, I made my way to the path and waved. Hugh drew back on the reins and halted the cart. I pointed at Brighida, and he nodded and then sat back to wait.

Martyn jumped down and put an arm around my shoulders. So many things he could have said; but standing so close, such a comfort, he needed not speak. And we too waited.

When Brighida finally looked up, Hugh went to her. As he helped her to her feet, she looked down once more at her mother before stumbling away. I took her hand to lead her to the front of the cart, but she shook her head and instead climbed into the back.

"Martyn—" I pointed to the bundle and the jug I had left on the ground and motioned with my head for him to bring it to me.

I lifted the jug to Brighida's lips. "Drink."

When she had taken a swallow, I set down the jug and tore off a piece of bread and handed it to her. She wiped her blood-stained hand on an empty woolsack and took it. As she ate, I wondered why Michael Gough had taken Claris's blood. What he had said to Brighida. And why he had spared her.

CHAPTER 2

The men gently lifted Claris and carried her toward the cart, Martyn holding Claris's feet while Hugh held her torso against his chest, his arms looped under hers, his tunic now as bloody as the cloak that covered her.

Brighida and I moved to opposite sides of the cart as Hugh climbed in between us and laid Claris on the empty woolsacks I had spread to receive her.

"May I?" Martyn took off his cloak and held it over Claris.

Brighida closed her eyes in thanks, and Martyn laid it over that blood-soaked cloak. He got down from the cart and brought up the gate. "Do you need me to stay back here?" he asked.

I shook my head and laid a hand on Claris. "Just go slowly."

It seemed to take forever for Hugh to get his horse to turn the cart on that narrow path with its rocks and ruts, its trenches on either side. This terrible thing had happened halfway between the village church and the fields that abutted our farm, on a path we walked nearly every day through the copse that grew the foxglove and comfrey that Brighida and Claris had lovingly picked for their healing infusions. As we passed a shoulder-high shrub with long, slender leaves, I could almost hear Claris ask, "Roots, Brighida? Or leaves?" And Brighida, I knew, would have recited her answer exactly as she had done on so many walks to and from the village. "Comfrey. We use both roots and leaves. For healing the bones, soothing the skin…"

The path ended abruptly where the fields began, and we rode between tall hedges that divided barley from wheat fields. A woman tending the barley leaned on her hoe as we passed. Her gaze sought Brighida's, and I noticed her limp when she took a step toward the hedge. *Ill*, I thought. *She wants a cure.*

"Say nothing, Megge," Brighida murmured. She lifted her eyes to the woman and shook her head, the merest movement, and the woman, perhaps seeing the dried blood on her face, the pallor, the white lips, crossed herself and took a step back.

The horse hauled us across the creek, stumbling on rocks and making the cart lurch from side to side. Brighida and I moved in tight against Claris to steady her body when it began to roll. I looked down at the nearly dry creek bed with its tidy stepping-stones that had always seen us so easily across. Never had I dreamed, as Brighida and I had leapt from one to the next as children, that we would one day be crossing this creek as we were today.

With a final heave, the horse pulled us out of the creek bed and onto softly rolling pasture. Our pasture. Dotted with sheep. Their pen and barn were on my side of the cart, the herder's hill ahead of us on Brighida's side. At its summit, Alf sat upon on my rock guarding the sheep as they grazed. I looked beyond him to Bury Down grove, where Claris soon would rest.

Ahead of us . . . home. I let out my breath. Home. What had once appeared a simple, tidy cottage of shingles and thatch had been revealed, through fire, to be a fortress of rock and slate.

Light shone from the window. Smoke rose from the chimney and drifted across the pasture. But when I had left, just as the sky had begun to go pink over Bury Down, the cottage had been cold and dark.

Lowenna, I thought and breathed my thanks.

Martyn's mother rushed outside as we arrived and took me in her arms.

"Alf told me you had gone to the copse as dawn broke. And why you had gone," she said. "'Twas him, wasn't it? The imposter abbot. The blacksmith, Michael Gough. He did this."

I nodded and let her hold me a moment longer, then pulled away. I had to warn her.

"There's blood, Lowenna." I tapped the side of my neck. "So much blood."

Lowenna went to the door while her sons helped Brighida out of the cart and then gently lifted Claris out.

"In here, Hugh." Lowenna hurried into the workroom and as they neared, extended an arm toward the table. "Lay her there."

The long table was bare but for the cloth I had hastily folded to serve as a pillow and placed there before going for Brighida.

On the loom was a length of fabric made of white and black threads Brighida had spun and that I had woven into a silver-grey cloth as fine as a cobweb. It was as wide as the span of my open arms and twice as long as I was tall. It would do. I dipped my hands in the bucket of water by the hearth, wiped them on a clean cloth, and began to take the fabric off the loom.

Martyn and Hugh laid Claris on the table and then slipped away. Lowenna drew back the cloaks and studied Claris's bloody hair, her slashed throat, her blood-soaked dress. She looked at Brighida with infinite compassion, her expression revealing none of the horror I was certain she felt, then slowly pulled the hood back up.

Brighida's breath caught. As she wept, I left the loom and went into the cookroom to give her a moment with her mother.

Lowenna followed me and stood with one hand on the hearth as she tried to compose herself. Though she squeezed her eyes shut, the tears still fell. After a moment, she wiped her face on a towel and bent to whisper in my ear. "The earl must be told what's happened here. Hugh and Martyn must report this . . . horror . . . and see to it that Gough hangs."

I recalled the way Earl Edmund had spoken with Claris outside the castle when we were all leaving after Michael's first attack on our family. It was the day the earl had made Martyn our protector. He had spoken so softly to Claris, and she had reassured him that there was still time for his wife, Lady Margaret, to conceive. How intimately they had spoken. He would surely grieve this terrible loss. And Lady Margaret . . . who would cure her barrenness now?

When she was once more in control of her emotions, Lowenna went to the table and filled a cup from a jug she must have brought. "Wine," she said as she handed it to me.

She crossed to room and whispered something to Hugh, then went back into the workroom.

Hugh went to the door, where Martyn stood looking toward the grove. "Martyn, unhitch the mare and go get Alf. Tell him he's to ride to Restormel to alert the earl. He won't need the cart. Horseback will be faster."

Martyn nodded though he had not looked away from the grove. It came to me then that Mister Gynneys and Hugh were the only living men who had ever seen the clearing where the women of Bury Down were laid to rest. Mister Gynneys had helped us bury Aleydis and Morwen in graves he had dug. And Hugh had spread Mother's ashes there. Now, Martyn too would see.

"I'll be going out to the barn once Alf's off, Megge," he said. "There's work to be done."

A coffin to build, I thought.

"I'll tell Alf what to say to the castle guards so they'll let him pass," he went on. "Gynneys, Hugh, and I will see to the rest. Alf will be back tomorrow to help . . ."

. . . to help bury Claris, I thought and looked into the workroom at my inconsolable cousin.

Lowenna had laid a hand on Brighida's shoulder. After a long, silent moment, she said, "I'll take care of her if you wish, Brighida. Go rest. You'll be tired."

Knowing Brighida would refuse her, I winced. Only women of Bury Down could care for our departed. How it would hurt Lowenna to be told no.

My cousin shook her head. "No, Lowenna. Thank you." She absently reached out and stroked Lowenna's sleeve. "We'll all take care of her."

Without looking away from her mother's cloaked form, she called into the cookroom, "Megge. Bring some warm water."

Stunned, I ladled warm water from the kettle into a large bowl, then looked into the workroom at Brighida, who was still staring at the covered figure lying on the long table. Deep down she must have sensed that though she'd been trained in the rites of Bury Down, she could not tend her own mother's body. But though Lowenna was capable of caring for a body, she had not been trained in our rites. She wasn't one of us.

I dropped two cloths in the bowl and carried it into the workroom. Lowenna gently took it from me, carried it back to the cookroom, and set it on the table.

"Come here, Brighida," she called into the workroom.

When my cousin looked into the cookroom, Lowenna bade her sit at the table. She put a cup of wine in her hand and then washed her face with the warm water. Then her neck, her arm, her hand. "You'll want a clean tunic, won't you? And some of your mother's scented infusion." She looked at me and tipped her head toward the door.

Understanding, I said, "Let's go to the lodge."

Brighida's eyelids were swollen. It seemed she was struggling to keep them open. She swallowed hard and then nodded.

I mouthed, "Thank you" to Lowenna and led Brighida to the door.

She lingered on the doorstep. "I should be in there with Lowenna."

"Hush now." I put my arm around her shoulders, drew her outside, and took a deep breath of fresh air. "You needn't do anything now. You stayed with her in the woods. You kept vigil."

So tired her feet plodded, she let me guide her down the hill toward the lodge.

"Lowenna will do only what is needed. The rest can wait. You'll speak words over your mother. Lowenna will simply do . . . the necessary."

As we passed the roost, I reached into the barrel and scattered some grain for the chickens hoping their chatter would raise Brighida's spirits. She did not notice and simply allowed me to lead her where I would. As we walked, I spoke nonsense to her, crooning a tale about chicks and sheep, as Morwen had always done when I needed to be soothed.

We made our way down the long, steep path and by the time we had entered the lodge, Brighida was leaning on my shoulder. I helped her off with that spattered shift, guided her down onto the pallet, and took off her shoes. She lay back, and I covered her with soft blankets and hides.

"I'll rise in an hour or so, and we'll speak words over my mother." She smiled up at me and a moment later fell into slumber.

CHAPTER 3

I had not slept the night before, having spent it in the company of the Mentors as they revealed both my past life and the duties that lay before me. Nor, I realized, had I slept the night before that, troubled as I had been about my fight—for there was no other word for it—with Claris.

She had revealed to Brighida and me her deepest secret, her one-time love of Michael Gough, and when I had seen in her eyes that some part of her loved him still, I had used her words against her. Then I had used her twin sister's death at Michael's hands against them both. I had been harsh. Cruel. The words I had shouted now echoed in my mind: *You and Mother could have been two powerful women. Yet you chose to be two halves of one weak one.*

Yet, the very next morning, Claris had forgiven me and had taught me the meaning of the symbols on the cover of my inheritance, *The Book of Seasons*. She had spent that morning—her last morning in this life—illuminating the symbols that would lead me to my destiny. And then she had walked away from the cottage having completed her duty, certain that I would complete mine. If she had gone about her usual work with Brighida—studying *The Book of Time*, consulting the skies, and looking into the ether—she might have known what was to be and might somehow have defied fate—though she had argued just the night before that that could not be done.

I looked down at the sleeping Brighida. Her soft, even breathing made my eyelids heavy. My strength waned, my arms hung at my sides. I could not pick up my feet to leave the lodge and go help Lowenna.

Such a friend to this family, I thought. *So like one of us.*

My mind refused to hand me another thought. As if I were once more a girl of six, I lay down next to Brighida beneath the pile of hides and blankets. She moved closer, so her back was alongside mine, and I was overcome by a wave of slumber. Unresisting, I let it carry me under.

I had not been asleep long when something woke me. Something, it seemed, in the very air around me. Someone was in the room.

I lay rigid and tried to still my breathing and slow my tripping heart. The lodge was dark, but I felt someone standing over us. I thought I could hear them breathing.

The Blacksmith, I thought.

. . . *I will see to you*, I had promised.

It was time.

I reached beside my pallet and gently, quietly patted the floor until my hand came down upon my shearing scissors. Gripping the handles in my fist, I threw back the covers and leapt to my feet, ready to plunge the points into the blacksmith's throat.

But before me was not the blacksmith. It was a column of smoke, grey and black, that roiled as if seething with rage.

I stood taller, shears still at the ready, and spoke in a voice I hardly recognized, a voice calm and forthright. "What would you have of us?"

"Naught of her." The rumbling threat came not to my ears but to the place where dreams lived, and I knew that *her* meant Brighida.

"What, then, would you have of me?"

Brighida stirred in her sleep and mumbled, "Be gone."

With a clap of thunder, the cloud dispersed taking with it the rage that had filled the lodge.

I looked at the door. Closed.

That thing came in without opening it, I thought.

I flung it open, and the golden afternoon light revealed my cousin awake and looking at me with concern. "Come, sit. Tell me what's troubling you."

"Didn't you hear? Didn't you see . . . it?"

"See what?" She pulled her blankets up to her chin and looked around the room. "Was someone here?"

"It was . . ." What had it been? "I saw only smoke. A great column of smoke. But then you spoke in your sleep. 'Be gone,' you said. And it . . . vanished."

"Ah . . ." She sat up. "This smoke, did it speak?"

"Only after I did. And I heard it only with my dreamer's ear."

"What did you say to it?"

"I asked what it would have of us."

"And?" she waited. "What did it say?"

"Only that it wants naught of you."

She nodded, and I began to sweat despite the coolness of the lodge. "What?"

"Did *it* remind you of anything, of any*one*?"

"I saw only a great, towering cloud of smoke. Black. Grey. But that presence. It reminded me, somehow, of the imposter abbot the day he came for the books. Do you remember? He was like a tower of smoke. Cloaked and hooded in black, even his hands were gloved. He never showed his face. We never saw his eyes. And though he trembled with rage when Mother and Claris refused him the books, his voice rolled like thunder. Just like that cloud. But what I saw today? It was no living man."

She sat so still. "What you saw was a totem."

"A what?"

"A spirit. Likely the unstill spirit that rules Michael Gough. The same spirit that once ruled Colluen the blacksmith."

I nodded. "The spirit that murdered Murga."

"No, Megge." She put up a finger. "The unstill spirit did not murder Murga. Colluen murdered her."

"But it murdered our mothers."

"The imposter abbot—" Brighida swallowed hard. "The blacksmith Michael Gough murdered them. Of his own will, but at the spirit's goading."

"But he did not kill you though he could have done so with ease. Why did he not?"

She twisted a corner of her blanket as she thought and then seemed to settle on a reply. "Because I was not my mother. And, perhaps, because I did not possess what he wanted."

"Wait." I put up a hand. "What Michael Gough wanted, or what the unstill spirit wanted?"

"They both want the same thing, but for different reasons. You must understand, Megge, that Michael knows naught of the unstill spirit or its power over him." She pushed back her hair and sat up straight as if to assume the master's role.

"The unstill spirit, upon encountering a kindred—someone in the living world who wants what it wants—usurps that person's will and then goads him, inflames his passions, makes his own desperation rule him. And Michael wants our books, though I know not for what purpose a blacksmith would use them."

"Mother always said that the unstill spirit coveted our power to return to the living world at will," I said. "Would Michael Gough want the books for the same reason?"

"Perhaps." Brighida got up and found a clean tunic. "But I believe he has his own reasons."

"Last night, though, he did not come for the books. He came for your mother's—" I could not bring myself to say that word. "Why had he wanted it?"

While Brighida slipped on her tunic and an apron, then looked about for her shoes, I dressed in silence.

And why, I wondered, had he not come for the books when he must have known I would be alone? Brighida had mentioned *rites*. Had he some blood rite to perform that night? Had he another task? One more compelling than the one that had consumed him for years?

I could summon no reason, but I knew one thing with certainty. He would return for the books. And he would return soon.

CHAPTER 4

Brighida picked up her mother's slim vial of scented water. Wearing an odd expression, tenderness warring with hurt, she pulled out the rolled-cloth stopper, sprinkled a few drops on the pallet that had been her mother's, then replaced the stopper and slipped the vial into her pocket.

As we walked up the path to the cottage in the gathering dusk, I broached the questions for which I still had no answer.

"Why did Michael Gough not come for the books last night? Could it be they no longer interest him?" Even I could hear the childish hope in my voice. "Or that they no longer interest the unstill spirit, and so it no longer goads him? What changed, Cousin? What made him seek . . . something other than the books?"

"Megge. Stop. What happened last night had naught to do with the books or the unstill spirit. The blacksmith was taking revenge on my mother. He was serving his own purposes. And perhaps he did not seek out the books simply because he was ill." The frustration in her voice subsided. "Do you recall the cough that first brought Lowenna to us?"

I winced as I recalled the gob of yellow phlegm that had flown out of her mouth when Mother had ordered her to cough.

"Well, the blacksmith's cough was nearly as bad." Her impatience returned. "But I've other matters on my mind now. Please stop asking me these questions."

When we reached the cottage door, she said, "Lowenna will have tended my mother's body. But you and I have a final service to provide to her spirit before . . ." She stopped, her hand on the latch. Head bowed, she breathed slowly for a moment. "Before we take her to the grove in the morning. So tonight, we've work to do. While I make preparations in the cottage, perhaps you can go for some dried oak and a rowan branch."

Brighida went inside while I walked up the herder's hill to the tiny hut Alf and Mister Gynneys had built to store drying wood after Michael and his men had burned Mother's hut to the ground—with Mother inside.

I found a short rowan branch, then split an oak log into four long, slim pieces and walked back to the cottage, the wood piled in my doubled apron. Brighida's back was to the door, her head bent over her task at the sideboard. A sheet hung over the entrance to the workroom.

"Is Lowenna still with her?"

"She must have gone home. She saw to Mother with great care. Bathed and swaddled her."

I set the wood down next to the hearth and reached for the edge of the sheet.

"You needn't go in. Her spirit is no longer there. It is with us now as we prepare to bring her peace." She nodded toward the hearth. "Lowenna left us a kettle of stew. Eat."

I had no appetite. Nor, it seemed, did she, for both bowls Lowenna had left out for us were still clean. Shoulders hunched, she pressed down with her pestle, crushing something very small in a tiny bowl. *The Book of Time* lay open on the table alongside a lighted taper and three tidy piles of dust: yellow, green, and brown.

"Tonight's rite, the final rite the women of Bury Down perform for our dead, is one of rebirth, of releasing the old. Tonight we take up my mother's unfinished work. We free her from her cares and her . . . burden."

"I know what her cares were—seeing to our wellbeing and to that of the women she tended. But what was her burden?"

Pain crossed Brighida's countenance. She looked away. "Please move the kettle so I can lay the fire."

I swung the kettle away from the peat, and she laid the wood atop the embers, rowan over oak.

I struggled out of my dirty apron and hung it on the peg alongside the ratty old cloak Morwen had once worn. Though she had been gone for so long now, I still could not bring myself to move it. Just looking at it comforted me.

"What must we do?"

"Take these." She handed me three bowls, deep blue, each the size of my cupped palm. I ran my finger over the smooth surfaces.

"Fill each with one of the these." She pointed to the neat piles on the table and then emptied the white dust she had just ground into a bowl the color of blood.

"Why is that one different?" I asked as I filled the blue bowls: one with flower dust the color of saffron, one with leaf dust the deep green of late summer, and one with what looked like delicate twigs snapped into tiny pieces.

Brighida tapped a finger on the rim of each bowl. "Flower, leaves, and stems of the horned poppy. They bring rest to the traveler's spirit. And this, of course," she picked up the red bowl filled with white dust, "is hyacinth flower."

As the scent rose from that dish, it conjured Claris's loving presence.

Fear gripped me. Would this ceremony, intended to give her spirit rest, take from me the comfort I had always felt when she was near?

Brighida touched my arm. "Not even death could take her from us. This ceremony simply breaks her bonds to the living world. Her unfinished work we will now take upon ourselves."

"What work of hers remains unfinished?"

"My mother's charge was to teach me all I needed to know in order to fulfill my own charge. And to do that, there is much I do not yet know that I must now come to on my own."

"And what is *your* charge?"

She smiled. "To help you fulfill yours."

"But already I've taken up my book. What more must I—" And then I remembered what Morwen had told me I must one day do. "It is for me to unite the books," I said.

"Perhaps," Brighida said. "But that is not your charge in this life."

What else can it be?

She must have read the question on my face, for she did not wait for me to ask. "It is your charge to free us from the tyranny that has gripped us since the dawn of time."

"What?" I shouted. "Free us from *tyranny*?" In my mind's eye I saw men fighting battles with axe and spear. "But that is the work of kings."

"No, Megge." She shook her head. "That is the work of the Lady of Bury Down, for the tyranny I speak of, which has forever plagued us, is the power of the unstill spirit to usurp the will of those in the living world. This tyranny has claimed the lives of both our mothers and of countless others. It has claimed even your own, when you lived as Murga. Ending it is your charge in this life."

Before I could speak, she took my right hand and touched the tip of my forefinger to the dust in the red bowl. One by one, she dipped each of the others into one of the blue bowls I had set upon the table until one fingertip was saffron, one green, and one covered with specks of brown.

"Fulfilling this charge," Brighida said, "shall imbue you with the knowledge and wisdom, and the power and courage, to serve forevermore as Lady of Bury Down."

She gently opened the fist I had clenched and brought my fingertips together so the white, yellow, green, and brown powders mingled. "Take a breath."

I inhaled sharply. The dust, bitter on my tongue, rasped in my throat and lodged deep in my chest. My eyes slowly drifted closed, and my vision filled with the faces of those I had loved: Mother, Claris, Morwen, Aleydis, and others I knew only through Morwen's tales—my great-grandmother Gytha; her husband, Adaem; their daughter, Natalje; her husband, Arjen.

One face was missing. Now I tasted fear.

"Murga." I searched Brighida's face. "I don't see her. Has she abandoned me?"

Brighida shook her head. "She's part of you now."

And through Murga's rheumy eye I saw her hilltop settlement—Bury Down hillfort in ancient times—its beehive huts clustered within a high stone circle, its men and women toiling in fields under a blazing sun. And then day became night, and constellations began to spin as my spirit soared over rivers and moors, beyond burial cairns and standing stones, and ever deeper into the past until finally I reached ragged cliffs at whose feet churned a blue-green sea.

"You know them, don't you, Megge of Bury Down?" asked a voice that was silk over silk. "These cliffs of Kernow."

I could not see the woman who spoke, but I knew that voice. And I knew those cliffs.

"Once, they had been your home," she said as if coaxing me to remember.

I felt her beckon and yearned to go to her. To those cliffs. To that crashing sea.

My chest filled with longing and a glimmer of recognition—not of person but of spirit—and I bowed my head. "Lady."

When finally I had returned to our cottage—and our time—I opened my eyes. Brighida had lit her mother's green candle and stood it alongside the stub of the taper that had been burning throughout this rite. The rising smoke from the two flames swirled and met in the space between the candles, then rose in one strong column. She spoke quietly.

"It is done, Mother. You're free."

CHAPTER 5

I felt different now, awed by duty and drawn to those rugged cliffs and the woman with the silken voice.

Brighida stacked the blue dishes, set all three into the red bowl, and carried them to the hearth. She held them out to me, then inclined her head toward the fire. "We're nearly done."

One by one I emptied them into the fire. As the dust touched the heat, it sent up colorful sparks and spicy scent. When I emptied the red bowl, the hyacinth dust, still fragrant, filled the room with Claris's essence, making it feel as if she were still with us.

"How is it," I asked, "that you and your mother have a scent that conjures your very spirit while my mother and I have none?"

Brighida swung the kettle of stew back over the fire and picked up her long spoon. "You believe you have no essence of your own?" She stirred the stew. "And that your mother had none? Close your eyes."

I closed them.

"Think of your mother in her healer's hut. See her at her work."

I saw her squatting next to a low fire in a pit just outside that hut, her back to me as she stirred something in a small crock.

"What do you smell?"

It's not a smell, I thought smacking my lips, *but a taste.* I rolled my tongue over the taste of metal and heard Mother say as she lifted a cooling ball of silver metal from her crucible, *Tin, to bring you courage. To bring about dreams.* Into molten tin she had stirred zinc, *for spiritual revelation.* And bismuth, *to ease the transition from the physical to the spiritual world.* Just as I had done that long-ago day, I once more tasted a tang as, with my dreamer's eye, I watched her blend the metals that made the stone now hanging at my throat.

"Metal," I said.

"That's right. She made your stone just as she made the fine metal strips we use to create healing images."

"But what of me?" I sniffed my hands, my shoulders, my tunic. "What is my essence?"

Brighida laughed. "You don't smell it?"

"Smell what?"

Her face went soft. "Of course you don't. Likely you lost the scent long ago. You stopped noticing it."

I brought my sleeve to my face and inhaled deeply. "What scent?"

"Why, sheep, of course. You smell of your sheep. Of their pen. You're a herder, after all."

"But I was once a great seer."

"Whatever else you are—and might once have been, and might one day become—in this life, I shall never catch the scent of sheep without conjuring your spirit."

Brighida stirred the stew and lifted the spoon to her lips. "It needs salt."

She had moved from sacred rite to cooking stew in but a moment. Or was her day but one long rite?

I shook a palmful of salt from the crock on the sideboard and held it out to her. She took a large pinch and scattered it over the stew. She stirred it, then tasted it. "Better." Over her shoulder, she twitched her head toward a bowl sitting on the table. "Put the rest in that bowl."

I opened my hand over the bowl and brushed the salt into it. Brighida leaned over and murmured over it.

"Now set it outside."

"Set it aside?" I picked it up, wondering where to put it, and set it down on the sideboard.

"Not there." She pointed to the door. "Outside. Set it on the ground just outside the door."

"*Outside?* Why?"

"It will protect you."

"Protect me?" I fingered the silver stone at the base of my throat. "From what?"

"From disturbances from the ether."

I picked up the salt and moved toward the cottage door. Through the open half came the rhythmic rasp of saws cutting through wood. *Hugh and Martyn,* I thought, *at work on Claris's casket.*

I looked into the sky. *She's free now. Free to rest and prepare to return to the living world,* I thought. *But will she come back alone? Or will she always return with her twin?*

Without turning away from the night sky, I asked, "Since Mother and Claris were twins in this life, are they eternal companions as well?"

"What do you mean, Megge? We are all eternal companions."

"No—they were different. They were as one in the womb. Were they also one in spirit? Had one spirit been divided in two in the womb?" I turned to her now. "My mother was brusque while yours was patient and kind. Mine healed the body while yours healed the mind and spirit. Two women, one healer. They completed each other. What one lacked, the other possessed. When one died, the other soon did as well."

"Yes, twins are different. You said it very well. One spirit divided in two."

"So, if twins become separated, does each feel that he or she is somehow . . . lacking? Does each seek the other?"

"I suppose they must."

I shook my head. How was that it I did not know the nature of our lives and our traveling companions? Perhaps it was simply as Natalje and Claris had said: *We are all one.*

But did *we* include the unstill spirit?

A cloud bank moved in, and the last trace of light along the horizon went out. The clouds gathered and grew upward until a tower loomed over our cottage. The skin at the back of my neck pricked.

I took a deep breath and demanded, "What would you have of me?" Then, still holding the bowl of salt, I stepped outside to face the spirit.

A breeze came up, warm and soft as a sigh, and the thunderhead drifted into the night.

"Set it down," Brighida called.

I searched the deepening skies as the cloud dispersed.

"The salt," she insisted while pointing at the bowl in my hand. "Set the bowl outside the door and come back in. It's gone. The spirit is gone. Surely you feel that."

I bent and set the bowl on the ground just outside the door. Coming inside, I closed the lower half of the door and watched the sky as the stars came out.

"It's time you knew, Cousin." She set two full bowls of stew on the table and motioned for me to eat. "The unstill spirit is ever with you."

"Ever with me?" Ravenous now, I shoveled spoonfuls into my mouth. "Do you mean in my dreams? Those dreams of—"

"Your violet-eyed giant." She smiled. "You always believed it a dream when you met the unstill spirit as you slept. But those were not dreams. They were moments in spirit. We—our mothers, Morwen, Aleydis, and I—kept the spirit from you when we could. But it found you when we were not able to protect you. For who can truly protect the dreamer?" She sipped the heady broth.

"But we stilled its voice to your waking ear."

"You did? How?"

"My mother taught me from the day I accepted my book how to hear the unspoken, see the unseen, and speak in the silent language of the books. You saw me always at study, or so you believed. But I was often at work quieting the ether and engaging the unstill spirit so it could not frighten you."

And yet that voice so often had found me. *Murderer.*

"I know it was the unstill spirit whose voice frightened me whenever I touched *The Book of Seasons.* I always heard that voice whisper, 'Murderer.' But when else has it been near?"

"Do you recall the time you came upon me, apparently hard at my work, and I said, 'My milk is gone,' and you suddenly felt weak, as if you would faint?"

I nodded.

"We both had entered a moment in spirit; the unstill spirit had ensnared us both. Only Morwen had the strength to break the spell. She feigned a cough, but in truth had said, 'Be gone.'

"Later that day, when I told my mother what had happened, she taught me the secret of salt: that it can keep at bay unwanted voices from the ether."

"I saw you whisper over that bowl of salt before you gave it to me. What did you say?"

"A simple incantation. 'Unstill spirit, be gone.'"

"That's what you said in your sleep this afternoon. 'Be gone.'"

She smiled.

"Even in your sleep you are doing the work of a seer," I said. "Why, though, does he taunt me? What does he want of me?"

"You still call the unstill spirit *he.* But the spirit is neither *he* nor *she.* Only in the living world does the spirit—any spirit, Megge— abide for a time as *woman* or *man.* Why does it taunt you? That is for you to learn. We've long believed it seeks our power. But only Murga ever truly knew."

"Will I understand this when finally I unite the books?"

Brighida set down her spoon. "Listen with care, Megge. Yes, it your destiny to unite them. If you so choose. But understand this: there is more to the unstill spirit than any of us knows. Our mothers were charged with bringing us to accept our books. But they were also charged with keeping you from uniting them until you had learned who the unstill spirit was, what it wanted, and what would happen if the books came together. *And* would happen if they did not. You must be very sure you can accept the consequences before you decide whether or not to unite those books."

Resting her hand on the table, she pushed to her feet. I followed her outside and down the path to the lodge as hammer blows continued to ring out. Would either of us sleep tonight knowing what we must do on the morrow?

The half-moon shadows beneath her eyes spoke of fatigue, but she stopped and raised her forefinger.

"There will be signs when the unstill spirit is ready to reveal itself to you. My mother has told me that I will know when the time is at hand, when what must happen has begun."

"What does that mean?"

Her smile was a weary one. She shrugged. "It means that I will simply know. I will see the signs and know what we must do. Trust me."

At dawn, the jingle of harnesses and the creak of cart wheels coming from just outside the cottage drew my eye to the door. I looked to Brighida. "Are you ready?"

She nodded.

Hugh, Martyn, and Lowenna got down from the driver's bench. I opened the door for Lowenna as Hugh and Martyn released the gate at the back of the cart.

"Where's Alf?" I asked Lowenna.

"With the flock. He got back late and worked with his father most of the night." She lifted her chin toward the grove, where Alf and Mister Gynneys had likely spent the night digging Claris's grave. "He's letting the sheep out to graze now. He'll be along."

"What word has the earl sent back with him?"

"He's ordered Martyn and Hugh to return to Lostwithiel to lead the search for Gough. They leave on the morrow."

Brighida looked away as Hugh and Martyn slid a lovely oaken coffin out of the cart and carried it toward the cottage. Lowenna held the door open, and Hugh backed into the cookroom carrying one end of it.

"Steady, Martyn, not so fast." He bowed his head and stepped beneath the drying rack, nudging the table aside so he could turn and enter the workroom.

Lowenna waved her hand, stopping him. "It's too long."

Carefully, Hugh turned around, re-grasped the coffin, and lifted his chin toward the door. Once outside, they lowered it to the ground.

Lowenna and Brighida spoke quietly near the hearth and then nodded in agreement. Lowenna went outside and told Hugh, "You'll have to carry her out."

"Carry her . . ." He held out his forearms as if they held a sleeping child and looked to his mother. *But this is Claris*, his expression seemed to say. *And she's . . .*

I glanced into the workroom and was awed by Lowenna's painstaking work. She had wrapped Claris's body tightly in long strips of cloth and covered her with her crimson cape, now her shroud. *All so perfectly done and with such care*, I thought, *with such respect. How did Brighida know she could trust Lowenna with such a task?*

"Megge," Brighida whispered. She twitched her head toward the door. Hugh sat just outside, his feet planted in the dirt, his face resting on arms crossed over his knees. I went out and sat beside him. He lifted his head, his face so white I thought he might faint.

"Lowenna," I called into the cottage. "Some ale, perhaps, for Hugh?"

Laying a hand on his shoulder, I spoke softly into his ear. "She's tended to her, Hugh. Your mother bathed and tightly swaddled her. It won't feel as if you're carrying Claris herself, nor even a body."

He took the cup Lowenna offered and looked at me over the brim as he drank. "It isn't as if I've never—" He drank again. "Just yesterday I—"

I held up both hands. "You're one of the earl's men," I said. "You know what it is to carry a body. Yesterday, you had no time to think. You just did what was needed. Today is different. For all of us."

As he got to his feet, he nodded and handed me the empty cup. "Martyn." He jerked his head toward the workroom.

Brighida stood back, then leaned against the sideboard as the men passed with her mother. She turned away and looked up at the curtained shelf as if trying to sort through and comprehend things that were beyond her grasp. The ether was silent, but I could almost feel the Mentors weep for her.

While Hugh and Martyn carried Claris out to the cart, Brighida began her own rites. She emerged from the cottage wearing over her tunic the gauzy crimson cape the women of Bury Down reserved for rites and special healings. In her hand was another. She held it out to me. "Your mother's."

I drew it over my shoulders, surprised at its weight, and let the hood fall over my back.

With Lowenna, we followed the cart up the hill to the grove, each plodding step taking us closer to our last moment with Claris. Brighida fell behind, her head held high as she whispered into the ether. Was she saying goodbye to her mother? Or was she rehearsing the words she would speak over her as she was laid to rest?

She stopped suddenly and covered her face with her hand as her chest heaved. Lowenna drew a soft cloth from her pocket and put it in my cousin's hand. Brighida wadded it, brought it to her face, and cried into it, bending at the waist, her sobs muffled by the cloth.

"She's exhausted, poor mite," Lowenna said. "Has she slept?"

I shook my head. "Not long enough."

We waited until Brighida's shuddering breaths told us she was nearly done. After a moment, she straightened and exhaled, looking from Lowenna to me, then nodded and resumed the long, slow climb up the slope.

From the grove came the *shoosh* of a shovel digging into soft earth, Mister Gynneys still preparing the ground to receive Claris.

Please let him finish, I thought, *before Brighida can see.*

When the cart halted at the top of the hill, Martyn lifted the latch and the back of the cart came down. There it was. The gleaming box that held my sweet aunt. Something balled in my chest as I remembered Martyn polishing the alder wood he would use to repair our loom. Such care he had taken in measuring, whittling, and tapping each piece into place. In rubbing beeswax into the wood to make it glow. How like him to have rubbed beauty into the box that would hold our cherished Claris.

When he and Hugh began to slide the coffin out of the cart, my belly tightened as if I would vomit. But the purge was grief, not sickness. Arms crossed over my middle, I bent forward and let the tears come. Lowenna passed me a clean cloth. I straightened and wiped my eyes in time to see the backs of the men disappear into the deep green shadows of Bury Down grove.

Brighida nodded to Lowenna, and the three of us stepped over the remnant of the great stone wall that had once surrounded a thriving settlement. Lowenna touched the leaves of the sentry rowan as we passed and then took my arm as we entered the grove over mossy ground slick with leaves and treacherous with roots as thick as my wrist.

Just ahead of us, the men carried Claris's coffin to the site Mister Gynneys had prepared—a shady spot next to the tall stone cross that marked Morwen's resting place. They set the coffin down upon two thick ropes lying on the ground next to the grave, then stepped back, heads bowed.

Brighida pulled up her hood so it covered her hair and both sides of her face. I could not see her expression as she neared the casket, reached beneath her gauzy cape, and slipped her hand into the pocket at the hip of her tunic. While murmuring over the grave, she withdrew her mother's vial of hyacinth-scented infusion and, with her thumb, pushed out the stopper. Sweet scent filled the air as she extended her arm over the deep hole and, murmuring her mother's name, emptied the vial into the grave.

That murmur gave way all at once to bursts of speech: "... your own daughter." And, "... secret to the grave."

This is no sacred rite, I thought, *no last farewell.* Nor was it grief that made Brighida cry out. It was anger. Betrayal. She was demanding answers.

She shook out the last drops and then opened her hand and let the vial fall into the grave.

Mister Gynneys waited until Brighida's breathing had slowed and then went to her in silence. When she looked at him, he held out his hand. In it was a bit of wool tightly twisted into the shape of a cross.

"Might I bury it with her atop the casket? To bring her peace."

Brighida opened her mouth to speak—to object, I feared. Would she remember, I wondered, the comfort Morwen had drawn from her Christian beliefs? Would it occur to her that Mister Gynneys too might take some small comfort in this gesture?

Brighida met my eye, and I was almost certain she had had the same thought. She nodded, and Mister Gynneys laid the fine grey cross atop the coffin.

"And this." He opened his other hand. In his palm lay another symbol made of tightly twisted wool: four intertwining rings that matched the silver ring I wore on the long finger of my right hand, the ring Morwen had once given Alf, who had returned it to her when she was nearing death. The ring she had then given to me as she said, "I'm satisfied with you, my Megge."

Four intertwining circles, I thought. *The circles of life, of death, of transition, of rebirth.*

"The guardian's knot," Brighida whispered. "Thank you, Mister Gynneys."

He laid it beside the cross.

Brighida straightened and nodded to Hugh and Martyn. This was almost over.

But I didn't think I could leave the grove. How could I leave someone who had truly loved me, who had never spoken an unkind or impatient word to me? Now, like my mother, Claris was a Mentor abiding in the ether. But that thought gave me scant comfort, for never again would I see her in the living world.

The men arranged themselves around the coffin so each was standing near the end of one of the thick ropes that lay beneath it. Before they could bend to pick up their ends and lift the coffin, Lowenna touched Brighida's elbow. "Are you ready?"

She nodded.

Alf walked over to her, laid his hand on her back, and guided her away from the grave. I stayed behind as he walked with her and Lowenna to the edge of the grove and then left them and returned to the grave site.

He touched a fingertip to his crooked lips and then to the soft grey guardian's knot before picking up the opposite end of the rope his father held.

Hugh nodded at Martyn and then at Mister Gynneys and Alf. As they lifted the casket, I looked into the grave, at the vial that would forever lie beneath Claris, and tried to understand what had driven Brighida to shake out the last drops of her mother's scent and cast her vial into the dirt at the bottom of that deep, black hole.

CHAPTER 7

Lowenna opened the cottage door and helped Brighida inside. She waited as I went in and then left, pulling the door closed behind her. Brighida pushed back her hood, then slid the bolt at the bottom of the door into the hole in the floor.

"Why are you locking it?" I asked. We never locked the door during the day, nor even closed the top half. Did this have to do with her anger toward her mother? I wondered. Had she harsh words for me as well?

She bent to the hearth and spoke softly as she lit a candle. "My mother left you something." She straightened and set the candle in Morwen's old tin lantern. Its light revealed none of the hurt I had seen on her face at the grave site.

"Something for me? When?"

"She told me about it before we left for the village. She knew what was meant to happen to you that night. And she knew the moment you spoke your vow. Just as I did. Just as all the Mentors did." Her expression softened and her voice lost every trace of the anger she seemed to have felt in the grove. In its place was warmth so like Claris's own.

"And then the Mentors observed a long moment's silence," she said.

That terrible silence, I thought as I recalled how alone I had felt after speaking my vow.

"When they did not welcome me after I swore my oath, I thought I must have spoken the wrong words. Or that they didn't want me amongst them. And then, when I looked into the candlelight and saw your mother lying on the ground at your feet, I believed they were welcoming her into their midst. I thought that was the reason for their silence, for their not welcoming me as—" I drew a breath but could not finish.

"As one of us. A woman of Bury Down."

There. She had said it. Brighida had called me a woman of Bury Down. Finally. Something seemed to swell inside me, to fill my chest. I felt suddenly taller, more substantial. Worthy.

"My mother and I knew before we left for the village—we had always known—that that was the appointed night for you to speak your vow. I hoped you would do your duty." She smiled. "I felt certain you would. My mother had no doubt. Her step had been light that afternoon anticipating the celebration we would have when she gave you her gift."

She reached up to the shelf above the sideboard. I got up and helped her take down *The Book of Time*. She gathered it into her arm and nodded toward my chair. "Please, Megge, sit."

I sat.

Afraid to move, I only breathed as she laid it before me. I glanced at it and then back at her.

"*The Book of Time* is now yours. With its power you will draw to yourself those who are meant to surround you in times of need."

I thought of all the people who already surrounded us. "Like Lowenna, Hugh, Martyn, Alf, and Mister Gynneys?"

Brighida sat at the table beside me and nodded. "Most of us have walked together before, but this life—and these times—are different from any we might have shared. The need for Mentors in the living world is greater than ever before. In your world most of all.

"All who surround you were called and given skills to learn, a task to perform, a life to lead. Some of us know why we are here. Some even know who we once were. Most, though, do not. And even I do not know all who will one day awaken to their charge and come to you."

You are not alone, Megge, Natalje had promised. *Never alone.*

"Lowenna? Was she called?"

Brighida smiled and nodded.

"Does she know?"

"When she met me at the door yesterday, I knew she had been awakened."

"Awakened?"

"Suddenly made aware. By circumstances, by memory, by dreams, or by the Guardian herself."

"Like Morwen awakened me the night of my vowtaking?"

"Just like that." She watched my face, her eyes patient, then went on. "When it happens, it is as if the person has been asleep all their life. Suddenly they realize who they are and what their purpose is. It all comes back to them. It's how Lowenna knew how to tend a woman of Bury Down. I know this because I awakened to her at the same moment. It's how I was able to leave my mother in her care."

"Lowenna is a Mentor," I said. "Is that what you're telling me?"

"Yes. She was once called Derwa."

"Derwa? I've never heard of her."

"Derwa was Gytha's mother, a holder of *The Book of Time*, but not a great seer as her daughter would become. Derwa's—Lowenna's— spirit is that of a mother. She returns to the living world always as a mother willing to put her family at the service of Bury Down.

"Long before Derwa's day, her spirit had lived here as Irene, the wife of Odo, Bury Down's manor lord in the days of the Conquest. They endured hard times with their eight children. Times of war, times of struggle. Times very much like those to come. Lowenna will draw on Irene's strength and Derwa's sight to help us through."

I closed my eyes and tried to understand. "And Martyn and Hugh?"

"They are what we call *Companions*, people in the living world chosen to fulfill a task. Hugh and Martyn are Companions by virtue of having been born to a Mentor. Others become Companions by virtue of their acts in a former life. They've shown their mettle, proven themselves worthy of serving the Guardian. They come to their task in this life unawares. But if they fulfill their charge, they may take their vow on their last day of life to return to the living world when called upon to serve as a Mentor."

She brought me a cup of ale and nudged *The Book of Time* closer to me. "I will explain to you what I can about what lies ahead, but there is much you must come to on your own, much that even I do not know. But do not fear our friend Lowenna, for she is still 'our friend Lowenna.'" She smiled. "Not a ghost, not a wraith. A Mentor."

"And Hugh and Martyn . . . Companions," I said, repeating the word though unsure I fully understood this new meaning.

I finished my ale, and Brighida took the cup away. She once more drew her crimson hood over her hair, then drew my hood up as well. Standing tall, she looked down into my eyes. "You have accepted *The Book of Seasons* and vowed to protect it and the power that sustains the Mentors."

I bowed my head.

She laid her hand palm-up on table next to *The Book of Time*. "Do you accept this book, which will endow you with the power to cast your thoughts, your visions, and your commands to those who will receive them and serve you?"

. . . cast your thoughts, your visions, your commands. Though I could not have known the full import of these words, I said, "I do."

"You will one day be faced with a decision: whether or not to unite the books. Only when you understand the consequences of doing so—and of not doing so—must you decide." She allowed that to hang between us. "Will you take your oath to learn what you must before making this decision? And will you accept the consequences when you do?"

"I will. But how will I learn what these consequences are?"

"By keeping the last of the three promises you made when you looked into the candlelight and saw my mother lying at my feet in the copse. Already you have kept two. You have seen to my mother's needs and have comforted me."

It was time to see to the blacksmith.

The rumble of the cart sounded outside the door.

"The book, Megge."

While Brighida unlocked the door, I put *The Book of Time* back on the shelf. As I pulled the curtain over it, Lowenna slipped into the cottage, blew out the candles, and handed them to Brighida. She was putting them away when Martyn came to the door.

"Mother, Hugh will take you home if you wish."

"I have some needs to see to at home," Lowenna said, and my chest tightened. She was leaving us alone. "Provisions to make for my husband. The earl has duties for him that'll keep him away for some time." She looked at me. "Can you manage without me, Megge?"

Already she had spent two days tending to me and Brighida. She alone had tended to Claris. Having done all the work I should have done, she was wan. She needed some rest.

Though all the duties of the house and farm that would now fall to Brighida and me threatened to overwhelm me, I nodded. "We can manage."

Hugh rested a hand on the top of the door frame and looked in. "Alf says he'll stay for as long as you need him." He glanced at Brighida. "It seems he's in no hurry to be gone."

"Won't his father need him?" I asked.

"'Twas Gynneys himself who told him to stay. Though he needn't have, if you ask me. Alf wouldn't have left you."

I wanted them all to stay. My eye strayed outside, to Martyn, his back bent over the side of the cart as he reached inside for something. *If only he would stay*, I thought.

"My husband will be gone for some time, but I shall come back whenever you need me while he's away." She turned to leave but then looked back at me. "If you'd like, that is."

I felt as if my breastbone had swung open and the light had come in.

"Oh, yes." Breathing was suddenly much easier. "Yes. There's always a place for you here."

Lowenna swept past me on her way to the door.

I looked outside. Twilight. It would soon be dark and Brighida and I would be alone. Would we hear Michael Gough if he returned?

As Lowenna went out the door she called, "Martyn will stay here with you tonight."

My breath caught.

Brighida raised her hand and waved Martyn in. He shouldered past Hugh, a full woolsack under his arm.

"Thank you, Martyn." Brighida touched his shoulder. "I'll sleep better tonight knowing you're here."

"So will I," I said. *So will I.*

He placed the sack on the floor, and it fell over spilling blankets and clothes.

"Let me help you," Brighida said. While Martyn picked up his clothes and put them in the sack, Brighida picked up a blanket and carried it into the workroom. "You can sleep in here."

"We'll be off then." Hugh guided his mother out the door and helped her up onto the driver's seat then went around to the other side and slung himself up.

Martyn too would soon be off, tracking Michael Gough and his men. I knew we would be in danger until he had found them and brought them to face the earl. *But tonight*—I closed my eyes for a moment and thanked the Mentors for sending us this wonderful family—*I shall sleep soundly, for we are safe.*

A clatter came from the sideboard as dishes tumbled off the shelf and rolled about the cookroom floor.

"My fault!" Martyn set aside the bowl he had taken from the shelf and stooped to pick up the ones that had fallen. "I'm sorry, Megge. Hunger must be making me clumsy. I've not eaten and thought I'd have some stew."

I knelt beside him to help gather the dishes. So close now, close enough to touch him, I stared at his broad shoulders, his muscled arms, his long, strong legs. Surely he could best Michael Gough. Though Michael was bigger than any man in the village, save our own stone mason and his son, Martyn was younger. Stronger, too, I was sure. And he was trained in weapons of battle.

Lifting his head, he met my gaze. I roused myself from those thoughts and got up from the floor. As I filled his bowl with stew, I gave myself a stern rebuke. *Stop this dreaming. He's here to help, nothing more. And he cannot stay.*

I handed him the full bowl and poured him a cup of ale. It had gone nearly dark outside, and I could hear the whistles Alf used to guide the sheep back to the pen. Martyn took a seat at the table and began shoveling the stew into his mouth as if he hadn't eaten in days. Perhaps he hadn't, I thought, so busy had he been tending to our needs. I brought over another full ladle and emptied it into his bowl. He nodded his thanks, and I silently filled bowls for Brighida, Alf, and myself.

Brighida came into the cookroom and sat at the place I had set for her.

"Martyn's going to stay with us tonight," I said, forgetting in my excitement that it was she who had helped him in with his belongings.

"Yes, I've made up a pallet for him." She smiled warmly at him. "We've missed you, Martyn. And I've hardly spoken to you since . . ."

Martyn held up a hand, then laid it on Brighida's. "It is good to be back."

Alf looked in the door, and his breath hitched when his gaze fell upon those joined hands. He looked quickly at me and said, "I've penned the sheep. I'll leave them in for the night." He looked back over his shoulder as if about to turn and run.

I tapped the bowl across the table from Brighida. "You must be starving."

"We all are," Brighida said as she pulled her hand from Martyn's. "Come, sit."

Alf took off his cap and sat, his gaze tight on that bowl.

Brighida nodded at Martyn, then turned her soft gaze toward me and Alf. "You've all done so much for me—and my mother—these past days. I can't think how to thank you."

Martyn shook his head and held up a hand. "No need. We're nearly kin." He glanced at me, holding my gaze. My chest went hollow.

I recalled the day I saw him sitting at his loom, Vivienne Penneck standing behind him with her hands possessively on his shoulders. Later, when asked him if they were betrothed, he had scoffed and said they were like brother and sister.

Like you and me, I had said.

And he had slowly replied, *You are no longer a child. And I am no longer a boy. You and I . . .* but he hadn't said what we were.

CHAPTER 8

Late the next morning, after Martyn and I had broken our fast, he looked out the door, then hurriedly began to gather his things.

"Hugh's just arrived. Alf will stay here and see to the sheep while Hugh and I ride out to Restormel, speak to the earl, and get the hunt started."

"What will you tell him?" I asked.

"Tell him?" He looked at me as if he hadn't understood my question. "It's what the earl will tell *us* that matters. How many men he can spare, how many weapons and horses, how much time. Alf's already told him it was Gough who killed Claris. Is there something more the earl should know? Something you'd like me to tell him?"

I lowered my voice. "Did Brighida not tell you anything more?" *That Michael had taken a vial of Claris's blood? That he had said something so fearsome that she could not tell even me?*

"What more might she have told me?" Martyn asked.

I shook my head. "Nothing, Martyn." Those secrets were Brighida's to tell.

Brighida walked into the cookroom and picked up her cleaver. She studied it as if it held the answers to all her questions. Then, she took down the cutting board Martyn had made for her, the one with a nail sticking up in the center, slammed a turnip down on the nail, and began to peel it. Martyn and I just watched as she deftly sliced off the peel, top to bottom, in nice, even strips, and then—*Thud! Thud! Thud! Thud!*—sliced it with the cleaver into four pieces that fell away from the square still impaled on the nail.

I joined her at the counter, peeling and slicing alongside her. When we had finished, she set aside the cleaver and began to sharpen her longest knife on the whetstone affixed to the sideboard.

After watching her for a moment, I put an arm around her shoulders. "You haven't yet eaten. Come. Some porridge."

She shrugged off my arm and kept sharpening that knife. *Shoosh. Shoosh.* Pause. *Shoosh. Shoosh.*

Lowenna appeared at the door with Hugh and watched Brighida for a moment before taking three loaves out of her doubled-up apron and setting them on the table. Silently, she turned to Martyn, laid a hand on his broad back, and guided him out the door. Leaving Brighida to her task, I followed.

"We've brought your horse," Lowenna said to Martyn and lifted her chin toward Hugh, who was carrying buckets of water to two horses. "I will stay here with the girls. If you go now, Hugh says you will arrive at the castle before dark. You'll need to hurry. We were just in the village asking about Michael Gough. No one has seen him, but Mistress Trelawney saw Tinker Penneck driving that donkey cart down the road toward Lostwithiel. With him was a man wearing what looked like a monk's robe." She mimed pulling up a wide cowl.

"It's not likely that Tinker's in the company of a man of God. We all know who that was. If you leave at once, you can arrive at Lostwithiel before them and alert the earl. He can send men with you. Please don't confront Michael yourselves. Don't try to fight him. He's—"

"We *will* confront him." Martyn's breath came hard through his nose. "Along with Tinker and whoever else is in that cart." Still breathing hard, he looked at her worried expression then exhaled slowly. "But I don't intend to fight him. And not because I am not his match, but because I would kill him. But it would be far too swift a death. And then I would be the hanged man." He turned to go. "We'll arrest him. Let the courts try him. Let him sweat in the earl's gaol while he awaits death."

"Aye, let the earl mete out his punishment," Lowenna said patting his back. "Go now. They will surely pass through Lostwithiel, and then you shall have them."

"More likely, they're on their way to Bodmin. And from there, to the cliffs, where Gough's lived these many years." He shuddered. "Though where he hides himself out there is anyone's guess."

I put up a hand. "Why did you shiver just now?"

"If you've never been to the cliffs, you'd not understand. It's a mysterious place, the north coast. Those women. Those rites. But never mind. We'll see to him."

Rites?

Martyn went back into the cookroom for a moment and picked up one of the loaves. He took a good long swallow of ale from the jug and turned to leave.

"Martyn." Brighida held up her knife, turning it as she examined it. Its edge glinted in the sunlight.

"Take this." She put the handle in his hand. "You're more than his match. And a quick death is of no consequence to me. He will die anyway. Better it be now, before he can do more harm." She took her small knife out of her apron pocket and turned back to the sideboard, humming as she began to slice carrots.

"This is a butcher's knife, Megge." Martyn laid it on the table. "Watch over her," he whispered as he passed me on his way out the door. "She is not herself."

He mounted the horse alongside Hugh's and was gone.

He was right, of course. Brighida was not herself. *A quick death is of no consequence to me.* She, a woman of Bury Down, sworn never to take a life, would ask Martyn to do so?

But it would not be the first time someone had taken a life on behalf of the seer of Bury Down. As Murga, I had summoned Anwen from Tintagel, and after Colluen had taken my life, she had taken his.

The north coast, Martyn had said. *A mysterious place.* And what had he meant by *Those women. Those rites?*

Blood rites?

From Brighida's telling of Claris's murder, it sounded as if Michael might have taken that blood to perform his own rite.

Ancient rites . . . they've naught to do with us . . .

No, Brighida, I thought as I walked up the herder's hill. *They've everything to do with us.*

PART TWO

CHAPTER 9

I was sitting on my rock eating a piece of bread around midday when Alf walked out of the pen and across the pasture. The day was clear, the wind for once warm, so I did not call out to warn him to bring a cloak as I so often had to do.

He climbed the hill slowly, his lips moving as if he was rehearsing what he was about to say. He stopped just before reaching the top of the hill and looked up at me. He stood that way for a long time, trying, it seemed, to bring himself to speak.

"My father," he finally said, "often tells me of the time, when I was but a babe, that Morwen looked down on me, put her finger in my hand, and smiled when I grasped it. He says she took me into her heart as she took in only one other." He smiled that crooked, snarling smile.

A settling came over me. Just as Brighida had known what had happened when Lowenna was awakened, I knew what had happened to Alf.

"She came to you."

"Aye." He shrugged. "That is, I believe she did. A woman's voice woke me from a dream, a musical voice, and I would take my oath I saw Morwen's face and felt her hand on mine. She told me I was to go to you." He frowned as if trying to sort through that memory. "She said that I had been . . . chosen. Long ago. And that I was now to go to you."

I closed my eyes and saw beyond him the shadow of a man wielding a sword. Then, clearer now, a noble upon a garlanded mount. Then a brown-garbed monk copying sacred scripture. Finally, a hermit gazing into a cauldron, plumes of smoke shrouding his face as he breathed over it whispering incantations. Murmuring, praying, he plucked grey and white hairs from his beard and dropped them, one by one, into the brew.

"Chosen for what, Megge?" Alf asked.

He asked the question with such innocence, I wondered if he was aware of these past lives. My former life, as Murga, had come to me in visions, in dreams. Had his many lives ever come to him?

"Tell me, Alf, have you waking dreams?"

He pursed his lips as best he could and breathed out very slowly. "Do you mean, do I see glimmers of things that are not there? Dreams, though I am still awake?"

"Yes."

He nodded, his eyes now on mine, but I knew that his dreamer's eye was seeing not what was before him but what was beyond this world.

"What is it you see, Alf?"

"A hill that overlooks the sea." He frowned, looking deeper. "I see it from afar, from a ship at anchor beyond a quiet cliffside cove, men all around me awaiting a raised arm to bid them lower the boats and row toward shore."

As Alf spoke, I too saw the sea, a cove, a cliff—the same ones I had seen the night Brighida and I had performed the final rite for Claris. And again I heard that silken voice. *You know them, don't you, Megge of Bury Down? These cliffs of Kernow.*

But the cove I was seeing was not quiet, and there was no ship anchored beyond it. The water churned with an approaching storm.

And then I began to see something more. Someone on the beach at the foot of the bluff. A man. A naked young man running into a cave at the base of that cliff.

I gulped air and shook my head, and the cliff and the man and the vast, tossing sea were gone.

That wasn't Alf's dream, I thought.

He slowly sat on the ground. I slipped off my rock and sat in the grass beside him.

"How long have you had the sight, Alf?"

He cocked his head.

"Waking dreams. How long have you had them?"

"This dream? All my life . . . this dream of the sea. That ship." His gaze went soft and he shook his head. "Never have I been to the sea, yet always have I had that dream."

"And when you awoke from it today, Morwen told you to come to me?"

He nodded.

"What else did she say?"

He shook his head. "She said little, but though I was awake, she sent me another dream. A dream of rain. Long, hard rain. Then cold. Then drought. And yet more rain. Blighted crops." He grimaced and turned his face away. "Murrain."

"Murrain?"

"Pestilence. Dead flocks and herds. And then disease. Starvation. Villages gone to ruin."

Famine.

"Did she speak to you of this long-ago famine?"

He shook his head. "'Twasn't a long-ago famine, Megge. 'These are times to come,' she said. 'That ship. Those rains. The days of hunger.' And then she bade me go to you."

So, Morwen had shown me what Alf had been—a warrior, a prince, a scribe, a hermit—to assure me of his mettle. And she had shown him what was to come. A journey by ship to that cliffside cove. Murrain and pestilence. Famine. Whether a Mentor or a Companion, Alf was being awakened to his charge.

"And what do you understand, Alf, from what you have seen and heard?"

"That we've more to do in this life than guard and shear this flock."

CHAPTER 10

That night at the evening meal, thinking about the blight which Morwen had predicted to Alf, I felt compelled to prepare for what was to come. "Who will teach me all I once knew as Murga?"

"No one can teach you that. You must come to it on your own. And it is already inside you," Brighida said. "But I shall help you learn to read your books. And have no fear. You'll learn quickly."

"And while we are at this work, who will tend the sheep? Who will do my weaving? Your spinning?"

She laughed. "You'll master your lessons far more swiftly than I did mine. The first, most vital, pages of these books, after all, were Murga's words to Bryluen. *Your* words. *Your* incantations."

"But how will I ever learn them all before the coming famine, the 'hard times' the Mentors warned me of on the night of my vowtaking? The suffering I am meant to see us through."

"Not you alone, Megge. And the famine the Mentors revealed to you is on a distant horizon."

"You know of it?"

"Of course. What the Mentors revealed at your vowtaking they showed me years ago, at mine." She took a bite of her cheese. "But it will be some time before all the forces of man and nature—war, rains, cold, drought—come together to bring about the great hunger you've returned to see us through. By then, your power will be as much a part of you as your breath."

She pushed the jug of ale toward me and spoke as I filled a cup. "So study your books. Go to your rock and guard your sheep. Watch the skies and dream. For as you do what comes naturally, your sight will return. As will your power. And those called to help—or those you summon to help—will find you."

"Alf was called," I said.

"Yes?" She drew out the word.

"Morwen came to him today. She told him he had been chosen."

"Does he know his charge?"

"Not yet."

"He's always seemed but a boy." She shook her head. "But I've often wondered if there was more to him than we knew."

"There is more," I said slowly. "Much more. Today I saw his past. So many lives. Worthy lives. Lives I believe he may draw upon to serve us."

"Another Companion," Brighida said.

"He told me of a dream he often has. A dream of the sea, of a cliffside cove. As he was describing it, I caught glimmers of the cove. I saw a naked man standing at the edge of the sea gazing into a cave at the base of a cliff: the same cliff I saw in a vision the night we performed the transition rite for your mother. What can that mean?"

Brighida frowned for a moment as she thought. "Close your eyes, Megge. Look out over that water. Tell me what you see."

Leaning back in my chair, I closed my eyes and summoned a vision of that young man. But this time I saw two.

"There are two," I said. "Two young men bronzed from the sun and sturdy as oaks, each the very image of the other. Twins. One of them is me.

"The warmth of the summer sun washes over me, and a brisk wind rushes by tasting of salt. Gulls scream and waves wash against my legs, pushing me forward then dragging me back as my brother and I run naked from the water and collapse onto a beach strewn with egg-shaped stones the color of the thunderhead rolling in over the sea.

"He picks up a handful and throws one at me. Then another. I shout and dodge until a roll of thunder warns us to take cover from the storm about to be unleashed.

"Lightning flashes, and my brother pelts me with still more stones. Laughing, he taunts the sea, 'Come get me.' Then he picks up his tunic, slips it over his head, and dashes into the cave the roaring sea is advancing toward.

"A flash from the sky lights the mouth of the cave. As I pull my tunic over my head, I look inside, at a colorful, shallow bowl filled with water that drips from daggers pointing downward from the cave's ceiling. *Sacred water*, I think. *Healing water.*

"'Here!' My brother's voice calls from the depths of the cave. 'A second chamber.' Lightning flashes, and I see him standing before a fissure at the back of the cave. 'I'm going inside,' he calls.

"The water's rising. Waves are churning at my knees. 'The tide,' I want to warn, but I can't call out because a yearning is clutching at my throat. I turn back to that font. *My font.*

"'*Only one of you may forever serve,*' whispers a voice at my ear. '*Let it be you. Drink now at the healer's font and live.*'

"I dip my hand into the cold, clear water. With a roar, the sea hurls itself into the cave. Before it takes me under, I bring my hand to my mouth and drink."

The font, the cave, and that churning water faded. All went black behind my closed eyes.

"It's gone. The dream is gone." Feeling as if I had just risen from the depths of the sea, I tried to catch my breath. "But that man. That man in the cave. That man was me." My voice rose as my words tumbled out. "I was *him*, Brighida. It was I who stood in the wind just now. Who tasted the water. Felt that yearning. I was that man. I drank from that font. Why has no one ever told me of this past life?"

"Perhaps no one knew!" She touched my arm. "*I* did not know. No one has ever told me of a life you once lived as a man. As a twin." She bit her lip in frustration. "Even your life as Murga has been shrouded in the veil of forgetfulness, as has *my* life in those days. Whenever I am on the brink of remembering that life, it becomes a mist that burns away as I watch." She paused. "Much like this dream."

"No, Cousin. That was no mere dream."

That, I knew, had been a moment in spirit.

CHAPTER 11

"Why is my past hidden from me?" I shouted the next morning into clouds dyed pink with the dawn. "I've taken my vow. I hold both books. All of Murga's secrets. I hold within me her power. I've vital work to do, have I not? Yet all I receive are glimmers. Hints. Mysteries."

I slid off my rock and paced, and with each step planted my stick harder into the ground. I called into the sky, "I am Murga. Should I not know these things?"

"You are Megge," came a calm voice.

"Morwen?" I pushed back my hood and looked all around, cocking my head to hear.

"Bryluen. Murga's pupil. Morwen, in an earlier life."

"That's what I said. *Morwen*. Morwen was once Bryluen." I sought her with my dreamer's eye but saw no one. "She was once . . . you."

"This is what I have come to help you understand. Yes, Morwen and I share a spirit. Like me, she came into the living world unawares. She did not know all I knew until she found Gytha and awakened. Then she understood. She came to know who she once had been."

"But what if she had never found Gytha? What would have happened then?"

"Child." Morwen's voice calmed the pounding in my chest. "I was bound to find her. We are drawn to the ones we're meant to find. We choose them before ever we leave the ether. As our spirit searches for them in the living world, they search for us. There is a prickling within us that stills when we find them. We feel somehow at peace. This settling is how we know them."

I rested on my rock for the rest of that morning, and as I watched my sheep graze, I mused about Morwen. Just after midday, I noticed someone at the foot of the hill. I squinted. It wasn't Alf.

Shading my eyes, I watched as a tall man in a long, hooded robe, his face cast into shadow, began to climb the herder's hill.

The blacksmith!

The sheep, deep in their grazing, paid him no heed though he reached out now and then to stroke a fleecy back.

I slid off my rock and stood behind it, then reached inside my pocket and took out my knife. I held it at my side as he approached.

Too slender, I thought as he neared. He pushed back his hood. This was not Michael Gough.

His eyes, soft brown and heavy-lidded, were on me now. He closed them and bowed his head in greeting. His tonsured pate was golden brown and spotted from the sun. There in the center of his shaved scalp was a ragged-edged spot as large as the pad of my thumb and slick with salve.

He straightened and regarded me in silence for another moment. His wide lips held no rancor, his countenance neither judgment nor wrath.

"That one's but the newest." He rubbed the skin next to the sore with his forefinger.

I looked down, ashamed to have been caught staring.

"I am called James," he said. "Brother James. From the priory." He spoke as if he thought I might not know the garment.

He waved a hand toward my rock. "May I rest here?"

"Of course." I slipped my knife back into my pocket, then picked up my jug and held it out to him. He bowed his head in thanks and then drank, coughed, and handed it back to me.

"This isn't from the alewife." He smacked his lips, a question on his face. "It tastes of ale, certainly, but also a touch of," he wrinkled his nose and sniffed. "Pepper! Of nasturtium!" A smile of triumph lit his face.

"My cousin adds it," I said. "But it is the alewife's brew. She brings it to Brighida in exchange for—" I stopped. *Heretic. Blasphemer.*

He held up a hand. "In exchange for healing."

I backed away. Why had I sheathed my knife?

He pushed away from the rock. "I've not come as an accuser, lady, but as a supplicant."

Lady?

"My name is Megge, Brother James. What is it you would ask of me?"

"Someone once asked me to spend time with you when the day came. To teach you my skills if you wished to learn them. My arts."

To my knowledge, none of us had ever spoken to the monks. Except . . . "Morwen?"

He smiled. "A woman who truly knew the spirit, though in ways few Christians do." He watched my face. "I too loved Morwen. We spent many a happy hour over a honeycomb and a jug of mead."

"How she loved her mead," I said. "And her afternoons at the priory. She often spoke of the beehives."

"She knew bees, did your aunt," he said. "She knew, as well, the mysteries of the ages. And though she spoke of knowledge, wisdom, and power beyond this world, she respected the teachings of the Holy Ghost."

"Wait, Brother James." I held up a hand. "You said Morwen asked you to teach me your skills. Morwen wanted me to become a monk?"

Smiling, he shook his head. "She asked me to offer to teach you my *healing* skills should you ever ask to learn them."

Healing? "But I haven't asked."

"And so I've come to offer." He got to his feet. "Your mother and aunt are gone now, and village needs a healer. Your cousin is adept at brewing herbal teas and reading the stars to calm women's fears, but they also need a midwife, someone to see to their . . . womanly ailments and their babes. And there are others too who desperately need a healer."

I thought about those dark, fetid rooms where Mother had toiled and laboring women had screamed and bled and sometimes died, or their babies had, and I knew I was wincing.

"You needn't answer now, Megge. Just know that if it's a teacher you want, you've but to ask." He waved his hand over me and murmured his blessing, then made his way down the slope.

I sat on my rock and watched him leave.

He is a fine man, Megge, a man of his word. Morwen's voice was all around me.

I closed my eyes and lifted my face to the sun.

Though I felt sure I was not meant to be a healer in this life, I knew he was meant to teach me something. As I watched him pick his way down the slope, a settling came over me.

I jumped off my rock. "Brother James, wait!"

CHAPTER 12

s I passed the sheep pen the next morning, Alf called out, "Where are you off to?"

"The priory."

He looked beyond me to the fields that abutted the copse. "Are you going to take that path?"

"There's but one path I know of to the village. I've no choice but to take it."

"Alone?" He shook his head. "I'll go with you."

"Thanks, Alf, but I'm not afraid to take it alone."

I waved as I set out, but as I walked through the copse, I looked away when I passed the spot where Claris had lain. I could not bear to see the ground I felt sure was still stained with her blood.

I nodded to the few villagers I knew who tended the fields. If I one day became a healer, would they ever see me as anything more than my mother's willful daughter, the stubborn girl who had refused her mother's tutelage and loathed the birthing chamber? Would Lady Margaret accept me as her healer? Would I ever have the wisdom—or the courage—to offer her guidance or counsel?

The evening before, while Brighida worked at the spinning wheel and I at the loom, I had tried to imagine the countess climbing the slope in the dead of night, her ladies-in-waiting carrying torches to light the way to the grove, that she might seek my help. It seemed impossible that such a great lady would come to the grove for midnight cures.

"Why does Lady Margaret not summon us to Restormel Castle for her cures? Certainly it's her right to do so and within our power to go. Yet she's climbed that slope in the dark and the cold countless times, over many years."

"We heal in the grove, Megge," Brighida said as she spun. "It's there we cast out the afflictions of the spirit. There, beneath the oaks and the stars."

But not all healers do, I thought the next morning as I paused outside the priory's great door. Twice my height, it was made of solid wood and boasted a heavy brass ring.

Oak, I thought and nodded. *It's not a tree, and this is no grove, but there is oak here.*

I lifted the ring and let it drop. The door opened, and a boy in a long white frock nodded and extended an arm. "This way."

As I followed him down a long corridor, I took my coif out of my pocket and brushed off the fleece and dirt clinging to it. Young men in robes passed me without a glance, their hands busy with strings of beads or laden with basins or stacks of cloth.

The stone floors gleamed. The unadorned walls of brilliant white plaster shone. The young brother paused at a doorway. "In here."

As I passed into the room, he withdrew without a sound.

"Megge." Brother James bent over a woman lying on a table. Over his robe he wore what looked like a cooking apron. His sleeves were gathered just above the elbow with a bit of rope so his hands and forearms were bare. He spoke without looking up.

"See this?" He lifted the scalpel that had just sliced the skin over a walnut-sized lump on a scrawny elbow. I looked at the woman's face expecting to see tears.

"Nellie!"

Nellie Trelawney opened her eyes and tried to sit up.

Brother James clutched her arm and held it steady. "Be still, Nellie."

"A lump that size," I said. "How it must have pained you."

She waved her other hand. "It's but a lump. It's grown some, but it hurts not at all. But it won't let my elbow bend. The good brother has offered to see to it since—"

Shame made me lower my eyes. *Since there's no healer at Bury Down.*

Mother would have cared for her in her healer's hut. Or on the cookroom table, as she had cared for Harold Penneck after Tinker had shot an arrow through his leg. How he had keened.

"You feel no pain, Nellie?"

"A miracle," she said, her smile grateful. "Just like the miracle your mother and aunt performed when I was barren. Oh, forgive me, Brother James, I meant no offense."

Keep them talking, Mother used to say. *They'll feel less pain.*

But Nellie had no pain, I reasoned, and I didn't want to talk. I wanted to see this painless lump. What had Brother James given her to keep her from feeling his knife?

As Nellie chattered about her children, I watched Brother James work. With the blunt, back end of the knife he peeled back the skin over the glistening white nodule. He shook his head, the movement so subtle I noticed it only because I had once seen Mother do the same when a child she had just seen into the world lay silent and slack in her arms.

This was no miracle.

When he had stitched the skin, and the lump he had removed was sitting in a basin, he washed his hands and dried them on his apron. "I wish your mother were here."

"My mother?" Astounded, I had to remind myself to close my mouth. "You knew her?"

He stopped and looked at me. "You don't know, do you?"

I shook my head. "Know what?"

"She cared for the worst of them."

"The worst of them?" I waited, but he did not reply. "The worst of who?"

"You'll see."

We bade farewell to Nellie and set off down a corridor lined by a row of stools on which sat men in grey robes, many with hands bound in poultices. Others held crutches, their feet swaddled in thick dressings. A sharp-jawed man in a dun-colored tunic and heavy boots stood at the end of the row staring at his hands. As we approached, he held them out to Brother James.

"It's my fingers, brother. They've no feeling. It came on just before planting," he said. "Now I can't hold my scythe."

Brother James took him aside. "How long were you away, Jago?"

"The whole season. We only just harvested."

"And while you were away from home, did you sin against your wife?"

"Sin against Esther? No, Brother James."

The monk patted the bewildered man's shoulder. "I'll hear your confession later. Think, Jago. What might you might have done to bring on this punishment?" He glanced down the row at the men in the gray robes. "You know why they're here, and you fear you've the same malady. Do what you can do to atone."

"But I haven't—" The man looked down at his hands and then at Brother James. He wanted to object, I felt certain. To press for a cure. But when he opened his mouth to speak again, no words came out. He turned and walked down the corridor with an odd gait, his toes tipped up as if he were walking on his heels.

Mother would have touched his fingers, I knew. She would have turned his hands over, looked at his palms. She would have looked at his feet, would have asked him to walk away from her and then back toward her. What she would have been searching for I did not know, but it began to occur to me that I had noticed more at her side than I had realized.

Later, when Brother James and I were alone, I asked, "Without looking at his hands or skin, you would blame him for his ailment, call him an adulterer?" For that, I was certain, had been his accusation.

His expression, all at once weary, told me he had heard that question before.

"The Church," he said in a way that made me wonder if he actually believed it, "teaches that the worst diseases are caused by sin. I am bound by the laws of the church and so I must counsel Jago that until he has righted the wrong that brought this on, he'll not be cured.

"If his hands remain numb after he has confessed his sin and made amends, I will send him out into the parish orchard to work with the brothers. There, the fresh air and hard work will steady him, give him time to reflect, and make his nights a time for sleep. For when the sick are tired from work, their minds are at peace and their bodies will mend."

"But what of herbs?" I asked him. "What of incantations spoken beneath the planets and the stars?"

"They too have their place in healing . . . for those who believe in them."

"But I've seen Claris's infusions settle a churning gut. I have seen women tortured by itching skin cured by applying poultices, not by confessing a sin or righting a wrong. Look at my cousin, Brighida. Her burns were cured with salves and poultices, her legs made strong by rubbing the muscles and stretching the limbs. Are you telling me her cure came only from belief?"

"Please, Megge. I don't dispute your family's healing arts. Certainly not your mother's. How we miss her." He fell silent.

How we miss her? While I was guarding and shearing the sheep, Mother had been tending the sick of the parish?

"But I saw no birthing women here. Who did she tend? What

sickness did she cure?" I leaned forward to press him for an answer. "What did she heal that you could not?"

He did not reply right away, but as we neared the refectory he spoke thoughtfully. "Here, we see to those with the direst of diseases—the lepra, with its sores and lumps and deadened or lost limbs."

"Are you saying that Jago is a lazar?"

"Weakened hands in an otherwise hearty man. Pale fingertips. Sores and cuts on his forearms that have failed to heal. Bruises that bespeak injuries he did not feel. Thickened patches on his face. And, no doubt, feet as bad or worse." His smile was tired. "Did you notice that he walked as if his feet pained him? Your mother would have."

"Of course I did, Brother James. And I know that my mother would have made him walk to and fro and then examined his feet, his knees, his hands. And she would have set about curing him. Not with garden work but with true remedies."

"You sound so like her." Brother James smiled as he shook his head. "But the Church teaches that to be cured, if a cure's to be had, the lazar must confess his sin of fornication. He must be absolved. He must right his wrong. If this fails to cure him, he may go to the lazar house just outside the village. I shall take you there, if you wish. There a lazar may live a prayerful life, interceding for the souls of others. But it is a life of death. Slow, unutterably painful death."

He pulled out a chair for me at a long wooden table and poured me a cup of mead, his voice wistful as he added, "But your mother, who was not bound by the laws of the Church, had another way."

"Another way?"

"She eased their pain as they neared their end." He put up a hand. He would say no more, I knew.

"How did she ever come to serve the Church?"

"Never would she have said she served the Church." He smiled and shook his head. "No, she would say she served those who needed her skills. Her surgeon's skills. When first she came to us—a miracle, it seemed—I knew little more than prayer, the Church's remedy. I was near despair. I had confessed my lack of knowledge to Morwen as we shared a honeycomb and a cup of mead." He shrugged. "The next day, your mother appeared at the priory with that pouch of hers. And that scowl. How she scolded me! She said I could pray all I wanted, but still my patients would suffer and rot and die in misery. 'Is that what your god would have?'"

I could almost hearing Mother's voice and see her unroll her pouch and set to work. I poured myself and Brother James another cup of mead.

"She told me that if I wanted her help, I must be willing to become a healer's pupil. An apprentice of sorts."

I winced and put down my cup.

"She taught me how to cleanse a wound, concoct her healing salve, and remove a lump that threatened to fester or that grew into a joint and crippled the sufferer."

Like Nellie's lump, I thought.

"She spoke no incantations that I know of," he said, "but used herbs and poultices to bring relief. And when we could not cure them—and who could cure these wretches?—she eased their suffering. She eased their way. How I—how *they*—miss her."

Imagine, I thought as I walked home through the copse, *calling those sick with this dread disease fornicators and making them confess and—what was it Brother James had said?—right the wrong that had caused the affliction.*

And what, I wondered, was that sore on Brother James's scalp? Was it the lepra? Had that salve smeared on it been one of Mother's?

But if lepra was caused by fornication, how could Brother James have been stricken with it? Yet, he had spoken as if he too lived with the disease.

A life of death he had called it. And Mother had cared for them. *How I—how* they—*miss her.*

Though Mother had rarely spoken of the disease except to assure a woman that an itchy patch of skin was not lepra, she must have known a great deal more about it if she had imparted such skill and knowledge to Brother James. But what had he meant by "She eased their way"?

There was more I was meant to learn about Mother's work, something she had never taught me. Something Morwen believed I needed to understand. That was why she had sent Mother to Brother James and why he had come to me and taken me into his infirmary.

And why I planned to return on the morrow.

"We heal in the grove," Brighida insisted when I told her where I had spent the day. She swung away from me holding a wide wooden bowl heaped with grain against her middle. She set it down on the sideboard, next to her pestle, then sat at the table and patted the stool beside her.

"Come, sit." She poured me some ale. "Why would you go to the priory to be taught when their healing, as they call it, is no more than extracting penance and tithes and making the villagers do their work for them?"

"How would you know that? When did you ever set foot in the priory?"

"I talk to the people of this village. And I know how healers throughout time have sought to cure. How clergy, clerics, and conjurors spin their tales. 'Believe this,' they say, 'and you will be cured. *If* your soul is clean. And *if* you do your penance. And *if* you've tithed your wages. And *if*—and *only if*—you go back in time and undo the foul deed that brought this sickness upon you.' Tell me, Megge, how does one 'undo' fornication?" She spoke so fast now and with such venom that I could hardly believe it was my gentle cousin I was seeing and hearing. Her face had gone pale, her lips as tight as Mother's. "Morwen sang tales about cripples, suddenly cured, hanging their crutches on the church wall. Do you recall?"

I nodded.

"Did it ever occur to you that the reason they no longer needed crutches was not because they had been cured but because they had died of their disease? Because that's what your mother always said."

"My mother? Never did I hear her say such a thing." I leaned forward. "And why was I never told she worked amongst the lazars?"

Brighida sat back and laughed. "Megge, you refused to become a healer because the birthing chamber repulsed you. The birthing chamber! Have you ever visited a lazar house? Seen a lazar? Smelled the rot? Never would you have taken up your book if you believed your mother would have made you go to a lazar house to help her take off a finger or a foot. Yes, she worked amongst them. Why, it was she who taught Brother James the skills he uses even now, while the Church dismisses us and calls us heretics."

She sat back from the table and exhaled hard. "We have lived amongst these villagers for a thousand years, healing them under the planets and stars, listening to their woes. We understand them and their ways and their needs. We know how to heal them. When they can be healed. The priests—with their sins and their confessions and their *atonement*—have naught to teach you." She got up and went back to the sideboard. She picked up her pestle, scooped some grain into a stone bowl, and began to grind it. "When you have learned what you must from our books, it will be for you to decide what you will teach *them*. You've a long journey before you in this life, Cousin. But it begins here, at Bury Down."

CHAPTER 13

righida said little that evening as she spun and I wove, and remained quiet as we walked to the lodge that night, so I reflected on Brother James's skilled hands removing that lump, his quick eye taking the measure of Jago, likely a lazar. Mother had taught him well, and Morwen had sent him to me. He had something to teach me, and I was going to learn what I was meant to know.

I'll break my fast early and go back to the infirmary to begin my lessons, I promised myself.

As I passed the pen early the next morning, my thoughts on what I might learn from Brother James, I noticed Alf repairing the fence. He raised a hand in greeting. I lifted my chin in response.

"There'll be cheese this morning, Alf, and a fresh loaf of bread. Will you join us?"

His eyes roamed over the pasture, the slope, and the hills in the distance. "Aye. I'll be pleased to. And Hugh will be along. He's brought his father back from Lostwithiel but wants to talk to you before he returns to the castle."

"Martyn too?" I tried to hold back my smile.

Alf shook his head, but then smiled. Not the tender, lovelorn smile he always seemed to wear when he saw Brighida, but the roguish grin of a boy who believes he's found out a secret.

The top half of the cookroom door was open, framing Brighida's back as she bent over the sideboard and skewered an apple on her cutting board. "Don't just stand there watching me," she said and began slicing. "Come in and set the table. I've put the kettle on for gruel. We've a guest coming."

As I set out the plates, I thought about Hugh's return. "Do you think he's captured the blacksmith? Is that what he's coming to tell us?"

"I don't know why he's coming."

Surely, I thought, *once the blacksmith's captured, he'll hang. And when he does, the killing will stop.* I almost felt relieved; and then I thought, *Or, will it?*

The answer set my gut churning: It would not. The unstill spirit would find yet another kindred. Unless . . .

"Brighida, is there a way to destroy an unstill spirit?"

"No. A spirit never dies." She set down her knife and looked at me.

"Then we must make ready for Michael Gough's death, for when he is hanged, the unstill spirit will be free to find yet another kindred—perhaps one even worse than Michael."

"Yes . . ."

"And we don't know who that might be."

"Likely someone else whose rage against us it can harness."

We looked at each other and said in unison, "Tinker Penneck."

Alf tapped on the door. "I hate to disturb you . . ."

Brighida took a breath. "We'll talk about this later," she said quietly.

"Nonsense, Alf," I called. "Come in." I looked out the door. "Where's Hugh? Did he come to tell us that he's captured Michael Gough?"

"Nay, Megge. 'Twasn't that he came for. He'd have told me." He sat at the table, and I set before him the loaf of bread and jug of ale that he would take with him to the slope. Brighida filled a cup with ale and handed it to him.

"He's at his parent's cottage." Alf drank deeply and continued, "He'll be along."

"And Martyn?"

Alf shook his head slowly. "He's still away, searching out on the north coast. Do you know how many miles of cliffs there are out there? And how many sea caves Gough can hide himself in? I should have gone with him. I could have helped him if there were trouble."

"And what if there were trouble here?"

He took another swallow of his ale and cocked his head. "Megge, why is Michael Gough so intent on harming your family? Why will he never stop killing?" He pounded the table. "Must I worry day and night about Brighida—" A burst of spittle flew across the table as he spoke her name. "About the two of you, I meant. You and Brighida."

He got up. Forgetting his bread, he made haste out the door. "I have to go back to the pen. You've only to shout if you need me."

Brighida and I looked at each other, and Brighida's expression of bewilderment told me she had not a clue that Alf loved her.

Hugh arrived moments later, knocked, and then stood as he always did, with one hand resting on the doorjamb. His blond hair looked rough—tousled and dirty—as if he had not touched it in days.

"Hugh!" I took a bowl to the hearth and ladled gruel into it. "Come, sit."

He glanced outside, then held the door open. Lowenna came in carrying a loaf of bread and a jug and set them on the table.

"The earl's asked you to come to Restormel, Megge," Hugh said.

"To Restormel?"

"You've not seen him since we left the castle after my injury," Brighida said. "Much has changed since then."

"Today? But I'm meant to return to the infirmary."

"The Earl of Cornwall has asked for you," Brighida said. "You've no choice. Brother James can wait."

"What could the earl want with me?"

"You're now head of the household," Hugh said.

"Head of the household?" I glanced at Brighida.

"You're the elder of us, Megge. It's you the earl will deed the land to. And to you he'll grant the boon."

"The boon?"

A boon is a gift, Claris had once explained to me.

Lowenna said, "This is a private matter. I'll leave you." She was nearly to the door when Brighida stopped her.

"There's no need to leave, Lowenna. We've no secrets from you. Nor from Hugh or Martyn or Alf. We're family, we six." She pulled out a chair for Lowenna. "Every ruler has deeded this land to the seer of Bury Down since long before the days of Odo and Irene. When Gytha passed, Earl Richard deeded it to my mother. She was mere minutes older than Megge's, but she was the elder. Now, the land and the boon will pass to Megge."

"What is the boon?" I had to understand. "I once heard Agnes Gough and the old women at the church whisper about it, but Aunt Claris said they were mistaken. That there was no boon and had never been one."

"Sit here, Megge." Lowenna got up and gave me her seat. Standing behind me, she began to untangle my hair. "Hugh, step outside for a moment, please. Brighida, bring your cousin a warm, wet cloth. She'll want to freshen herself for the journey."

"Perhaps my mother believed you too young to understand," Brighida said. "There is a boon." She dipped a cloth into the kettle of warm water and handed it to me. "Face and neck, hands and arms. And—" she mimed washing under her arms.

"For caring for the women of the village, we are accorded all that grows on our land. We owe no duty on what we produce—vegetables, herbs, healing flowers—nor on our fleece. And for our counsel to the earl, we are freed from the burden of fealty, so no son of ours will ever be called in the event of war." She looked now at Lowenna. "These terms were dictated long ago by my great-grandmother Gytha. It was she who advised Earl Richard to befriend the pope." Brighida smiled. "And because he did, he was named King of the Romans. Thanks to Gytha's wise counsel—and to the earl's great intellect and piety, of course—he became the richest man in England. Richer, even, than his brother the king. Gytha saw to it that her descendants would be safe and that the writ would pass from generation to generation."

Lowenna smoothed my hair and then swept it back off my face. Rather than braid it, she twisted it into a long rope that she coiled at the nape of my neck. She tucked the end securely underneath, then patted it. "A wise woman, your great-grandmother. But Edmund—"

"Yes." Brighida nodded. "Edmund is still without an heir. If he has no son when he passes, and the king appoints one of his friends Earl of Cornwall, then our agreement may have no standing."

Now I understood why Mother and Claris were so desperate to help the Lady Margaret conceive and carry a child to term.

"You'll want to change your clothes." Brighida opened the door to the cupboard beneath the sideboard and withdrew a crate. She lifted the lid and took out a long, sleeveless garment of a color I had seen only once, in that dream of an endless sea. Light green, edged in gold. "One of the garments Polly gave you."

"When I outgrew all my clothes!"

"No doubt all these gowns would fit you now."

"A surcoat," Lowenna breathed. "And it matches this gown." She drew from the crate a light green gown with a woman's bodice and long, narrow sleeves that came to a point over the wrist.

"It'll be much too . . . long," I said, putting up my hands and backing away. "It'll cover me from shoulders to boots."

"Let me help you." Brighida slipped my tunic off and pulled the dress carefully over my head. She laced it up the back, then touched my shoulder to turn me around.

Brighida nodded and Lowenna sighed. "Oh, Megge. You look lovely. And it's not at all too . . ."

Crossing my arms over my chest, I looked at her warily.

"... long," she said. Haven't you noticed? You're nearly as tall and ... womanly ... as your cousin now."

"I've been making her tunics larger and longer," Brighida said. "But since they're all so alike, she's never seemed to notice."

I had noticed. I just disliked how much my body was coming to resemble hers.

Brighida held up the sleeveless coat, and I slipped my arms into it. It was heavy, its inner surface smooth and cool.

I turned.

She smiled at me, nodding in pride. "You look like royalty, Megge."

Hugh pounded on the door. "We must go!"

"Go, Megge." Lowenna waved a hand toward the door. She put the loaf of bread and the jug she had brought into a basket with some cheese and held it out. "Take this. It's a long journey."

I clung to the door jamb. "I've never spoken to Earl Edmund. I was a child when last I saw him. Surely he sees me as but a little girl."

"Do not fear, Megge. You look nothing like a little girl today."

"How do I even address an earl?" My voice sounded panicked even to me.

"With 'Your Grace' and a curtsy," Brighida said, dropping low and bowing her head.

I tried it as Lowenna opened the door.

When Hugh saw me, his breath caught. "Megge."

I rose from my curtsey. "I'm ready, Hugh."

He stared for a moment, then twitched his head toward the cart. "Aye. It seems you're ready to meet the earl."

I took off the coat and carefully folded it. "I'll put it back on when we arrive." I could not stop stroking the smooth, cool lining.

"Go now, Megge," Lowenna said. "Secure this place for your-selves and those to come. I'll be here with Brighida until you return."

As we started down the road toward Lostwithiel, Hugh nei-ther looked at me nor spoke to me. This was not the Hugh I knew. Friendly, often teasing, Hugh was warm, attentive, even to a mite of a girl, as he so often called me.

"I brought bread."

Had I awakened him from deep slumber I could not have startled him more. "Bread, you say?"

"What were you thinking? Something important, it seemed."

"A bit of business in Tintagel. Martyn's gone to see about it. Naught to worry you over." He clucked to the horse and shook the reins, seeming to force his thoughts back to me, to the cart, to our destination.

"He's not a bad sort, the earl." He cocked his head. "He's got a soft spot for the women of Bury Down." He clucked again to the mare and pulled her head to the left to go around a wide hole. "He speaks of you as if you were men. Barons. Counselors. Not a family of women."

"But Mother and Aunt Claris *were* his counselors. And heal-ers for the women of the castle and the village. Perhaps he knows their value—*our*—value." It felt strange to count myself amongst the women of Bury Down, but wasn't that why I was riding with Hugh, after all? I had to accustom myself to saying it. "We've coun-seled every Cornish leader since the dawn of time. Might that be his reason for according us respect?"

We. Us. Yet never had I counseled an earl.

"'Twas that I was saying. You're not like a family of women. You've the gods about you. That's what they say in the village, the castle, even as far away as Aldestowe. Except out there, on those cliffs, they say, 'The women of Bury Down walk with the goddess.'" He looked at me again. "And today, more than ever before, I'd have to say I agree. But I've felt that ever since the day I met all of you. I don't mind saying you four women scared me senseless. That mother of yours," he shook his head, "accosting me while I was repairing the cart's broken axle. I looked up and saw that face." He drew back his lips in a grimace. "'Never tangle with this one,' I told myself. 'She'll have you for her supper.'"

Through my laughter I said, "And you! Why, you stood up, and your size nearly made her swoon. Never before—or since—had I seen her so at a loss for words."

"What would she say now, I wonder," Hugh said, his eyes on the road as he took care to miss the rocks and ruts that were aplenty. "You, in this fine garment, riding off to the castle to speak with the Earl of Cornwall on your family's behalf. Head of the family." He tipped his head toward mine. "That's what he called you when he sent me to fetch you. 'Bring her to see me, please. Margaret of Bury Down, the head of her family.'"

Margaret of Bury Down.

"I was named for the countess," I said. "No doubt he sees *Megge* as a child's name." But I was no longer a child. And so, for the earl, I would be Margaret.

I sat taller, and my face composed itself differently. I felt as if my eyes were wider open, my lips softer. My hands had stopped picking at each other and lay still in my lap.

Glancing over at Hugh, I noticed that his gaze was once more directed into the distance.

CHAPTER 14

Earl Edmund strode into the great hall, a rolled parchment in his hand, and my curtsy brought my face so near it I could smell the ink. He touched my elbow when I rose.

"Margaret." He inclined his head. "Please accept my condolences on your terrible loss. First the loss of your mother, and now your aunt." He shook his head slowly. "A terrible loss. How we shall miss them."

"Thank you, Your Grace."

"Never would I have known you for the child you were when last I saw you." He smiled as he took my measure. "You've become as lovely as ever your aunt Claris was. And it is my hope that you'll one day be the healer your mother was. He shook his head sadly. "How we miss her here."

I did not know what to say, so I bowed my head in thanks.

"My father admired and took the counsel of your great-grandmother Gytha, to whom he accorded dominion over Bury Down manor. And I was guided by her granddaughter, your kind aunt, Claris. And by your mother, of course," he hurriedly added. "May you," he said as he handed me the parchment, "to whom I now accord this dominion, live long in service to the people of your village. Even as you continue to serve the crown." As I reached for the deed, he looked into my eyes. "I and my house are at your service, Margaret of Bury Down."

"Your Grace." Dropping into another curtsy I accepted the deed, my head bowed longer than necessary as I fought back the waves of relief and gratitude that threatened to show themselves as tears.

When I rose, the earl looked briefly at Hugh and then back at me. "There's one more thing. It does you little good to raise all those sheep if you can't sell the cloth you weave from their fleece."

He's going to take my flock!

"Oh, but Mister Tucker sells our cloth."

"Ah, Tucker. A good man. He trained Martyn, I believe. And Martyn trained you. I'm told you've surpassed them both, Margaret. You've become a master of the craft."

"Martyn took samples of your work to the guild," Hugh said. "He told them of your years of instruction. But it was your weaving that earned you membership in the guild."

The earl smiled. "Even with a boon and a parcel of land, a landowner needs an income. As a master weaver, you've a profession for life. Why, you could train your own apprentices."

"And sell my own wares?" No more listening to Mister Tucker's barbs? No more accepting mere pennies while he pocketed the lion's share of the money my work brought in?

"And sell your own wares. We've fairs in Bodmin now. Take your fine cloth there." He did not add, "Where you'll not have to compete with Tucker."

I curtsied low again and bowed my head in gratitude though I knew there'd be no need to journey to Bodmin. Women who came to us from Bodmin for cures often asked if they might purchase the cloth I wove from Brighida's "goddess thread." Until today, I had to send them to Tucker's market stall to buy it.

When they learn that I am a guild member entitled to sell my wares, I thought, *they will come to Bury Down for more than cures.*

When I rose, the earl was gone and Hugh was smiling at me. "Looks like you're now the master weaver," he said.

I looked at the deed that granted me dominion over Bury Down.

"Hugh," I asked. "What is *dominion*?"

"*Rule*," he said, taking my elbow. "It means you've the right to do with it what you will. It is under your rule."

He led me through the great hall and out to the stables, where he hitched his horse to the cart and helped me up onto the seat.

"Where will you go now, Hugh?"

"To the village, to await Martyn and some others I'm expecting from the coast. If they don't arrive in a day or two, I'll head back there. Gough hides himself in those cliff caves better than a rat on a ship, but it may be they've caught his scent."

"He's likely with Tinker Penneck. And he won't hide Tinker for long," I said. "For Tinker won't be hidden away."

Hugh smiled, his expression one of surprise. "That's right, Megge. And that's how I intend to find him. Through Tinker."

CHAPTER 15

This endless search, I thought as I watched the fields go by. How could I ask Hugh and Martyn and the earl himself to keep at it while I stayed behind and did nothing to help? Perhaps by uniting the books and unleashing their power, I could find Michael Gough myself.

Consequences, I heard Brighida say and gritted my teeth.

Somehow, I had to learn what would come of bringing them together. Such enormous books, I thought. How I would even accomplish such a feat if I chose to do so?

"Aren't you going in?" Hugh asked.

I was startled to realize that we were at the cottage. "Brighida will have a meal for us. Come inside, Hugh."

He shook his head. "It's late."

"Then I'll say good night now. Thank you, Hugh." I picked up my surcoat and climbed down from the cart slowly so as not to damage it or the parchment Earl Edmund had bestowed upon me.

Brighida sat at the table with *The Book of Time* open before her. Eyes closed, she murmured, then opened them and looked at the page as if to confirm that she had truly committed the incantation—or the lesson, or the constellation—to memory.

"Brighida." I spoke quietly to bring her back to the waking world without frightening her. As she looked up and closed her book, I handed her the parchment, then carefully returned my glorious surcoat to its crate. "Earl Edmund gave me dominion over Bury Down."

She nodded without looking up from the deed. "*Dominion* means—" She spoke as if teaching a pupil her lessons.

"I know what it means, Brighida. It means *rule*. It means that we decide what we shall do with our manor. He called Bury Down a manor, Brighida."

"I would have said *authority*—that we have authority over our land—but *rule* is also correct."

"Already I have authority over our books." I took a deep breath. "And if we are to find Michael Gough, I believe it's time to unite them so we might use their power to bring him to justice."

With her lips still working as she studied the Latin words on the deed, she stroked her cheek with her forefinger. Then, as if just realizing what I had asked, she looked up. "Unite the books?"

I touched the cover of *The Book of Time* and looked up at the shelf holding *The Book of Seasons*. "How can two such enormous books be joined?" I mused aloud. "Surely the bindings would break . . ."

"The books themselves are not to be joined into one great tome." Brighida laughed as if it had never occurred to her that I might think such a thing. "It is what they hold—their knowledge and wisdom—that must one day be united. Murga's great incantation, '*Scientia nupta sapientia potestas est*,' means 'Knowledge wedded to wisdom is power.' And with power comes duty.

"Power such as Murga wove into her writings, and which will be unleashed when their knowledge and wisdom come together, will no doubt come with a duty far greater than any woman of Bury Down has ever borne. A duty, perhaps, which you will choose not to shoulder."

"As I chose not to shoulder the duty to heal? Is that what you are saying? Or as I chose, out of cowardice, not to shoulder the duty to save my own people when I, as Murga, was their seer?" Gripped by remorse, I shook my head. "Why did I not take the life of that horrid Colluen when he began to turn the settlement against me? Surely I had the power to do so. Instead, I allowed him to let everyone starve, and then allowed him to execute me."

Brighida closed her book. "It was not for cowardice that *Murga*—not you, Megge, but Murga—did not kill Colluen. It was for a reason." She paused until I had stopped shaking my head and then spoke slowly. "How many times must you learn this lesson? The women of Bury Down do not kill. Not an animal, not a child in the womb, not even a man who would kill us himself. It is not—and never has been—for us to take a life."

"No, Brighida, we allow others to do that work for us. Anwen killed Colluen." I was breathing hard. "Tell me, did I call her from the cliffs to protect Bryluen and my writings or to do for me what I could not do for myself?"

"Enough." Brighida slapped the table and got up. "Enough. Anwen acted of her own accord."

I spotted the long knife Brighida had sharpened and had put into Martyn's hand. I picked it up.

"As Martyn would have done had he taken this knife *you* gave him?"

CHAPTER 16

"It's late, Megge."

I took off my gown, packed it away in the crate, then put on my tunic. I followed Brighida outside, and we walked down to the lodge, each wrapped in her own barbed silence until Brighida whispered my name and pointed toward the sheep pen.

A light swung back and forth from a lantern carried by someone meandering from place to place.

"Alf's still at work," I said.

"This late?" Brighida's lantern cast shadows upward on her face, bringing into relief a troubled countenance.

As we neared the lodge, I heard her muttering, and then crying, and I realized she was not merely troubled. She was suffering, and not because Alf was still working so late into the night. Something else was on her mind.

I touched her shoulder as she opened the lodge door. "What troubles you? I meant no insult. And even if you had meant for Martyn to—"

She looked at me not in anger but in grief, in frustration. This, I realized, had naught to do with me or my careless words.

"She's gone now. She can't explain." She took a deep breath and began to weep.

"What, Brighida? What can she not explain?" I rubbed her back as she bent forward, her back heaving with her sobs. Had I not known, I might have thought she was laughing, unable to catch her breath for her mirth, as the force of her misery took her over.

"Please, tell me what's wrong."

She said nothing, so I set the lantern between our pallets and left her to her release. There, in the shadows, she cried until the sobs became but huffing exhalations. She raised her head and seemed to stare at the ceiling as she mastered herself. She breathed long and deep before finally straightening.

"He's still nearby, Megge," she said. "I can feel it. He's not at the cliffs. He's somewhere near. And he—he said—he called me—"

"What? What did he say? What did he call you? What secret are you keeping from me?" Then I remembered one thing she told me he had said: *Daughter of a whore.*

"Brighida, did he call *you* a whore?"

She shook her head, winced. "I cannot speak of it."

"Why not? Why won't you speak of it?"

"We're not safe, Megge."

"Of course we are. Alf's keeping watch. You've seen for yourself. He's up in the pen, still moving about. He'll not sleep tonight, you can be sure of that. And Mister Gynneys will be back in the morning. Rest now." I helped her off with her tunic and pulled a soft shift over her head, then settled her under a pile of warm hides. "We're safe here."

CHAPTER 17

"Megge," Alf called into the cottage the next morning.

"Come in, Alf. Break your fast."

Still half-asleep after a restless night dreaming of monks and Mother and those incurable lazars, I got up from the table, where I had been toying with my bowl of gruel, and went to the kettle.

"No, thank you." He motioned with his head toward the sheep pen. "We've a problem. I could use your help."

All at once fully awake, I picked up my walking stick. "Brighida," I called into the workroom, "I'm going to the pen with Alf. Then I'll be off to the infirmary."

"Not today, Megge." Brighida came into the cookroom carrying a small pouch. "It's time you learned to read the stones. We've healings to do tonight."

"We've a lame ram." Alf's tone was apologetic.

"Another time, Brighida," I said and left with Alf.

At the back of the pen, a young ram limped on three legs, its back right leg tucked into its belly.

"What's it done to that leg?"

Alf shrugged. "It was lame this morning, but I see naught amiss."

Alf steadied its head while I ran my hands gently over its haunches and leg. No broken bones. No lumps.

But there.

Along the inside of that back leg, just above the pastern, were traces of dried blood that Alf might have mistaken for mud. I rolled my thumb over the bone. The ram jerked its leg, bleating and pulling away. Just beneath the skin something long and slender lay along the bone.

"There's something in there," I said. "Hold him."

I went for the pouch I kept in the barn, unrolled it, and took from one of its pockets a square of cloth and a small pot of the salve Brighida and Claris had made to heal sores. Alf held the ram as I stretched out its kicking leg and wrestled it under my arm.

I pressed my finger to a small cut in the skin and forced the tip of the stick out, then gently pulled on it. It did not come free. Bleating, the animal writhed, but Alf held fast. I looked closely at the short length that had come out. Tiny cuts had made the bark fan out like a row of arrowheads. This hadn't been an accident, I thought. Someone had intentionally hurt this animal.

I could see in my mind's eye the light of Alf's swinging lantern as he crossed the pen the night before. Back and forth it went, in a long, bright arc. An arc, I realized, that had been too long to have come from Alf's arm.

It seems he hurts animals for pleasure, Claris had once said of Tinker Penneck. *Keep your eye on this one.*

"What is it, Megge?"

I hesitated. If I told him I thought that Tinker had likely done this, he would leave for Restormel at once to alert the earl, and Brighida and I would be left alone.

"It's barbed." I ran a finger over the exposed stick. "The barbs swelled inside the leg and opened outward, like arrowheads. If I pull it, I'll tear both skin and muscle."

"How long is it?"

"I only see a short bit outside the skin, but it reaches nearly to the hock. I'll have to deaden the skin, enlarge the hole, and pull out that stick."

The ram pulled in a frantic effort to free its leg. I tightened my grip. We needed more hands. I closed my eyes and silently summoned the Mentors. *"Scientia nupta sapientia potestas est—please, we need help."*

"What are you doing, Megge?" Alf asked, then started to get up. "Here. Let me try."

A shadow fell over us.

"Atropos," came a deep voice tinged with humor. "What is it you're after clipping this morning?"

"Mister Gynneys." Had I somehow summoned *him*?

He strode across the barn to the shearing stall. "There they are!" Shears in hand, he turned to leave. As he passed me, he paused. "What's that you're doing?"

I lifted the leg to show him. "The stick is barbed. It won't come out."

"Nonsense," said the shearer. "Hold that leg." With one hand he pulled a slim blade from a sheath at his hip; with the other he stretched the leg out. And with one brisk swipe, he opened the skin over the stick. "'Twasn't deep, and it won't bleed long."

I swabbed the wound with Brighida's salve, covered it with the cloth, and held it tight.

Mister Gynneys wiped off the stick and held it up to the light. "It's been whittled to a point and sliced all along its shaft." He showed it to his son. "Who's been in this pen, Alf?"

I looked at Alf. He shook his head.

"No one," he said. He kept his eye on that stick as he held the ram and stroked its neck. "I penned the flock last night and stayed right here," he pointed to his pallet atop a bed of straw, "keeping watch. No one came in."

"You mean you fell asleep and *saw* no one."

Alf looked back down at the ram.

I lifted the corner of the cloth I was holding to its leg and examined the wound. Blood oozed but was not pumping.

"Hold him another moment longer, Alf." I made to rise.

Mister Gynneys held up a hand. "I'll get it." He went to my pouch and pulled out a rolled bandage. "Hold that cloth to the wound." He wrapped the leg with the bandage so it held snugly, then split the end with his knife and tied it down. He held out his hand to Alf. Alf took it and got to his feet while stilling the ram with his other hand. I stood slowly, reluctant to let go of that leg lest it bleed.

"It's snug." Mister Gynneys took my hand from the ram's leg. "Leave the dressing. You and I have other matters to discuss. Come."

He picked up the shears he had come for and walked out of the barn. I followed.

"What matters, Mister Gynneys?"

He walked me to the barn door, where he must have set down his basket of supplies before entering the barn for his shears. It was filled with candles and salted fish.

"You've not provisions to last a fortnight, my son tells me. There's work enough here for four strong men, and you've but three. With Martyn and Hugh away for God only knows how long, that leaves one—Alf—and you two girls."

"*Girls?*"

We were grown. I was Megge of Bury Down. I had spoken vows. I was not a child.

"By God, I meant no offense." He scrubbed the top of my head with a callused hand so big it covered both my crown and brow. "But you're orphans now, aren't you? The two of you. Great ladies you might be, but can you till the ground and plant and gather? Can you slaughter that ram when its leg festers?"

My breath hitched. *Slaughter it?*

He lifted his chin toward the barn. "That was a boy's prank. But dangerous enough. It stinks of Tinker Penneck." He tilted his head as his eyes took mine. "You've handled it well enough, lass, but could you hold your own against him and that blacksmith out of Tintagel should they come to call again?"

My breathing came fast as I scanned the fields, the slope, the distant hills as if his words might have called forth the unstill spirit.

I blurted, "But Martyn and Hugh—"

"Are about the earl's business." His whiskered face gentle, his brown eyes soft under brows going grey, he spoke quietly now. "Though you have Alf with you, I fear for you and your cousin. Someone got past him here last night."

"Yes, but—"

He put up a weathered hand. "A good boy, my son. Best herder you'll find." He paused, nodding to himself. "But a boy. And you wouldn't know about boys, having grown up with naught but women folk."

"When we met Martyn, he was but a boy."

"Martyn's different." Mister Gynneys shook his head. "And I'll not say an ill word about my son." His expression softened. "Don't worry, Megge. I see you like him, and you're loyal. But haven't you noticed? He sleeps hard."

"What does that mean?"

"He sleeps *hard*. Like one dead. Haven't ye noticed?"

I remembered seeing Alf dozing on the slope one night. He had fallen asleep while guarding the sheep, and I had thought it was my stealth that had kept him from waking when I climbed the slope and sat beside him.

"He would protect you with his life. That he would. But he's young. And young men sleep hard, is what I'm telling you. I was once the same. Oh, I learned, didn't I? How to keep watch for a day and a night and a day." His lower lip stiffened with pride for a moment. "Hugh and Martyn used to take the watch for him—to let him sleep—but they're away now and will be until your mother and aunt's killer comes to justice."

I brushed away the sudden tear.

"And they will find him, Megge. They will."

I nodded.

"But until they do—well, he said it himself—Alf heard naught though that ram was being skewered." He leaned on his herder's stick. "Alf cannot do this alone."

I drew a breath. "But I can—"

"Nor can you, Megge." He watched me for a moment. I tried to appear resolute.

He turned to go. "I see you think you're fine here, so I'll leave you. I'll be up the Swallows, then."

He was leaving! He was nearly to the creek when I noticed he had forgotten his basket.

"You left your basket!" I picked it up and ran after him.

When I caught up to him, I took hold of his sleeve. So grateful was I for his presence, so fearful of being left alone again, I could not speak. He waited for me to calm myself, his staff planted in the dust, his great paw tight around it, his empty woolsacks slung over one shoulder.

"You forgot your candles," I said. "Your fish."

"A mistake," he said. "I bought too much to carry back up the Swallows. Keep them."

I read the lie on his face. "You bought this food, these candles, for us."

He turned and started walking again.

"You said we've matters," I called out to his back. "What other matters have we to discuss?"

He lifted his staff toward my rock on the herder's hill. "For one thing, I've seen you out here, perched on that rock in the heat, the rain, the ceaseless wind."

Now it was my lip that jutted. "I'm a herder."

"Even a herder needs shelter, girl."

"We had a hut." The hut Mother had burned in.

"I know you did. Didn't I build it myself?" He nodded toward the slope. "Now you need another. And you need another herder to help you with that flock." His voice rose. "Look at those sheep languishing in that pen, Alf so tired he can barely speak, and you wrestling with things you know naught of."

"I was caring for that ram. We are healers here, Mister Gynneys.

Healers and—"

"Oh, aye . . ." He drew out the word. "Great healers and seers. Once upon a day, your mother and aunt were our healer and seer. Now, your cousin reads the stones. But you just saw for yourself: you're no healer. Not yet, anyway. And are you a seer? Can you see who it was skewered your ram? Because even if you can't, I can."

"I know who did it." My voice was ragged. "I know it was Tinker."

"And you didn't come for me. Can you not see what more's to come?"

Tears brimmed and then rolled down my cheeks.

"Look at you. Why, the first time I laid eyes on you, you were twice the woman you are now. Naught but a child that day, you took up the shears as well as the goddess you reminded me of. But can't you see? It's been nearly a fortnight since your aunt Claris passed. You've been on your own, you two girls. Tending a farm, tending the sheep, with not a soul tending you."

"Lowenna—"

"Aye. And thank God for her." He wiped my cheek with a thick, rough finger. "But you've smudges beneath your eyes. You cry if I look at you. Have ye slept?"

I shook my head.

He waited a moment and then turned to leave. "Aye, there's work to be done here, but I see you've too much pride to ask for my help."

"Pride? It isn't pride, Mister Gynneys." I looked into his eyes and waved my arm over the hill, my rock, the pen with its rails in need of repair, and the sheep—all those sheep to tend and feed and guard and shear—and my voice cracked. "There is so much. So much to be done. The cottage and the chickens to care for. The sheep to guard. Fleece to spin. Have you seen Brighida's hand?" I held mine up as if it were a claw. "We both need help." Frustration colored my voice, making it sound harsh. I softened it. "I never dared ask you. It seemed too much to ask. I didn't know how." I looked down at that clawed hand. "Nor would Brighida ever have asked."

Wilted now, I said, "I think I'm tired. Until now I didn't know how very tired I was. But it wasn't for pride I didn't ask, Mister Gynneys."

"There's our Megge." He tousled my hair.

"Will you stay?"

"Aye, and I was wrong to make you ask. I only meant to rile your Cornish enough to bring you back to us. Go on to your pallet." He chuckled. "Alf's had a good night's sleep. We'll see to your sheep. And we'll get word to Martyn and Hugh that young Mister Penneck's about."

"But I'm meant to go to the priory today. To the infirmary. Brother James is going to teach me—" I looked at him dully as sleep threatened to overtake me.

Alf came out of the barn brushing straw from his tunic and dirt from his knees.

"Take our Megge to your pallet, Alf. She won't make it to her own." Mister Gynneys took me gruffly by the arm and led me over to my friend. Alf walked me into the cool, dark barn. Seeing that pallet atop the pile of straw nudged the sleep within me. It rose from my chest, stilling the clamoring voices within me, and took me under.

CHAPTER 18

"Megge." Brighida shook my shoulder. "Wake up. You've slept the day away." As I struggled to wake, she plucked straw from my clothes and hair. "There is a full moon tonight, and I've spent the afternoon readying the grove. I meant to prepare you for tonight's healing, but Mister Gynneys told me you needed your rest."

I had slept the day away? I looked outside. Nearly dark. "The infirmary—"

As I sat up, she held out a small jug and a cloth-wrapped bundle. "Eat quickly while I explain what's to happen tonight."

I took a long drink of ale and unwrapped thick slices of bread and cheese.

"Women will come to us for all manner of healing. No doubt, they will have been told what happened to my mother. They will come to see me, but they will not expect to see you. So, for now, watch and learn. In time, as we study the books and as you spend time with women in the grove, you will begin to catch glimmers of their lives. The sight will come to you."

"But—"

Before I could protest, she helped me to my feet and brushed crumbs from my cloak. "They're arriving now. It's time."

I took a long swallow from the jug, set it on the ground beside Alf's pallet, and followed Brighida out of the barn.

The light from a dozen swinging lanterns drew a line from the foot of Bury Down hill to a point just below the summit. Brighida, accustomed to making her way to the grove in the dark, tipped her head toward the herder's slope.

"This way." She pointed to the path leading away from the one the women were taking. We crossed the pasture and started up the slope to my rock, the same path I took every day of my life. Carrying only our walking sticks, we climbed the hill swiftly and reached my rock before the first lantern reached the sentry rowan just outside the grove.

"There they will gather and await my call," Brighida said.

When the first lantern stopped moving, Brighida pointed toward the back side of the herder's hill, just behind my rock, where Mother's healer's hut had once stood. "We will descend the back of the hill and enter the grove from there."

The leafy canopy, though having taken on autumn hues, was still thick enough that the moonlight barely penetrated it. Nevertheless, Brighida strode surefooted through the tall grasses at the back of the hill and led me into the oaks as if she had forgotten why we had stood in this grove only days before.

Night closed over us, the cool, damp air silent but for the chorus of peepers and the calls of night birds. A root snagged my boot, and I stumbled into Brighida. She felt like a sack of rocks.

"Brighida, what are you carrying?"

She lifted a finger to silence me as we entered the clearing at the heart of the grove. As we passed the granite cross that marked Morwen's grave and the fresh dirt that marked Claris's, the full moon cast shifting light and shadows over Brighida's face, as calm and serene tonight as her mother's had always been. Was mine as pinched and tight as my mother's? I touched my lips.

"They'll come to us by way of that path." She raised her arm toward a narrow opening in the grove. "One at a time. You may not know them, as little time as you spend in the village, but I know them all. And soon you too will not only know them, but you will know who is approaching before ever you see them." She smiled. "Stop frowning. Trust me, Cousin."

She pushed back her hood and shook her head. As her unbound hair fell to her waist, golden wisps caught the meager moonlight and lifted in the breeze, turning Brighida into a luminous cloud.

She unfastened her cloak and laid it on the ground, then spread it to reveal the many bulging pockets that covered its inner surface.

From a small one she withdrew a fire kit and lit the kindling already laid in the pit beneath a small kettle that dangled on a chain from a tall metal tripod. Then she lifted a cord that spanned her chest from right shoulder to left hip and produced a leather wineskin. From it she poured fragrant, spiced wine into the kettle. Two pewter cups, shallow chalices gifted to the great seer Gytha by Earl Richard, already sat on one of the logs that encircled the pit.

Next, she drew from a long, wide pocket a folded cloth of dazzling blue, embroidered with bright seeds and shells that shone and glittered in the moonlight. She carried it to a wide, flat stone. Though it held no markings, I knew what lay beneath it. Brighida shook out the cloth and let it fall over Gytha's grave.

The peepers went silent.

While murmuring an incantation, she glided back to her cloak, knelt, and drew a small leather pouch from another of its many pockets. She put it in my hand and from another pocket pulled out six narrow strips of metal so thin they curved in her palm.

"Take care with these." She held them up to the moonlight. "Do not crease them. They are the last of the strips your mother crafted."

She laid them in my palm. So light were they, I could hardly feel them against my skin. I gently closed my thumb over them while Brighida withdrew from that bountiful cloak a slim grey rod roughly the length of my splayed hand from the tip of my thumb to the tip of my little finger. She held it up. The polished stone rod tapered into a pointed tip of silver metal.

Women's voices grew louder outside the grove, some low and confiding, others high and excited. Would their chattering break the spell my cousin was weaving?

"*Scientia nupta sapientia potestas est,*" she murmured, seeming not to notice. "Let us begin."

A woman I had not seen approach stood next to the fire, from which white smoke rose straight up into a cloudless sky.

"Please," Brighida said. "Sit."

She sat on one of the logs and waited. Brighida closed her eyes for a moment, her lips moving over an incantation, and then opened them and turned to her. "Your hood."

She pushed back her hood and turned her face to Brighida.

My cousin breathed deeply as she regarded the woman's countenance. "Those circles beneath your eyes—" She traced crescents beneath her own. "They speak of worry, of anxious nights, days of dread. What is it you would ask of me?"

The woman pulled her gaze from Brighida's, closed her eyes, and dropped her head.

A widow.

The thought surprised me. I did not know this woman. Why had I thought her a widow? I drew nearer. She began to speak in a voice so low I had to strain to hear.

"It's my man. He went north." She raised her head, her expression begging Brighida to understand. "He's not a fighting man, my lady, but a farmer. His father holds land north of the wall. Rich farmland, he's always said, and he's old now. And though my man's now a Cornishman, he's gone to join his family. To help them fight *our* king. He left under cover of night." She covered her face and wept.

Treason, I thought. *Her husband is a traitor.*

"Who else knows of this?" I asked.

She turned to me as I approached and sat beside her. Her thin face was taut, those violet smudges stark against blanched skin.

"No one, lady." She shook her head in small, fast jerks. "Not a soul."

"He has no other family here?"

"They're are all north of the wall."

I shivered and leaned closer to the fire. In its rising smoke I saw lands put to the torch, great flames leaping high in the night sky. I heard men scream as their limbs were severed and watched their blood flow into the scorched ground. I had to look away.

"She's gone white," the widow said to Brighida. "What's happening? What does she see?"

"You've family, here in Cornwall," I began.

She drew away. "Family? No—"

"Sons, Mistress. You've three sons."

She looked fearfully from me to Brighida and then back at me. "Aye. One nearly grown."

"Set them to work on your lands, for your man shan't return." Cold words. Not words of solace. But they rose from my chest and would not be stopped. "More work than they think they can bear. Tilling, planting. A new crop. Your eldest will speak to you of a grain that will grow in days of heat and cold. Dry times and wet. He has spoken of it to his father, who told him nay. But now is his time. Keep him at home. Give him his head. Let him and his brothers sow their father's land. 'Twill hold them here. And the grain will serve you in times of need."

Though I had delivered the words slowly, deliberately, they had come to me in a rush, had filled my chest and throat and pushed until the last had been spoken. I felt as breathless as if I had run up to my rock all in one burst. I had to breathe long and slowly to steady my voice, for there was more.

"Your man fought valiantly for his ancestors' land," I said quietly, seeing the man's face now, grimacing, sweating, mud-smeared, and streaming with blood and tears. "He called your name at the last," I said. "Amareth."

She dropped her head. As she wept, her squat fingers dug at her skin, pulled at her hair.

"Did no one come with you tonight?" Brighida knelt beside her and took the woman's wide, thick hand.

Amareth shook her head.

Brighida helped the stricken woman to her feet, led her to a log on the other side of the fire, and bade her sit while she ladled wine from the kettle and filled a cup. "Drink," she said and held the cup out to the woman, who clasped it in trembling hands. As the widow sipped, Brighida looked across the fire at me. Our gazes met somewhere in the midst of the smoke. She held mine for a very long time and, without looking away, nodded.

Brighida's expression was placid when she returned to me, her eye seeming to see something very far away as she turned and bade me follow.

Holding her pouch in one hand and the metal strips in the other, I followed her back to that glittering blue cloth. She laid her stylus at the center of it, then stood silently for a moment, eyes closed, and lifted her face. Moonlight turned it to stone.

She lifted her arm and opened her hand.

"The pouch," I heard her say though her lips had not moved. Her voice had come to my dreamer's ear just as the voices of the Mentors had the night I took my vows.

I opened the pouch and emptied it into her hand. Half a dozen stones, small and smooth, each etched with a symbol, tumbled into her palm. She ran her thumb over them, turning them over and over in her hand. She pushed one forward and held it over the glowing blue cloth as her lips moved over words not even my dreamer's ear could hear, then flicked it with her thumb.

It bounced, rolled, and came to rest at the edge of the cloth, where it caught the moonlight and glowed white against azure. I squinted. Upon it was a *Y* etched lengthwise.

"This symbol," Brighida's voice whispered into my dreamer's ear, "and its placement near the border of this plane—at its outermost reaches—tells of one from afar. Its tines, reaching like outstretched arms, signal a calling out. A search for one who is away." Her voice in my head paused and then repeated, "A calling out."

She dropped another stone. Small and perfectly round, it rolled halfway to the corner and stopped. I saw no mark upon it. Brighida picked it up and turned it over. Little more than a pebble, it held a symbol no larger than a grain of barley.

"Can you see its mark?" she said. "Revealed, it speaks of union, of a bond. Hidden, it foretells separation. Loss. Death. Ruin." She sat back on her heels. "But without casting a stone or invoking the Mentors, you knew this. You knew that her husband had died. You saw it."

"As if in a dream. My eyes were open and I was awake, yet I saw it. I watched him die."

"A moment in spirit," Brighida said. She picked up her cloth, folded it, and slipped it back into its pocket. "We are done."

"What about the other women?"

"Look around, do you see their lanterns? They fled. No doubt Amareth told them what had happened here." She held out her hand for the metal strips. "We won't be making any images tonight." She returned her stones and fire kit to their pockets, strapped the wine-skin over her torso, and pulled her cloak around her. "You've no need for me to teach you to cast stones. You need no stones. No symbols. You need nothing, nor anyone, at all."

"But I do. I know naught of your arts. Naught of the stones or the images."

"These," she patted the pockets of her cloak, "are but tools. You've the eye. The dreamer's eye. And the ear. As Murga, you captured the essence of spirit and brought it under your power. Power you, Megge, now possess."

Since childhood I had seen with that eye, the dreamer's eye. With it I had watched the world go small and seen in its place what once had been. *But tonight,* I thought, *I saw not what was, but what is: Amareth, a widow. A traitor for a husband. Three sons.*

And I had known, without having been told, what she must now do to protect them and to prepare for the hard times to come. What she must do to fulfill her charge as a mother.

The dreamer's eye, I thought. *May it one day reveal what I must know in order to fulfill mine.*

Brighida bent to the kettle and picked up the ladle. "There's enough left for two."

Not since my sixth natal day, when Morwen had given me a sip of her wine, had my lips touched one of those fine pewter chalices.

Our hands touched as I took the cup.

CHAPTER 19

The ether, silent and still, grew heavy. Grey smoke rose around me until a cloud towered over Brighida just as Colluen the Blacksmith had loomed over the back of a sickly young mother while I, Murga in that life, had wrested from her hand a half-full cup of grain.

A tendril of smoke broke free of that column and teased my ear.

—That life was not the first we shared.

Not the first?

I fought my way back to the living world.

"Take it, Megge." Brighida pressed the cup into my hand. She had neither seen nor heard the unstill spirit.

I took it but simply stared at it while wondering how many lives I had shared with that spirit and what I had to do to ensure that we never shared another.

"Drink," she said. "Then we must go." She bent and cast handfuls of dirt onto the low fire until it went out. "It's been a long day. I'm tired."

I brought the cup to my lips and washed away the taste of smoke.

I followed Brighida out of the grove and down the slope. When we reached the cottage, I was still wide awake. I knew I would not sleep that night and would spend the hours pondering those words.

That life was not the first we shared. Perhaps I could put the night to better use by preparing for the morrow's work with Brother James. I touched Brighida's sleeve.

"Let us sleep in here tonight."

"Here?"

"In the workroom. Martyn's pallet still lies beside the loom, and we've blankets and the hearth to keep us warm."

"But why?"

"I've slept all day, Brighida, and I plan to return to the infirmary on the morrow. Perhaps if I study the books tonight, I'll learn something that will help Brother James. A cure, a skill Mother might have honed. Something other than confession and atonement."

"We heal in the grove," she said again, then touched my sleeve and softened her tone. "But others do not, and their *cures*, as they call them, serve no one. See what you can learn that will help the ill of the village. Perhaps one day you'll indeed be a healer like your mother."

She slipped into the workroom and settled herself on the pallet before the hearth.

The ether was quiet, and I was alone. I filled a bowl with salt, murmured over it, "Be gone, Spirit," and set it outside the door. "I've no time for your riddles."

I took down *The Book of Seasons,* lit one of Claris's green candles, and searched until I found the page that Mother must have consulted while caring for those afflicted with lepra. It showed a man's body covered in sores, his brow thickened, his nose sunken, his fingers whittled to nubs.

I searched *The Book of Time* until I found a drawing of the same man with the same malady. Beneath him was a sketch of a flowering herb.

The next notation in *The Book of Seasons* was a meticulous drawing of that same plant. A woman was picking it in high summer, root and all—at midday, it appeared, for the blazing sun shone directly above her.

Should it be dried? I wondered. *Steeped? Eaten? Should its essence be taken in as a tea? Rubbed into the skin as a salve?* Curious now, I turned to the next page in *The Book of Time*. On it was a series of etchings showing in exacting detail how to prepare the herb for this use.

Not all entries were so beautiful, not all plants so exquisitely drawn. Many entries were simply strings of symbols, some but one. But it was clear that, by some coincidence, the books had grown in tandem, each answering questions posed in the other.

"Coincidence?" Brighida shook her head the next morning when I asked her. "No, Megge. That was Anwen's work. Throughout time, she has moved the books from heir to heir and whispered questions to their dreamer's ear so that their answers—their notations—would make the books fit together like lock and key, and provide the knowledge and wisdom you would one day need to answer your own questions."

I closed the books. "But how am I to learn all that is in these books? Many of the notations are images I can easily understand. Symbols I can decipher. But others are written, and I haven't your skill with letters—"

"You already know what you must do." Turning away, she reached up to the drying rack and pulled down a handful of crisp herbs, then crumbled them into a wide bowl. She cracked an egg with that one hand, its knuckles like knobs, and stirred it into the herbs. How did she ever do all this cooking and spin all that glorious thread with such a hand?

We both needed help. I needed not only Murga's power but also the knowledge and wisdom held in those books. So I needed to be taught how to read them. While Brighida could teach me the meanings of the incantations, she had not the time to sit with me as I learned each letter. And I could not ask her to use that knotted hand to teach me to write when she should be using it to teach an apprentice to spin.

I nearly asked myself how I would ever find a teacher and how Brighida would ever find a pupil. Then I heard Mister Gynneys's words, *Aye, there's work to do, but I see you've too much pride to ask for my help.* And Morwen and Natalje's promise. *Never alone.*

You already know what you must do.

"Send me the teacher," I whispered. "Send Brighida her apprentice."

CHAPTER 20

I was washing our bowls and cups at the well early the next morning when Alf waved as he walked from the pen to the slope. I ran into the cookroom and brought out the loaf I had put aside for him.

"Alf," I called. "I've bread for your midday meal."

"No need," he called back. He trotted across the pasture and came inside. "I've one here." Opening his sack, he took out a loaf with a fine golden crust. "From the friary."

"Friary?"

He sat at the table and accepted a cup of ale and a bowl of gruel. "In the village they call it 'the abbey,' but the Dominican friars— the *Blackfriars*, as they're called—would thank you to call it a friary. Nothing so grand as an abbey would suit the life they've chosen."

"Why, then, have we always called it 'the abbey'?"

"It once was an abbey. Benedictine. But the Benedictines abandoned it long ago when they established the parish with its priory and its infirmary in the village. Some Dominican friars came across it on their way north years ago. Though it was something of a ruin, they used it as a resting place on their way to and from the moors. As time went by, some simply stayed there and taught. It served as a humble home for them and the boys they took in.

"Over the past . . ." he looked to the ceiling, ". . . ten years or so, the young friars moved on until only a few old ones remained there." He took a long drink, then wiped his mouth on his sleeve and started in on his gruel.

"But ever since Gough murdered those friars on the moors a few years back and left the old ones locked in their cells to starve, more young friars than ever before have gone there to live and to help the last of the old men. They're in ceaseless prayer these days for the soul of Friar William, their eldest. He's dying, and they're holding vigil until he passes."

"Not hunting heretics?"

Alf shook his head. "They never have done. They're scholars. Teachers, the lot of them. They've no time for aught else."

"Will they stay?" I thought again of that ancient church with its wild orchards and unmown fields in need of the sickle. "And if they do, how will they live if they fail to tend their orchards and plant crops? What will they eat?"

"Oh, already they tend them. And they've a grindstone now, and ovens, so they bake their own bread, as you can see. They need little more other than their parchment, quills, and ink. They barter their bread and fruit for candles, cloth, peat, and fleece. And those of us they've served will always provide for them."

"'Those of *us* they've served? They've served you?"

"Aye, when my mother died of childbed fever. I'd been born with this—" he pointed to his cleft lip. "And you know what people believe of children born marked."

"Yes, they say it's evil given for evil done. Punishment for the sins of the mother or father." I winced thinking of a poor babe feared and blamed by the villagers for having been born with a flawed lip.

"Aye. My father feared for my life. And even had he not, he had work—shearing, herding, here at Bury Down and on other manors—and had to be away. How could he take care of a newborn babe?" He shrugged. "He left me in the friars' care until I could be of use to him. And they taught me to speak properly. To read." Now he smiled broadly. "Latin. I can read and write in Latin. I also know French and a bit of Greek."

I shook my head. "You're a scholar!"

"Aye, like my father." He gave me that crooked smile. "A learned shepherd."

"And what did the good friars request in return for your care?"

"At first, wool. It's why my father always took his pay in black fleece. As I learned to read and write, they taught me how to teach. I taught some of the younger boys. When I left the friars, they asked only for my word that when the time came, I would do for another as they had done for me."

"And have you, Alf? Have you repaid their good work?"

"Not yet." He shook his head, his eyes not leaving mine until, together, we shifted our gazes to the curtains that hid my books.

"I've seen you stare at your book," he said. "Are there languages you must learn in order to master its teachings?"

Something inside me began to hum.

"Much of it is written in Latin," I said and added hurriedly, "And Brighida knows every language there is. I've heard her practice them. But she's far too busy to teach me."

"I'd be glad to help," he said. "I once promised I would teach. You could help me keep that promise."

"To the friars."

"And to someone else."

I hesitated. "Morwen?"

"I've been thinking about her since last we talked," he lowered his voice, "about my dreams. 'Twas she who told my father to send me to the friars. She, too, who taught the friars how to feed me goat's milk from the finger of a leather glove.

Once, when she visited me at the friary, she said, 'A time will come when you'll be called upon to use the skills you're learning here.'

"I was a boy of six struggling just to sit still, to study, and to ignore the barbs of the other boys." He rubbed his lip. "I didn't even know what the word *skill* meant. 'Twas then she gave me her ring and whispered that I would one day serve another who wore it." He finished his ale and picked up his sack.

As he went out the door, I sat at the table fingering that ring and thinking about my book. Bryluen and Anwen had written Murga's incantations in Latin. Anwen had come from Tintagel, on the north coast, a land of harbors and traders, where many languages were spoken. Clearly, someone had taught her the language of the Romans. But who had taught Bryluen?

Murga, I thought. Murga had taught her.

I had taught her.

So, somewhere inside me lay that language, Latin, waiting to be awakened.

"Alf," I called after him. "Wait!"

CHAPTER 21

A few mornings later, Alf came into the cookroom carrying a stack of vellum sheets covered with writing. No mere scratches, these were true letters written in black ink by a scribe who had added gold and green and red flourishes to both the text and the margins of the page.

"Friar Joseph allowed me to bring these to you. A loan," he said. "But you won't need them for long, for I know you shall prove an apt pupil."

I laughed. Here was Alf, a herder and shearer, now my master at Latin.

"You chuckle, but you've seen my skills with shears, Meg. Now I shall astound you with letters."

I put up a hand. "Meg?"

He shrugged. "'Tis a woman's name, is Meg. Not a girl's. Does it offend you?"

I liked it but simply shrugged. "Call me what you will."

He picked up the page at the top of the sheaf. "We will begin with letters."

I cleared away the bowls and began to wipe the table, but he touched my arm. "Not here." He lifted his chin toward the slope, where the sheep were grazing. As we would do for many days to come, we settled ourselves beside my rock, and Alf taught me Latin letters. In the evenings I would go back to the cookroom, close the door, and find those letters in *The Book of Seasons,* written in the deepest pages in Anwen's sure hand.

It took time to bring order to the letters, but Alf taught me to write them in the dirt with a stick so he could teach me their meanings and help me turn them into words.

One afternoon, as I was studying in the cookroom and about to close my book, I noticed on the lower edge of the cover's inner face seven symbols lightly etched in Anwen's hand.

"Alf," I asked the next day, "what are these symbols?"

"These?" He squinted at them. "They're Greek." He pointed to each and spoke its name. "Alpha. Tao. Rho. Omega. Pi. Omega. Sigma." After a moment, he laughed. "It spells *Atropos.* Isn't that what my father always calls you?"

That evening, after Brighida and I had supped, she went to her spinning wheel and I to my book, where I fixed my eyes on those letters and forced myself to recall and repeat the names of all seven exactly as Alf had spoken them.

. . . Pi. Omega. Sigma. As I spoke that final letter, fatigue overtook me. I closed my eyes and rested my head on my folded hands. Into slumber I tumbled, deeper and deeper into a vast silence.

A rumble broke it.

A man appeared before my dreamer's eye, his feet planted in a thunderhead, his right hand gripping a lightning bolt.

"I gave you dominion over death," he roared. "And therefore over life. But you cast your power—and your charge—into the sea. And yourself into flame."

Fear rolled through me.

"Return now, Daughter, to the cliffs. Reclaim what you once renounced."

Daughter?

My father had been a mason. This man was no craftsman. Though his tunic was plain and he wore no crown, surely this was a king. And he had issued an order.

Return. Reclaim.

I shook myself awake and looked for Brighida. She was still in the workroom but now asleep on the pallet before the hearth. Climbing under the blankets, my back to hers, I fell asleep to that rumbling voice.

Return now, Daughter, to the cliffs.

And in my dreams a rolling sea drove itself into a cove at the foot of a cliff, and I heard that silken voice. *You know them, don't you, Megge? These cliffs of Kernow.*

CHAPTER 22

Now more intent on those seven Greek symbols than on the Latin letters, I studied them closely, squinting at each and comparing the letters Anwen had inscribed on the cover with others scattered throughout the book.

"Tell me, Alf," I said the next afternoon as I studied an inscription on a page in the middle of *The Book of Seasons*. "This fish." I pointed to an elongated circle with two legs sticking out from the right side.

"'Tisn't a fish, Meg; it's alpha, the first letter in the name *Atropos*. You've seen it before."

"It looks like *alpha,* but it has no line dividing it in half."

"It *is* alpha. Alpha has no line through it." He leaned forward and looked carefully at it, then opened the cover, and we both squinted at the first letter in the name *Atropos*.

"You're right, Meg. This alpha looks like someone's divided it in half."

It means something, I thought, *that Anwen drew a line through this letter.*

"What are you?" I asked, gazing steadily at that divided alpha until my vision began to blur. The room went small and silent. I turned my vision inward, and before me stood a queen.

Gowned in white, with gleaming black hair caught up in braids that looped over her shoulders and swirled down her back, she descended a path cut into the rocky face of the cliff I had seen in so many visions. She paused at the mouth of the cave I once had entered with my twin brother, then glided inside and raised her face to the cave's jagged ceiling. A drop of water fell from the tip of a long, white spear. It landed in the center of a puddle of clear water that filled a basin atop a stone pillar that rose from the cave floor nearly to her hip.

She dipped her left hand into that shallow stone bowl and sipped, then smiled and faded into the sea mist as two young men trying to outrun a tempest dashed into the cave. The first, discovering a fissure in the rocks deep inside, slipped into a second chamber. His twin, drawn to that font, tipped his head as if hearing a siren's song, then dipped his hand in the water and sipped.

"Meg!"

I came so suddenly out of the vision that I could feel my pulse pounding behind my eyes. Catching my breath, I looked up.

"You're tired," Alf said from the doorway. "You were asleep just now. It's getting late. I'm going to bring the sheep in."

I wanted to study, but looking into the workroom at the balls of yarn filling the basket beside my loom, I knew I would have to spend the rest of the evening weaving.

The workroom was in shadow, so I lit a candle.

"Thank you, Megge. I was just about to do that." Brighida looked up from her spinning wheel and dropped another ball of yarn into a basket full of balls all the same shade of gray.

I looked at the bags of fleece at her side—white and black, none grey. "How is it that you can make every ball the same shade?"

"How is it that you can weave it into cobwebs?"

Dipping her hand first into the bag of white fleece and then into the bag of black, she commenced to spin a soft yarn the color of fog. Though light as smoke, it was strong, and I used it to weave cloth so fine and soft the wearer could scarcely feel it. Shifts, undergarments, even fine surcoats were fashioned from the cloth Brighida and I made together.

Goddess cloth, some in the village called it.

I thought once more of that black-haired queen. *Or is she a goddess?*

I set the candle on the hearth and took my place at the loom strung entirely with the whitest thread Brighida had ever spun. The length of cloth I was making would one day cover the altar in the church.

"White," Dora had said as she ordered it. "The whitest of whites. And that fine weave only you seem able to create. It's for the altar," she said in a hushed voice.

"Won't the priests object?" I had asked her.

She had waved a hand. "What are they to say? A cloth as fine as this? Who could object?"

"Surely the *priests* will object to 'goddess cloth' adorning their sacred table."

She had laughed. "'Twas Prior Francis himself who coveted a length he saw in my shop. 'It's promised to the steward of Treveley manor,' I had to tell him. And you would think he'd be angered, but he only smiled and asked me to speak to you about making the church an altar cloth."

"It's Brighida's fine thread that makes this cloth what it is."

"Coveted." Dora nodded soberly. "They all covet it in the village. But it's so dear."

"Do you know what it costs Brighida to card the fleece, blend it, and spin it? And all with but one hand?"

Dora had raised her hands. "Oh, aye, Megge. I don't begrudge our dear Brighida her due. How that dear girl does it I'll never know. You know what it is to card wool, but have you ever spun?" She heaved out a sigh. "I have. Even with two good hands, I could never do the work Brighida does with but one."

Recalling Dora's words, I looked at Brighida now as I prepared to throw the shuttle. She had stopped spinning and was rubbing her hand up and down her leg as if trying to massage her knuckles.

"What is it?"

"It's this—this—abundance." She waved her arm toward the sacks of wool waiting be carded and spun, and I noticed the tremor in her hand. "We've a wealth of fine fleece, but too much, I fear, for a one-handed spinner."

As I stared at that hand—scratched and calloused and trembling from fatigue—I caught glimmers of the smooth, pale hands of a young girl. Clever fingers, slender and nimble, separated long strands of something . . . not fleece . . . then plaited them into thin, supple thongs as long as her forearm.

"Brighida," I said. "There's a girl . . ."

Her hand went still. She inclined her head. "What girl?"

Show me, I ordered, and I searched with my dreamer's eye for another glimpse of the girl I felt sure was meant to be an apprentice for Brighida.

But the girl I now saw, a young girl, her face tanned from the sun, had stubby hands as brown as a nut. This was not the same child. Her hair hung in plaits blurred from sleep. Or from neglect.

"I see her," Brighida said. "She's wearing a tunic frayed at the neck and arm holes, ragged at the hem. Too big for her."

"She's barefoot," I said, "and walking the market road alone."

"Not the market road." Brighida shook her head and then rubbed her brow as she searched inside the very vision I was trying to see more clearly.

"A road, yes," she said. "But not the market road. Not *our* market road. Look beyond her to the setting sun."

I looked past the child, the huts she was walking toward, and all the way to the abrupt end of the earth.

"Can you see the cliffs?" Brighida asked.

I nodded.

You know them, don't you, Megge of Bury Down?

Tearing my dreamer's gaze from the horizon, from *these cliffs of Kernow*, I let it fall once more upon the girl. She was pulling pebbles out of a deep pocket at the side of her tunic, all nearly the same shade: the purple-grey hue of a thunderhead. After selecting two the size and shape of a chicken's egg, and a flat one the size of her palm, she held them out to me in a grubby hand, her countenance calm as she stared into my dreamer's eye.

Then, as if something had frightened her, she went suddenly rigid. She turned, breaking our gaze, and ran into a copse just beyond the last hut in a long row of mean dwellings alongside a newly mown field. She disappeared into the shadows.

"Megge." Brighida gripped my arm. "Do you know what you've just done?"

"I didn't do it!" I struggled to emerge from that waking dream. "I only saw the girl—"

"You shared your vision with me." She released my arm but kept her eyes on mine. "Don't you understand? You saw that girl and then you opened your dreamer's eye to mine." She smiled, and then laughed. "You have surpassed me as a seer. Not only did you see, but you brought me into your moment in spirit." Her face went serious. "Not even my mother had that skill."

"You've never shared a vision?"

She shook her head. "What were you doing just before you entered into spirit?"

"I was looking at your hand. You had said you were tired of working, that it was too much for a one-handed spinner." I hated to say this part. "I pitied you."

"And then?" she coaxed.

"And then I saw the hands of a little girl. Not the girl you saw. This one had slender fingers, pale skin—"

"You felt something for me, and the vision came to you." Now she nodded. "To enter the ether, Megge, I must quiet my mind and cast a stone or a rune, or recite a summoning incantation." She stared at me for another moment. "I must *ask* to be shown."

I blinked.

"This happened before, in the grove," she went on. "When Amareth was suffering, a vision came to you of her man dying in battle." She shook her head as if astonished. "Your dreamer's eye, it seems, is always open, always at the ready. And now, you can open that eye so others might see."

"But we know only that we saw a girl walking on a cliffside road," I said. "The sun had not yet set in that vision, but it is nighttime here, so we don't know *when* she walked that road. Was it today? Yesterday? A year ago? And you did not see the other girl."

"Who was she?"

"I don't know, but when I looked at your hands and then at the nimble hands of a young girl, I believed she was the apprentice I've asked the Mentors to send you. But the girl you saw—"

"Wait. You asked the Mentors to send someone to help me?"

"Yes," I said. "An apprentice. But—" I pictured once again the bedraggled child in that tattered dress, who had suddenly gone rigid and fled into the woods like prey.

. . . but the girl we just saw, I thought, *is not meant to help us. We're meant to help her.*

CHAPTER 23

"It's late, Megge." Yawning, Brighida pulled her cloak around her. "Let's go to the lodge. We'll start afresh on the morrow and learn more about these girls."

I shook my head. If there was an apprentice meant for Brighida, she would find her way to us. I had no fear for the pale, slender-fingered girl I first had seen. I did fear, though, for the little girl in the ragged dress who had looked into my dreamer's eye and offered me her stones. I had to know where she was now.

"I'll come later." I lit the candle in the lantern and handed it to her. When she had gone, I closed the door, turned to the shelf, and reached for the curtain. Then I recalled her words and stopped. I needed no symbols, no incantations.

Show me.

The air in the cookroom seemed to go cool and moist. It filled with the sound of peepers and bullfrogs, the songs of night birds, the screeches of owls. I tasted forest loam at the back of my throat as I watched the little girl pass between two oaks. When she had come upon a thick, mossy log, she sat and pulled a knife from her tunic pocket. She cut a long, slender branch off a tender sapling and whittled the tip to a point.

Why, she can't be more than six or seven years old, I thought.

Stick in hand, she looked up and sniffed the air. Still sniffing, she moved toward an oak, brushed a hand back and forth over its roots to clear away the leaves and acorns, then dug in the ground with the stick. She ran her fingers through the loose soil, pocketed dirt-encrusted lumps, and carried them back to the log.

As she brushed off a truffle, I felt the dirt against my own fingertips. As she brought the truffle to her nose and breathed deeply, I smelled the musty scent of root, of rotted leaves. As she swallowed it whole, I felt it move down my throat so fast I hardly tasted it. Hungrier now than I had ever been, I felt desperate need clawing at my chest. I felt my fingers grip the rough bark of the oak log and my nails scratch at it as I struggled not to cry out, "Feed me."

Exhausted from that vision, I willed myself back to the cookroom, sat, and leaned hard on the tabletop, one hand cradling my head as the other stroked the seat of my chair. Smooth, it was no longer the rough, moist bark of a long dead log.

I stared unseeing at the wall as pity clutched at me for the hungry child, alone and cold, willing herself not to speak.

I went to the hearth and stirred the embers. Though I held my hands over the heat, I shivered as the damp air that had chilled that little girl once more seemed to envelop me. Cool, fragrant air I had only ever felt in the grove—

The grove!

I stood very still, not daring to move a finger or take a breath for fear any disturbance to the air—or the ether—might be carried on the wind to the grove and frighten the child hunkered on that log.

The cottage door creaked. Brighida looked inside.

"Megge, are you going to sleep in here?"

I waved my hand in front of my lips and shook my head.

"Be still," I whispered as I went to her. "She's in the grove."

She looked at me and frowned. "Who?"

"The girl. We're going to her."

"But it's dark."

"When has the dark ever troubled you?"

I covered myself with my cloak and took Morwen's from its peg. The child would be cold.

"Quiet now," I whispered as I eased open the door. "She'll be frightened. She's alone and hungry. She's suffering." As I spoke, I saw the little girl huddled on that log, her knees drawn up to her chest, her bare arms clasping her legs. She let her head drop so her face rested on her knees.

Brighida lifted the lantern, and we began the long climb to the grove. Before long, she was well ahead of me and all I saw were her back and her lantern's light.

I felt the sting of the wind that was blowing down the back of the child's neck and saw five bright stars hanging over the oak canopy above her.

She's there, Brighida, I called to her dreamer's ear. *Beneath Cassiopeia. See her!*

I cast the vision to Brighida as she passed the sentry rowan and slipped into the grove.

I waited.

A shriek as high and loud as a screech owl's broke the silence followed by the crack of brush and the pounding of running feet.

"She has a knife!" Brighida shouted.

Through the bushes at the edge of the grove came the child in the tattered, sleeveless tunic. I watched in dismay as she hurtled toward me. Realizing she was not going to stop, I opened Morwen's cloak, shook it out, and held it up before me.

Chest heaving, breath whistling, her speed never slackening, the child hurled herself into the cloak. The force knocked me to the ground. Only then, as she lay in the grass beside me, did she begin to cry in earnest. I wrapped the cloak around her. As I drew her to me, I felt her grab at the edges to cover herself.

Sitting in the damp grass with the panting child lying against me, all her weight pressed into me as if to draw the warmth of my body into hers, I wrapped my arms around her and pulled my cloak taut so it covered us both.

She smelled of moss, roots, dirt, and sweat. Her hair tickled my nose, and I felt a sneeze coming on. My breath came hard as I tried to hold it back, afraid of startling her. She huddled hard against me and pulled that cloak as tightly as she could around herself. After a long moment, she stopped trembling.

I squeezed her gently and whispered, "I'm going to sneeze."

As quietly and gently as I could, I let it come. Three more followed. I wiped my nose on my shoulder, relieved that the child hadn't cried or tried to run. Indeed, she had gone soft in my arms, her breathing slow and even. Soon, her head fell forward.

Why, she's sleeping. She's fallen asleep. What miracle is this?

As if I had caused the sun itself to rise over Bury Down, I felt pride and accomplishment mingle within me. My chest seemed to expand to accommodate some new fullness. I wanted to laugh and weep but did neither. Instead, I sat in silence on the grass and held the sleeping child who had crashed into my life like a wild boar.

When I looked up, Brighida was standing over me holding up the crude little knife the child had used to whittle her stick. She twitched her head toward it, then smiled gently and set the lantern on the ground beside me. She pointed toward the cottage and held up her hand to bid me stay.

"It's nearly dawn," she whispered.

Something about her had frightened the child senseless, so she was leaving her to me. I slid the lantern behind me so its light would not awaken her.

Brighida took off her own cloak and wrapped it around the two of us sitting as one on the herder's hill. The rising wind whistled through the grove as the child, now heavy with sleep, lay pressed against me. Her cheek, smudged with loam, was all I could see against the dark brown wool of Morwen's well-worn cloak.

I touched that cheek to brush away the dirt and felt a fine, raised line. A scar? So near her eye?

With my forefinger I stroked it. Yes, that was a scar. Perfectly straight and so thin I could barely feel it, it crossed the apple of her cheek from the center of her left eye to its outer corner. I looked closely. Three short lines, evenly spaced, dropped from the first. What injury could have caused such a mark?

I closed my eyes to think, but no answer came to me, so I bowed my head over the girl, pulled Brighida's cloak more tightly around us, and slept.

CHAPTER 24

I awoke to a red sky, crimson slashes over Bury Down, and a fist prodding my chest. The child was pushing away from me and grappling with the tangle of cloaks enveloping us. When she had freed herself, she struggled to her feet and stood, feet apart, eyes darting over the slope.

I got up and began to pick up the cloaks while she ran from one side of the hill to the other, craning her neck to look to the summit, the grove, and my rock, where Alf soon would sit guarding the sheep.

The smoke drifting up from the chimney must have caught her eye, for she fell very still as she regarded the cottage. The top half of the door was open, the cookroom dim.

She turned her head slowly and chewed on the inside of her lower lip as her gaze drifted from my boots to my tunic and then to my neck, where it came to rest. I touched the base of my throat. *My stone.*

She stared at the silver lump Mother had painstakingly made and bade me wear always. *To bring you courage.*

She reached down the frayed neck of her tunic and pulled from beneath it a long, thin cord made from braided threads. Hanging from it, tightly wrapped in those same threads, was a rough lump of dull grey stone.

"My mother gave me this." I touched mine. "Did someone give you yours?"

Without taking her eyes off my stone, she brought hers to her lips, kissed it, and dropped it back inside her tunic.

I held out a hand.

Her gaze rose, and I saw that her eyes matched her hair. Brown, with glints of gold. Her small face, full at the cheekbones but pointed at the chin, with a blunt nose scattered with freckles, might have been mine at her age. Short and sturdy, she came to me and took my hand.

A clatter rose from across the pasture as Alf let the sheep out of the pen and crossed the fields alongside them, the two buckets he carried in one hand rattling against each other. He brought his other hand to his face, put his thumb and little finger into the corners of his mouth, and whistled. Then he swept his arm down to his side, motioning the sheep to keep moving.

As she watched him, the child put her fingers to her mouth, as Alf had done, and blew. Only breath and spittle emerged.

The flock moved slowly toward the foot of the hill, bleating and coughing, with Alf now behind them, whistling, clanking, and waving them forward. The girl's face broke into a smile. She looked up at me, surprised and delighted, and the scar on her cheek curved so the three downward strokes looked like eyelashes.

"That's Alf," I said.

I looked once more at the cottage door. It was light inside now, and Brighida was stirring the kettle, her hair tucked up under a cap.

"My cousin's made the morning meal. Shall we eat?"

She nodded, her eyes still on Alf. But as she walked alongside me, her gaze roamed over the field, the pasture, and the sheep, finally settling on the rooster, the hens, and the chicks pecking grain outside the cottage door. She squatted in the dirt and watched them at their work, scratching, preening, and plucking grubs from the garden.

As a hen walked past her pecking the ground, she reached out and touched it lightly with one finger.

Brighida stood at the door, spoon in hand, and watched. On her face was an expression I had not seen since before Claris died.

She's pleased, I thought. *Happy.*

A passing cloud cast the girl, the birds, and the cottage into shadow. The sky quickly filled with the thunderheads which the crimson dawn had portended. The chickens hopped up their ramp and into their roost just as the first heavy drops hit the ground.

Brighida flung open the lower half of the door. "Quickly! Before it soaks you!"

Laughing, she motioned us inside with a sweep of her spoon. The child, though, seemed rooted in place. I reached down and gently touched her back. "Come along, we're getting wet!"

She did not get up, so I opened the cloak and shook it out, then flung it over my head and knelt beside her so it covered us both.

"Come!" The door was maddeningly close, but the child would not move. I could have picked her up but did not want to frighten her.

Lightning whitened the sky. A clap of thunder shook the earth. The girl trembled but stayed hunkered at my side. I moved closer to her, much as I would to a frightened lamb, then lifted the corner of the cloak and looked out. Alf was moving the flock back to the pen, where he would wait out the storm.

The driving rain leaked through the cloak and ran down my face. Under that cloak the air grew warm, and the fragrance of hyacinth mingled with the smell of sweat, dirty clothes, and unwashed child. She raised her head and sniffed the cloak. Squatting on her haunches, face lifted, eyes closed, sniffing, she resembled a wild thing trying to determine if the scent she had just caught was that of a predator.

I kept my voice low. "It's a flower you smell. Brighida's fragrance. And Claris's."

She sat very still.

"Claris was Brighida's mother," I went on. "My aunt. She was good to me. And Brighida is every bit as kind as she was."

The sound of feet splashing through puddles came from across the pasture. She cocked her head. I lifted the cloak just high enough for both of us to see Alf running toward us, hurried but not panicked, smiling that odd, crooked smile. I looked down quickly to see if his disfigured mouth had frightened the girl. I was stunned to see her smiling up at him as if she somehow knew him, her soft brown eyes now dancing with merriment.

She got to her feet as Alf neared and followed him into the cottage without a backward glance.

Brighida handed Alf a length of cloth I had finished weaving only days before. He wiped his face and hair with it, then handed it to the child who, still watching him, still smiling, dried her own face. She rubbed the cloth over her wet, dirty hair, then held it out to me and sat at the table beside Alf.

I knew only one other person who had been so taken with him, and this child could not have been more like her.

"Brighida," I whispered as she passed me on her way to the hearth, "I believe this little girl may be Morwen."

CHAPTER 25

"It's not her," Brighida insisted in the lodge the next morning, her voice quiet but her tone urgent. "She's not Morwen. She can't be."

"She can be. She is," I hissed. Bending over to smooth soft hides and warm blankets over the small pallet I had placed between mine and Brighida's, I stole a glance at the child playing quietly in the doorway with the purple stones I had found in her pocket. Though she had been with us for an entire day, she still had not said a word.

Brighida went to her and knelt beside her. "What shall we call you, little one?" She tilted her head and smiled; but the child, somber in Brighida's presence, put down the stones she had been piling in the dirt and got up. As she walked away, Brighida simply watched.

"Let's go to the sheep," I said holding out my hand. "Then we'll go to the springhouse and get some cheese to break our fast."

Her face brightened and she ran to me, the hem of the tunic we had hastily made for her brushing her short brown legs.

Over the child's head, I mouthed to Brighida, "I believe she is."

Holding her hand, I led her to the pen, just as Morwen had led me when I was not much older than this little one. She looked every bit like I imagined Morwen might have appeared as a child. And she seemed to know Alf the moment she laid eyes on him. Each time he approached, she ran to him.

Who else could she be?

As if to bear me out, she let go of my hand the moment Alf stepped out of the pen and ran to him and took his.

He smiled at me and raised his other hand as if to say, "I don't understand this either." He bent down and said something that made her run into the barn ahead of him, then waited until I had reached him and walked slowly with me toward the sheep.

"Ask her her name," I said.

Still watching her, he nodded and then followed her into the barn.

That she could be so fearful of Brighida yet embrace this man with the snarling lip, who smelled of hay and animals and manure, mystified me; yet there she was, bringing him a bucket she had filled with straw. And there was Alf, thanking her solemnly, taking out the straw, making a neat pile of it, and carrying the bucket back to the spring to be filled.

Like brother and sister, I thought.

And hadn't Morwen loved Alf? Hadn't she prophesied that he would one day serve me? Hadn't she herself seen to it that he would learn Latin and Greek from the Blackfriars so he could teach me?

I closed my eyes for a moment, hardly able to bear the sweetness of seeing the two of them together again.

Morwen. Even my thoughts were soft this morning.

"'Tisn't I." Morwen's voice was soft with pity. "It's in the ether you'll find me. Though, were I once more in the living world, my spirit would be ever attuned to yours. You'd need only summon me, and I would come to you."

Tears stung my eyes.

"You want what you once had, child. You're lonely. You miss me, though I'm ever with you."

"Who, then, is she?" My own voice startled me. No longer in the ether, speaking in silence with Morwen, I was speaking aloud, seemingly to no one, and those gold-flecked brown eyes were look-ing at me warily from across the pen.

I went to her and held out a hand. She took it, and we walked to the shearing stall.

"Let's sit here," I said hoping she would take comfort in the small space, the smell of hay and straw and fleece, the tools hanging neatly from nails hammered into the beams.

"Who are you, child? What do they call you?"

Still standing, she kicked the dirt.

"Alf," I called.

He straightened and looked at me. "Yes, Meg."

I pointed to him. "You see? He's called *Alf*." I laid my hand on my chest. "And I'm called *Megge*. What do they call you?"

She dug her toe into the dirt. Though Brighida and I had fash-ioned a pair of slippers for her, she would not wear them.

I leaned closer and took her hands. "Who is your mother?"

She looked around quickly, as if searching for her, and began to cry.

"Hush now." I pulled her to me and held her tight. "Are you hun-gry, little one?" I brushed wisps of hair back from her brow.

She nodded.

"Alf," I called. "Have you need of us?"

He shook his head and dumped a fresh bucket of water into the trough.

I took the child's hand. "We'll go help Brighida with the soup. And maybe you can tell me about your mother. And, perhaps, your sisters and—"

She screamed and pulled her hand from mine. Stunned, I look to Alf. He shrugged and shook his head.

I knelt before her and looked into her enormous, frightened eyes.

"What is it?" I wiped tears from her face.

She looked away.

What had I said? *Mother* and *sisters*. But I had said *mother* before and she hadn't screamed. "Is it . . . that word?" I whispered, "*Sisters?*"

She recoiled as if I had struck her.

I held up my hands. "I won't say it again. I won't ever say it again."

I gathered her to me, and she allowed me to hold her close. Her nose was running now, and I felt her wipe it on my shoulder. Laughter bubbled up as I remembered wiping my own nose on my sleeve, and my mother, aunt, and cousin all shouting, "Megge!"

I got to my feet and picked her up.

"Let's go get something good." Hefting her higher on my hip, I remembered what I had promised her earlier. "There's cheese in the springhouse. Let's go have some."

She squirmed out of my arms and walked beside me. As we passed Alf, she took his hand and pulled him along too.

"Fine," he said. "We'll have cheese. And I shall call you Amice, for I know we shall be friends."

CHAPTER 26

mice." I pronounced it as he had: *AM-miss.*

"The Latin word is pronounced *Am-ee-chay*," Alf said, "but let's just say *Am-miss.*"

Amice, I said to myself as I watched her put a small piece of cheese in her mouth. As she chewed, she took Alf's hand. I walked behind them to the cottage, thinking as I glanced at the sheep milling about in the pen that this would be the first time I had seen Alf walk away from the pen on a sunny day instead of trotting toward it to release the flock to graze.

"What brought you to Bury Down, Amice?" he asked.

When she did not reply, he tipped his head as if to show her he was listening. She ran to me and slapped my leg.

"It was Megge, you say?"

She pointed up the hill, to the grove.

"It was Megge and Bury Down grove you came to see?"

She nodded, still chewing, her eyes tight on his.

He looked at me and raised his eyebrows as if asking a question.

I nodded. "That's where we found her. In the grove. I had . . . seen her . . . walking along a road. But not our market road. A coastal road. Beyond it was a vast sea, with the sun setting on the horizon.

And then . . ." I shrugged, not knowing what had happened next. "We found her alone in the grove."

"How did you find this place?" Alf knelt beside her. "It's so far from your home."

She closed her eyes and with her fingertips rubbed circles in the space between her eyebrows.

"She must be tired," I said and took her hand. "Come, Amice. There's soup for us in the cookroom."

Brighida laid bowls on the table before each of us. Amice, no longer drawing away from her, ate heartily. I touched Brighida's elbow and motioned with my head toward the door.

When we had reached the roost, I spoke quickly. "Don't use the word *sister* in her hearing."

Brighida held up her hand. "Don't say *sister*? Whyever not?"

"It makes her cry. Now let me finish. Alf calls her Amice. He says it's pronounced *Am-ee-chay* in Latin, but we shall call her *Am-miss*."

"Amice." She smiled. "*Friend.*"

"He asked her why she came here."

"And she spoke?"

I shook my head. "Still too frightened, I suppose. She still answers with nods or by pointing her finger or shaking her head. But when Alf asked her why she had come here, she ran to me and slapped my leg, then pointed to the grove."

"She sought you out and somehow found our grove? How could she have found us?"

"I don't know."

"And she cries when she hears the word *sister*?"

I nodded. "Screams. It terrifies her."

"She's from the cliffs," Brighida mused, her eyes going narrow and looking far beyond me. "I had thought the Sisterhood a thing of the past . . ."

"Sisterhood?"

Without another word, Brighida went back into the cottage and took down her book. She laid it on the table and began to turn the pages. Her forefinger slid halfway down a page and stopped on a symbol. A straight line with three short lines dropping from it. She touched her left cheek. "She bears their mark."

"That scar." I fingered my own cheek.

She closed her book. "The Lady of the Cliffs, as they called her, had a mark beneath her left eye. Her novices marked their own cheeks in the same place." She looked at me, and I knew my face revealed my confusion. I hated to have to ask what that word, *novices*, meant.

"Novices are pupils, Megge. The lady's novices were young girls who learned from her and served her. She was said to have been kind and compassionate, a true healer. She died young. And so long ago, only the bards still speak of her. And the seers," she added, as if speaking to herself. "And the women of the cliffs."

A healer surrounded by pupils. I thought of Brother James and his acolytes. "This *lady* sounds like a priestess."

She shook her head. "She was a goddess."

"A goddess?"

Her laugh was refreshing to hear. "Do you not know what a *goddess* is?"

"Of course I do. I know about Atropos, the goddess who clipped the string of life. Mister Gynneys often calls me Atropos."

"Yes. But did you know that though she was charged with ending lives, she renounced that duty?"

Something tingled at the nape of my neck.

"She assumed the form of a mortal woman and fled her home, her sisters, and her unforgiving father by escaping on a trading ship bound for the West. When it landed in Kernow, she slipped away and made her home in a secluded cove along the rugged northern cliffs, curing the sick and teaching others the healer's arts. She came to be called the Lady of the Cliffs, and mothers sent their young daughters to live with her and learn from her."

"Like apprentices."

"Yes, like apprentices. But these were novices, for this was their calling, the one thing they would do in this life. The lady called them *Sisters*."

"So, the goddess Atropos," I said, "who was known for 'clipping the string of life,' chose to save lives rather than take them?"

"Yes. But the killing side of her gave her no rest. It gnawed at her. It never let her forget that she was not mortal but a goddess and that she had another charge to carry out. With no choice, and unwilling to take another life, she ended that mortal life, vowing as she left the living world to return with but one charge, the only charge she could bear. To heal."

"And did she?" I finally asked.

She shrugged and shook her head slowly. "No one knows. No one ever saw her again. But for a very long time, priestesses and conjurors performed a yearly rite that mimicked the goddess's death in the hope of bringing her back to the living world."

"A rite?" I felt myself wince.

"In it, a woman—a priestess—would take the life of the eldest of six Sisters—all virgins—on the same day of the year and in the same way that the goddess took her own. If the goddess did not return to the living world in the priestess's body, then a new girl—a very young girl—would be taken into the Sisterhood and given the goddess's mark. For the next five years, she would watch the other Sisters play their part. And when her time came, she would play hers. It's how the Sisterhood stayed alive. Always taking in new girls."

She had mentioned *ancient rites* the night her mother was killed, as she tried to comprehend why Michael Gough, a blacksmith, would have wanted her mother's blood.

"Brighida." I touched her shoulder. "Do all ancient rites call for blood?"

"Not all, but some do."

"Did the rites these priestesses carried out have to do with blood?"

She nodded.

I recalled what Martyn had once said about the north coast, where Michael Gough was thought to be hiding. *It's a mysterious place, the north coast. Those women. Those rites.*

"The one who sacrificed the eldest Sister," I said slowly, thinking of Michael Gough and considering now a terrible scenario, "was it always a woman?"

CHAPTER 27

Brighida did not reply, but her troubled expression told me she had heard my question and simply had no answer.

She bears their mark.

Trying not to imagine the unthinkable, but unable to expunge it from my mind's eye, I went to the door. "I've work to do."

It was time to learn who Amice was and why she had come. It was too late now to leave for the village, where someone might know of her family or might have heard of a child gone missing, so I walked out to the barn to select the fleece I would take to market the next morning.

Alf was in the pen changing the dressing on a lamb's back leg.

Suddenly wary, I asked, "What happened?"

"It wasn't Tinker," he said quickly. "She was in a rush to get into the pen last night. Tried to climb in between the lowest fence rails and scratched her hock on a nail." He dropped the soiled dressing and reached for his bag.

"Do you need the salve?"

He nodded. "I should have taken it out before I started."

I knelt and searched through the bag beside him for the small pot of Brighida's salve. Handing it to him, I asked, "I'm going to the village on the morrow. Have we fleece I can take to Tucker?"

He sat up straighter and looked into the shearing stall.

"A little. It's been so warm, and some of the ewes had such thick fleece, I had to do some shearing yesterday." He jerked his thumb toward a pile of fleece in the shearing stall.

"I've heard from Lowenna," he said. "She expects Hugh back any day now, perhaps with Martyn. They can carry to market whatever fleece you want to sell."

I had heard that before. That Martyn was coming home. Each time, I had been disappointed. I shook my head. "I've got to go into the village and ask about Amice. I can't wait for Martyn to come home." It felt as if a hammer had struck my chest with each word.

I took a rolled bandage from Alf's bag and handed it to him, then began to pick up handfuls of white fleece. When I had stuffed two small sacks to overflowing, I set a heavy stone on top of each to pack the wool more tightly.

"I'll come for these tomorrow and take them to Tucker. He was happy with the last batch of white and offered a good price for more of the same."

"Alone?" Brighida asked when I told her I would be going to the village the next morning. The fear on her face told me that she was not worried about my carrying heavy sacks.

"I'll be fine." I glanced toward Amice. "And you've got the little one to look after."

Brighida's eyes followed my gaze and nodded. "But the woods—"

She had not yet walked through the copse since that night. Whether she feared she would meet Michael Gough there or was simply unable to look upon the spot where he had killed her mother, I could not know. Rather than remind her that this would not be the first time I had taken that path, I squatted next to Amice.

She sat in a nest of fresh river rushes stripping fine hairs from a long, narrow plant and laying each strand flat on a space she had cleared on the floor. Her brow was furrowed and her lips pursed in concentration.

Brighida whispered, "She's been at it since midday."

It was nearly dark outside.

While watching her separate a vein from a frond without breaking it, I absently fingered the stone at my throat. My eye then went to the stone at hers. Leaning closer, I saw that both the cord and the threads wrapped around the stone looked as if they'd been made from fibers as long and fine as the veins she was separating.

Her painstaking work brought to mind the vision I had had just before I had seen her walking along that cliffside road. It was another girl's clever fingers I had seen separating and plaiting strands like these, but I had little doubt that both girls were doing the same work.

Rushes like these become brittle, I thought, *and would not serve to make thread. But the supple fibers of another plant would.*

"Could it be that Amice's mother and the women—and girls—in her family spin flax?"

Brighida got up from the table and went to the basket outside the cookroom door, where Amice's old tunic was bundled. She picked up the dirty, ragged cloth and examined it closely while rubbing it between her fingers.

"Linen?" She closed her eyes. "This may be linen. It's not wool. But it feels so different."

"Does flax grow on the coast?"

Brighida shrugged. "It grows on the moors, but I don't know where else."

"Gus Tucker sells it," I said. "He'll know where this cloth comes from."

"It's filthy." Brighida brushed dirt off the tunic. "But look at this." She held it up. "When you brush away the dirt, you can see the fine weave, the tough threads. Why, this was once a fine garment." She held up a frayed arm hole. "Or was meant to become one."

I took it out to the well and washed it in a bucket until the water went brown. When I had wrung it out and held it up, I saw a tightly woven garment made of strong, light-green threads.

"It's too big for Amice," I said.

Brighida took it from me. "A castoff, perhaps, from a bigger girl?"

"Or a garment not yet finished but worn regardless."

"Let it dry by the hearth and take it to Tucker tomorrow. He'll know who spins that sort of thread and who might have woven the cloth. At the very least, he may be able to tell you where it came from."

CHAPTER 28

"You say you think it's flax?" Mister Tucker brought Amice's tunic to his nose and sniffed. He shook his head. "Some weavers treat their flax with lye. New cloth can hold the scent." He brought it to his face again and breathed deeply. "This doesn't carry it, though." He handed it back to me.

I dumped my fleece onto the scales and stuffed the tunic into an empty woolsack.

"Where did it come from?" As he talked, he weighed and then bundled the fleece into one big sack. He wrote something in his ledger and slid some coins across the counter. I pocketed them.

"A child was wearing it. A stranger. Brighida and I are searching for her mother. We believe the girl is from a village on the north coast. Tintagel? Aldestowe, perhaps?"

Gus looked up. "Aldestowe, you say?" He held out his hand. "Let me see that again."

I took the tunic out of my sack and handed it over. He held it up to the light and passed it from right to left as if reading it. Then he laid it on the counter and hurried to a stack of cloth and lifted several lengths to the light. He studied each one, reading the weave and then bringing it to his nose and inhaling deeply.

"A woman brought these in only yesterday," he said. "I was busy. I hadn't time to look at them closely. I assumed they were linen, but Dora said otherwise." He looked around for his wife.

"Dora!" he shouted. "Megge's brought us something!" He held up the tunic.

"Megge!" Dora, who had been folding lace at the back of the stall, straightened, her fist going to a hip still lame after having been gored by a boar years earlier. She lumbered toward us, took the tunic from Gus, and held it up. "So unusual. The weave, the threads. Why, it looks something like the cloth we wove when I was a girl."

She picked up a length of light-green cloth from the stack Gus had shown me, then held the tunic next to it and, as Gus had done, breathed deeply, first of the new cloth and then of the tunic.

"It's had some wear, hasn't it?" She looked at it more closely, sniffed it again.

"But though it's unfinished and hasn't been gently used, it's rarely been washed. It still carries the scent of the sea." She looked at me now. "It's not linen. It's nettle cloth."

"Nettle?"

"Oh, aye. Once you get the leaves off, nettle is something like a reed, but not like Fowey River reeds. Nettles are long, slender plants that grow even taller than Hugh and carry the merest hairs that will burn you like fire. Ask Brighida. She'll know all about stinging nettle, even if not how to weave it."

She sniffed the garment again and then the green fabric. "We used sea water to rot it. Oh, you'd not detect the scent if you'd not grown up on the cliffs splitting that retted nettle stalk, carding it, spinning it, and weaving it like I did until the day Gus took me away from the coast and brought me here. But I'm a woman of the cliffs, after all. I carry the sea water in my blood to this day. I know it when I smell it."

A woman of the cliffs.

Before I could ask if she knew about the Sisterhood or the Lady of the Cliffs, she said, "I didn't know the lass who came with the woman who brought this cloth, but didn't she call to mind Brighida as a girl."

"Did the woman tell you her name?"

"It was unusual," Gus said. He ran a finger down the left-hand column of his ledger, then stopped. "Kaatje." He closed his ledger.

"And the girl was called—" Dora began, but Mister Tucker interrupted.

"Bretl? Brett?"

"Britlen." Dora looked up, her expression dreamy. "So pretty. Do you know the lass?"

I shook my head.

Dora set down the green cloth and handed me Amice's tunic, then took my hand and led me outside the stall.

"The woman—" Holding up a finger, she glanced back into the stall at Gus, who was already dumping the next customer's bag of fleece on the scales. "Oh, she was a lovely thing. Tall, slender as a reed, with hair the color of honey. Deep amber, nearly red." She swept her pudgy hands up her neck and over her head. "Covered with a wisp of a veil. A lovely, long neck she had. And the bluest eyes."

"You studied her."

"Aye. And who wouldn't? Who didn't? We women all had a good long talk about her—about the two of them—after they'd gone."

"Who else saw her?"

Dora pointed to the stall next to hers. "Nellie Trelawney, for one." She looked around the market. "The others are gone now. Must be at the ovens. But you can ask Nellie. She talked to the woman. I didn't."

CHAPTER 29

"Not that one, Nellie. The big one beneath it, if you please."
A woman in the next market stall was calling out directions and pointing to a stack of pots when I came in.

Nellie stooped to put back a small pot and select a bigger one. She rose with it and was turning to show it to the woman when her eye fell upon me.

"Megge!"

As she handed the pot to the woman, I tried to inspect her hands and arms without her noticing. I saw only the scar from the cut Brother James had made. The stitches he had placed were gone, but the skin was still red. *Healing slowly*, I thought.

I wanted to ask her about that lump but feared she would have told me how much she wished my mother were still caring for her, and I didn't believe I could bear to hear that.

"You look in the peak of health, Nellie."

She laughed and patted her belly. "And so I am." She leaned toward me and lowered her voice. "I believe I'm with child again." She lifted her chin toward the little boy asleep on a pile of woven rush mats and then down at her daughter, asleep in a cradle at her feet. "It seems your mother and aunt truly knew how to cure a barren woman."

"Aye, they did."

"If only . . ." she heaved out the word.

Please do not plead, I thought. *Please—*

"If only I had a midwife to attend the birth." She looked at me, her expression earnest, hopeful. "You were at the infirmary with Brother James. Are you truly learning the healer's craft?"

Before I could answer, her words began to tumble out like grain from a barrel. "He's not a midwife. We have none. Will you be with me when it's my time? Is that what you've come to tell me? That you've assumed your mother's mantle?" Her voice had gone high and now went even higher. "There are others about who call themselves midwives." She grimaced. "But they do more harm than good."

And there it was again. That warring within me. Mother's wistful voice always at my ear. *If only I had an apprentice.*

A lump rose in my throat, and my mouth went so dry I could not reply.

She waited and then turned back to her shelves. When she turned back, her tone was businesslike, her words clipped. "What is it you need then? A pot? A cup?"

I've hurt her, I thought.

And then I then noticed that another customer had come into her stall and was standing behind me. Nellie had been speaking to her, not to me. I exhaled hard in relief.

When she looked at me again, her expression softened into apology. "I shouldn't have begged, Megge. A woman is either a healer or she's not. You're a weaver. I only thought, when I saw you with Brother James, that you had chosen a new path." She smiled. "Now, what is it you need?"

"Thank you, Nellie." I wanted to embrace her for her kindness. "I've come to ask you about a woman—a stranger—who spoke to you yesterday."

"Aye," she said slowly and held up a finger to stay me.

Turning to her customer, who had chosen both a cup and a bowl,

Nellie accepted a coin and wrote something in her ledger. She stood watching as the woman left the stall, then took my arm.

"The woman." She raised an eyebrow.

"You saw her?"

She nodded. "When first I glimpsed her across the market road, all I saw was that hair." She swept her hands up her neck as if piling her hair atop her head.

"Was she with anyone?"

"A girl." She lowered her voice again. "A golden girl so like our own Brighida at that age."

"Did she speak to you?"

"No, the girl didn't speak—not to me. She went into Dora's stall with the woman, who carried a pile of cloth. The girl carried only a long stick."

"Was the girl her daughter?"

"I believe she must have been, they looked so alike."

"Dora said that the woman spoke to you."

"She only mentioned that she'd come to visit kin, and she bought three pots. Gifts, she said, for the Chandlers."

"The Chandlers are her kin?"

She shook her head. "She didn't come to see them. They're away."

"Why, then, did she buy gifts for them? And where is she from?"

"She mentioned Aldestowe." A squall made Nellie look away suddenly. "The babe's got to suckle."

"Nellie," I called to her back as she bent to lift the crying babe. "Her kin—"

She shrugged. "Ask Martyn. 'Twas he who brought her."

CHAPTER 30

artyn is back, and this woman is with him?

I rushed past the stalls Mother had forbidden me to enter—the workplaces of the fishmongers, tanners, and butchers—and was nearly overcome by the stink of entrails, feces, and urine that wafted out and by the carcasses and rotten meat piled ankle-deep along the edge of the road. I buried my nose in Amice's tunic as I hurried past, glancing inside each stall for a red-haired woman and a golden girl who resembled Brighida. But I saw only a leather-aproned man cleaving the bones in a slab of meat the size of my pallet.

I continued down the road toward the craftsmen's homes. As I was nearing the Chandler cottage, a small donkey cart slowed in front of it.

Sitting on the driver's bench was a fine-featured man in a bulky hat. Its brim, low on his brow, did not hide the face I knew at once. Delicate, with pale skin, a slim nose, and wide lips, Tinker Penneck's face twisted with rage as he halted his little cart and jumped down carrying his whip. He strode to the cottage door, fists bunched, and pounded.

"Kaatje!" He pounded again. "Show yourself!"

The cottage door flew open, and there stood a behemoth in a tunic of tanned hides, his huge arms bare, his heavy boots reaching nearly to his knees.

Hugh. I could not close my mouth for my astonishment. His beard looked wild. His expression conveyed wrath barely contained.

"Stay inside," he called into the cottage and closed the door behind him. He reached the cart in six long strides, then snatched the whip from Tinker's hand, seized the neck of his tunic, and hurled him to the ground. He let him lie there for a moment, then ordered, "Get up."

Tinker struggled to his feet and stood swaying like a sapling. He pursed his lips as if to spit. Then, looking up at Hugh, he held it in.

Hugh took a step closer.

Tinker swallowed.

Hugh grabbed a fistful of tunic and held Tinker at arm's length. "Oh, you're a dangerous one, aren't you?" He pulled him close enough to kiss, no doubt relishing the stink of Tinker's fear.

"Dangerous to women, that is. And to boys. Like the brother you crippled. And I hear you're skewering farm animals now—lambs, they tell me—under cover of night. Stunts. A boy's cruel prank. But then, without Gough at your side, you're no kind of man, are you?" With a shove, he released him.

Tinker stumbled backwards, breathing hard, his lips fighting to form words he had the good sense not to speak.

"What brings you to the village, Tinker? Are you here with your man Michael?" Hugh's voice, now almost friendly, nevertheless held menace. He stretched out his arm to take the hand of a regal woman coming toward him from the cottage, her reddish-gold hair swept off her face beneath a whisper of a veil.

"Or is this who you've come for?" Hugh took the woman's hand and drew her close. "Are you looking for my wife?"

Wife? Hugh's taken a wife?

Tinker's eyes shifted from Hugh's face to that of the beauty Hugh had just called his wife, a woman nearly as tall as Hugh and as grace-ful as ever Claris had been.

Her gaze went from Hugh's bearded face to Tinker's smooth one, and her back straightened, making her appear even taller.

Tinker sneered, then pursed his lips and took a breath.

He's going to call her a whore! I sucked in my breath. *To her face!*

Hugh's great paw shot out and clamped Tinker's throat, stifling the word before it could emerge. Tinker's hands clawed at Hugh's fingers, but Hugh held tight, his face once more a finger's breadth from Tinker's. The gathering villagers looked to one another but did not move.

"Kaatje knows all about you, Tinker. Aye, and the murdering cur you've hitched yourself to." He released Tinker and looked at his hand as if it were fouled. He wiped it on his tunic. His eyes went hard. "She's under my protection. Her daughter too." He looked toward the open door of the cottage, where a slender, pale girl with golden hair stepped into the sunlight, her head held high but her step uncertain, her hands behind her back.

The rest of the village must have thought the same thing I did—*Brighida!*—for, as one, we all sucked in our breath.

"Britlen," Kaatje's low voice drew the girl's attention. "This way. Use your staff."

The girl took from behind her back a long, slim staff and swept it from side to side before her. I squinted to study her eyes and noticed a white cloud covering the irises.

Hugh took the girl's hand as she neared and placed it in Kaatje's. Then, like a serpent, his other hand struck out and snatched Tinker's arm. Bending it behind his back, he pulled Tinker close. "Your face was the last thing she saw."

He marched the writhing, kicking, cursing Tinker toward his donkey cart and took down a coil of rope hanging from the side.

The butcher I had seen in the market pushed through the crowd, his bloodstained hand still gripping that cleaver. He held it at his side and gave Tinker a serious look that Tinker seemed to understand. He went suddenly still, and Hugh tied his hands behind his back, then hoisted him over his shoulder, strode to the back of that donkey cart, and dropped him in.

"Thanks, Charles," Hugh said to the butcher, who nodded and then turned and headed back toward the market.

The stone mason's son, Neville Angwin, nearly Hugh's size though years younger, ran down the market road from his father's shop, his tunic and his muscular arms covered in white dust. He pushed through the crowd and leapt into the back of the cart, pinning Tinker and threatening, "Lie still, snake, or I'll skin ye."

"Thanks, Neville." Hugh stepped up to the driver's bench and snapped the reins.

"Tell my father!" Neville shouted as the cart drew away.

"I see ye, boy," Mister Angwin called from his shop door. "That headstone'll keep."

The men in the crowd laughed and slapped one another on the back. "Edmund's men will get him talking!" one shouted.

"Are ye jesting?" another called out. "'Tis Neville himself will do that job!"

"You'll have that blacksmith before the night's out!" shouted another.

A cheer went up. When it quieted, someone touched my elbow.

CHAPTER 31

"Martyn!"

"Megge." He held my gaze as he squeezed my arm, and I laughed out loud. My arms went around his chest, all hard muscle, and my cheek rested on his.

After a moment, he released me. "Someone here would like to meet you."

With his hand on my elbow, he led me toward the lovely Kaatje and the golden girl at her side. He kept his voice low. "She's not truly Hugh's wife."

When we had reached them, Martyn extended an arm. "Kaatje, meet Megge."

Her eyes were the color Morwen had often had described as "the very blue of the Welsh sky I was born under." She stepped closer, and her outstretched hands took mine.

"Megge." Her voice, low and resonant, as if her throat were honeyed, was warm and welcoming, as if *I* were the newcomer. Bending from her great height, she kissed my cheeks. "Finally I meet the Lady of Bury Down."

"Nay!" I shook my head. "I've not yet—"

She squeezed my hands. "Megge, then." She released my hands

and took my arm. "Come, Megge. We'll have some food and ale to refresh ourselves. We shall talk. And then we'll set out."

"Set out?" I pulled away. "Where?"

She drew me toward the cottage. "We will talk inside." The door opened, and a stout little woman with the blackest hair I had ever seen appeared in the threshold.

I hissed to Martyn, "Where are the Chandlers?"

"They're away. In Aldestowe, with family. I spoke with them there and asked if we might stay in their cottage for a few days. They know why we've come and have allowed us to stay."

I looked now at Kaatje. "While you waited for Tinker to find you?"

Britlen nodded. "Aye."

"But how did you know he was here?"

"Gynneys sent word about the ram," Martyn said.

I turned back to Kaatje. "Why was Tinker looking for you?"

Not seeming to have heard my question, Kaatje took her arm from mine and linked it with Britlen's. Together they walked toward the little woman standing in the doorway. Kaatje touched the woman's meaty upper arm.

"Megge, I'd like you to meet Ffion."

I hesitated. "Fiona?"

"*FEE-on*," Kaatje said.

I bowed my head. "Good day to you, Ffion."

Her hand came up to her mouth as she stared at me, then she hastily bent as if to curtsy, but flinched and simply lowered her eyes. "Good day to you, lady."

"Nay, Mistress. I'm called Megge."

"Aye, 'twas that I said. 'Megge, Lady of Bury Down.'"

"She's asked us to call her Megge," Kaatje said gently to Ffion. She took my arm again and led me inside.

Ffion hurried in behind us and began dipping a ladle into a kettle of bubbling pottage and setting full bowls on the table.

Suddenly remembering the reason for my trip to the village, I opened my woolsack.

"Sit, lady." Ffion pulled out a stool.

Martyn smiled and winked at me, then led Britlen to the table and sat beside her while Kaatje sat next to me. The food before me smelled delicious.

Ffion took my sack, set it on the floor, and handed me a piece of hard bread. I dipped it in the pottage. While I waited for it to soften, my stomach began to churn and growl. Forgetting all about Amice's tunic, I ate until I burped and then looked at the kettle to see if there was more.

"Megge." Martyn reached over, lifted my sleeve, and encircled my wrist with his thumb and forefinger. "Look at you. I hadn't noticed until now." He pushed my sleeve up to the elbow. "Why, you're naught but bone." He studied my face. "Even your face has gotten thin. Aren't you eating?"

"Your hand's gotten bigger, is all." I pulled mine away.

Ffion poured ale into a cup and handed it to me.

"Brighida and I feed ourselves," I said as I drank the ale and set down the empty cup. "And your mother comes with bread and ale. We're not helpless, you know. I just haven't eaten since early this morning."

Kaatje tilted her head. "What brought you to the village today?"

I leaned over and took the tunic out of my bag. When I held it up, Ffion gasped. "You found her!"

"You know the girl who wore this tunic?"

"Nay, I don't know her, but I've seen her. A little girl. The dress was far too big for her." She thumbed the neckline. "And unfinished."

"I found her in Bury Down grove days ago," I said. "Alone. Barefoot. No cloak."

"I caught sight of her some time ago, dressed just that way," Ffion said. "She was walking the cliff road alone. I called out, but she fled. Like a rabbit she ran, like something hunted. And she was gone."

"May I see that dress?" Kaatje asked and nodded her thanks to Ffion when she handed it to her. She inspected it much as Gus Tucker had done. "This is our fabric," she concluded. She lowered it and looked at me. "All the women weave nettle cloth where we come from. I brought some with us to barter. But I didn't seen the child wearing this tunic." She looked at her daughter. "Nor, of course, did Britlen."

"Kaatje," I said, keeping my voice soft and tilting my head toward Britlen. "May I ask what happened?"

"She saw something," Kaatje said, having understood my unspoken question. "Something Tinker was doing. She's never told me *what* he was doing. Only that when he saw her and realized that she had seen him, he threw her to the ground, prised open each eye, and touched a hot poker to it. He warned her that if she ever told me what she had seen, he would come for me. Then he fled, leaving her in a sea cave to drown when the tide came in."

I touched Britlen's arm. "Tinker Penneck blinded you?"

She nodded.

Incredulous, I looked to Kaatje.

"It was a miracle I heard her screams and found her. Ffion saved her. For weeks, those poultices, those salves."

"Ffion, you are a healer?"

"Nay, lady," Ffion said. "We've none in our settlement, nor anywhere near. We do what we can."

Kaatje laid her hand on Britlen's. "Hugh came to our settlement two summers ago, just after Britlen was hurt. When he told us that Tinker Penneck and Michael Gough had burned your mother alive and nearly killed young Brighida, and that he was going to find and arrest him, Britlen finally told me that it was Tinker who had hurt her." Kaatje got up and went to the hearth, picked up the poker, and absently stirred the embers. "That very day, I left Britlen in Ffion's care and joined Hugh in his search along the coastline. I've been helping him ever since."

I looked upon her now as something more than a beauty. Though she had known what kind of man Tinker was and what he might do to her, Kaatje had persevered in a long, dangerous search and had traveled all the way to our village to bring him to justice.

I recalled the hatred on Tinker's face as he had pounded on the cottage door. And his rage at seeing Hugh put his arm around Kaatje and call her his wife, and asked again, "Kaatje, why was Tinker looking for you?"

She looked at Martyn. He nodded.

"He's my husband."

"Your husband?" I leaned forward. "You are married to Tinker Penneck?"

Kaatje nodded. "We were young. I hardly knew him. We weren't but sixteen when we wed, and we never shared a hearth. He preferred the company of Michael Gough. But I bore his child. And you've seen for yourself he still believes us wed."

I tried to imagine this regal woman with Tinker Penneck. But, as she had said, they had been young. Clearly, she had grown into a woman while he had remained a pretty-faced boy.

"But you said Tinker blinded Britlen." I looked from Kaatje to Martyn, and then back to Kaatje. "He blinded his own daughter?"

"Yes." Britlen answered, turning her face toward me. "When I was eight."

"Tinker had gone—mad." Kaatje lifted her hands. "That's all I can say. He went mad. He had deserted us long before that to be with Michael Gough. A detestable man. And Tinker too became detestable."

"Tinker was detestable long before that," I said. "My aunt Claris told us that when he was a boy, he would burn and drown animals for pleasure."

But that face, I mused, recalling it clearly. Nearly as fine and pretty as Brighida's or Britlen's. What must he have looked like as a boy? *An angel*, I thought. And as a girl, Kaatje likely believed him one. But now, though a man, he was still behaving like a spoiled child, not wanting Kaatje but not allowing another man to wed her.

I recalled how Tinker had spat the word *cuckold* when accusing Claris and his step-mother, Jenifer Penneck, of making a cuckold of his father, and I understood why Kaatje and Hugh had chosen this ruse to draw him out of hiding. How well it had worked! But at such risk.

"You were willing to serve as bait to lure Tinker."

"For blinding my daughter and murdering your mother? For so dreadfully injuring your cousin? Oh, yes," she said, nodding. "I wanted to kill him myself. I only wish Michael had been with him today. They both belong in the gaol." Her expression turned from anger to disdain. "But Tinker's a coward. When they threaten him with the gallows, he'll tell them where they can find Michael. And they'll both pay."

"You're so courageous, Kaatje," I said. "Coming here and facing Tinker, knowing what he might do."

"Nonsense. I was never in a moment's danger standing at Hugh's side." A softer expression crossed her face followed by one of resolve.

CHAPTER 32

Martyn looked out the door. "My father's finished his work and is waiting for us out on the cart." He turned to Ffion and smiled. "Are you ready?"

"Oh, aye. Let me just take care of these." She picked up the bowls. I picked up the cups and went outside with her. We rinsed the dishes at the well behind the row of huts, then went back inside and put them away while Kaatje unwrapped three bowls she must have just purchased from Nellie and set them on the table as a gift for the Chandlers.

Ffion took down an old brown cloak from the peg next to the door and wrapped it around herself, then picked up a basket covered with a clean cloth and opened the door. "I want to see that bairn while we are here, lady. I have to learn how she found her way to you."

"She won't be able to tell you, for she doesn't speak," I said, and heard Britlen suck in her breath.

"Doesn't speak?" Narrowing her eyes, Ffion cocked her head.

"Is it because she's frightened?" Kaatje asked.

"Perhaps, though even when she seems happy, she remains silent."

Kaatje and Ffion exchanged a glance as Martyn took my elbow to lead me outside. As Kaatje came out, Martyn's father stepped down from the driver's seat.

"Father," Martyn said, releasing my arm and taking Kaatje's. "Meet Kaatje."

"Mister Caerlin." Kaatje dropped into a curtsy.

"Haven't I been hearing your name from Hugh for a good long time now!" He smiled at her. "Let's get you home. Lowenna's prepared us a bit of supper."

It was nearly dark. "Mister Caerlin, can I ask you to take me home instead? Brighida will be worried."

He took my arm and helped me into the cart. "I spoke with Gynneys before I set out. He's with your sheep, and Alf's bringing Brighida and the girl. So I'll not hear a word about taking you home." He squeezed my arm. "You could use a good meal."

The "bit of supper" Lowenna had prepared was, in truth, a feast. Stew, bread, cheese, ale, wine, and something I had never before seen—golden colored balls of what looked like glistening bread.

"Sweets, Megge." Lowenna picked one up and held it out to me. "Taste it."

The outside was sticky with honey, but inside was something hard. I bit down.

"A nut!" I chewed it. "Sweet." I looked at Lowenna. "What kind of nut is this?"

"Hazel." She smiled. "Hazelnuts steeped in mead. Hugh brought them to me last month when he returned to report to the earl." She looked fondly at Kaatje. "A gift from Kaatje."

It seemed she could not tear her eyes from her visitor. Nor could she do enough for her. "Have another cup of ale, Kaatje. You look peaked, child. That long journey. Here's a damp cloth to wipe your face."

She hopes Hugh will marry Kaatje, I thought with deep fondness for this woman who had cared so tenderly for Brighida and me.

The door opened, and Brighida came in with Alf and Amice. The child's hair, washed and plaited, was crowned by a wreath of aster loosely woven with hawkbit so the purple and yellow flowers mingled. Her gaze roved over Kaatje's face, but when she noticed Britlen, she backed away and hid herself in the folds of Brighida's skirt. I went to her took her hand.

Ffion appeared at my side with two cups of ale.

"Ffion, this is Amice."

She gave one of the cups to me, and before I could say another word, squinted at Amice's face, then reached down to as if touch the girl's left cheek. Amice drew back, and Ffion lowered her hand and knelt beside her.

"Amice." Ffion's voice was tender. "Do you remember me? I saw you some time ago on the road near my cottage. You were all alone. You heard me call out, but you ran away."

Amice fixed wide eyes on Ffion but leaned into me.

"Have you no kin, child?" Ffion's kindly voice pressed. "No mother?"

Amice's countenance remained serious as she shook her head.

"No home?"

Amice shook her head.

I looked afresh at this little waif.

Ffion whispered over Amice's head, "It seems this motherless child was meant to find you."

Martyn and his father stood by the doorway smiling as they looked from Kaatje to Brighida. The women's laughter had filled the cottage until finally they had sat, still laughing and staring at each other, and began to speak in low tones.

Martyn and Alf remained in the cookroom eating the hazelnut sweets and watching the women, seeming to take pleasure in their talk of new homes, long journeys, and long-forgotten kin.

Small and round, with hair far too black for a woman with such wrinkled skin, Ffion too looked upon them, but with the tenderness of a mother or an elderly aunt. Tears pricked as I recalled Morwen's gaze, so like Ffion's, as her dimple gave away her delight when I had learned how to shear sheep "like a man" and recite the tales of my family "as well as any bard."

Ffion turned and looked around—searching, I suspected, for a latrine—so I touched her elbow and led her outside. I pointed to the privy Martyn had built the previous summer, a tall wooden box sitting atop a deep pit, with holes shaped like leaves cut into its sides and door.

"Thank you, lady."

"Please, Ffion, call me Megge."

Her glance, a quick one that met my gaze and then pulled away, made me flush as I recalled the way I had first looked at Lady Margaret, hardly daring to meet her eyes.

I was waiting by the cart when she returned.

"It seems Kaatje and your Brighida have a great deal to talk about," she said with a laugh. "And don't they look nearly like kin!"

"Are you Kaatje's kin, Ffion?"

She shook her head. "I was Kaatje's nursemaid. Of a sort. Her mother was seldom about when Kaatje was a bairn. Oh, and wasn't she a darling thing, a sweet child. But that mother of hers. She hadn't wanted another child so late in life, especially another daughter, so she left Kaatje to herself. Taught her naught. Gave her naught."

"And so you did."

"Aye, I cared for the bairn." Ffion shrugged. "My good man and I had no children of our own. I was barren, you see, and he died young. Little Kaatje was born in the hut next to mine. Her mother, a cold, hard woman, left her so much on her own, I began to see to her, and she became like my own daughter. When she was a girl, we worked the nettle in the summer and the spinning wheel and loom in the winter. Such a good helper she became." Ffion let her voice go low and her eyes wide. "But I lied to her, you see. I always told her that her mother had *asked* me to see to her care, and I always called myself her nursemaid. She's grown now. A woman. And she came to *me* when she needed help raising her own little girl.

"Oh, she's come to know the truth about her mother, of course, but not from my lips. And she's never admitted that her mother didn't love her."

A dagger pierced my heart as I recalled my own unloving mother, and I felt I would weep. I covered my face tried to fight off the sadness that rose within me as I saw Mother's downturned mouth and heard her call out to the winds, *If only I had an apprentice.*

"Lady!" Ffion bent down and touched my shoulder, tried to look at my face.

I shook my head and waved her away, but she wrapped her arms around me and held me.

In her comforting embrace, I could almost feel the nearness of Morwen, her little hands tucking me in at night when Mother had gone to Bury Down grove and left me behind.

"Don't cry for Kaatje, lady. She's grown now, and happy. And Tinker's been seen to. She and Britlen are safe. I feel sure they've found a home here with Hugh." She seemed to be thinking aloud now. "Soon they'll have no need for me."

Amice wandered outside and, noticing us, came to stand beside me, her expression serious as she looked at my face.

Another motherless child.

And it seemed she was now ours. I turned to Ffion. "Have you room in your heart for another bairn?"

Ffion was still waving goodbye to Kaatje and Britlen when Martyn urged the horse up the steep hill toward our cottage. Alf and Brighida sat opposite Ffion and me in the back of the cart while Amice sat on the driver's bench next to Martyn. She stared at him until he must have felt her gaze, for he turned his head slowly and looked down at her. She studied his face until he smiled, nearly laughed. Tears welled in her eyes, but before she could cry, Martyn held out one of the reins. "Would you help me drive this cart, Amice?"

She opened her mouth as if to speak, but quickly closed it and only looked at him.

When he smiled and tipped his head toward the rein, she reached out a finger and touched it. He laid the rein in her hand and closed her fingers over it. Letting go, he looked away from her as if studying the road ahead and then asked, as if he were speaking to me or to his brother or father, "Do you think we'll reach the cottage by morning?" He absently shook the rein he held in his left hand.

Amice looked straight ahead and, like Martyn, shook her rein. Though I saw only the side of his face, I caught the smile that touched his lips and the slight shake of his head and thought, *And now, she's won all our hearts.*

The cart hit a deep rut, jostling me against Ffion. I quickly righted myself and helped her sit up. Only then did I realize what I had done that night. Without thinking, without consulting Brighida, Martyn, or Alf, I had invited this stranger to live with us and care for Amice. It had felt so natural, I hadn't realized until that moment that I had assumed Amice would be living with us and that we would need help raising her.

I studied the back of Amice's wreathed head and watched her nod as Martyn spoke and look where he pointed, and knew my impulse had been right. Neither Brighida nor I knew anything about rearing a child. And it was clear to me that Amice was now ours to raise.

When we arrived at the cottage, Martyn took the reins from Amice, who was swaying now, likely half asleep, and brought the cart to a halt. He lifted Amice into his arms so her head rested on his shoulder as he descended from the high bench. Safe in those muscular arms, lying against that sturdy chest, she had allowed herself to surrender to sleep.

Martyn looked at me and gestured, one palm up, *Where shall I take her?*

"There's a pallet in the workroom. And blankets."

Alf ran ahead of him and opened the door. He smiled as Martyn passed him carrying the sleeping child. Brighida shouldered past Alf and knelt by the pallet to pull the blanket aside. Martyn laid Amice gently on the fleece-filled pallet, then took the blanket from Brighida and covered her. He pulled the edge of the blanket under her chin, then sat back on his heels and watched her for a moment before getting to his feet and going to his loom. His fingers played over the smooth wood, the taut weft yarns, the harnesses, all the parts he himself had built for the loom he warmly referred to as *the old monster.*

"I've missed this thing." His eye lingered on it, then he shrugged. "But no matter. I'll be back at it before long."

He's coming back! I stifled a laugh of happiness and relief.

"Now that Tinker's headed for gaol," Martyn said, "we'll soon have Gough. He's bound to be nearby. If Tinker was here, it's because they had something in mind. And before Neville's through with him, Tinker'll talk. The Tinker Penneck I know won't sacrifice himself—not even for Gough."

"Don't be too sure," Ffion said quietly.

CHAPTER 33

"What do you mean, Ffion?" Brighida asked, still full of good cheer from the pleasant evening. She filled cups with ale, then pulled out a chair for Ffion, took a long drink of her own ale, and sat at the table next to her. "Do you know about these two?"

Ffion took a long swallow and gave Brighida an appreciative smile. "You've a good alewife!" She wiped her lips with the corner of her apron. "Know about them? We all do out there. There's a difference in age between them, but they're like this." She held up a hand with the first two fingers pressed tightly together. "From the day Tinker turned up in Aldestowe, just a boy, they were of one mind. Wherever we saw Michael, we could count on seeing Tinker as well."

"But Tinker was born here," Brighida said. "His father is the carter. Tinker lived in our village until after his father married Jenifer. Jenifer *Gough*. Michael Gough's *sister*." Having finished her ale, she refilled her cup, her eyes now bright and riveted to Ffion's. "How did Tinker come to live in Aldestowe?"

She pronounced it *Aldeshtowe*. I wondered how much she had drunk at the Caerlins' that night.

"Why, 'twas Michael's mother herself, Agnes Gough, who brought him there after Jenifer married the carter. Seems that marriage enraged Agnes. Didn't she talk as if she hated her own daughter." Ffion finished her ale and held out her cup for more. When I had filled it, she took a long drink and went on. "Tinker couldn't abide Jenifer either. It's said that after his father married Jenifer, Tinker took his hatred of her out on animals. Rabbits, lambs—" She winced. "I can't speak of it. But from what you told us, lady, you know it's true."

"Why, though, would Agnes take him in?" I asked. "He wasn't her blood kin, and he was naught but trouble."

"I believe Agnes saw something of herself in the boy. They might not have been kin, but they were kindred spirits, you might say. They both hated everything and everyone but themselves." She took another long swallow. "Tinker was naught but a boy. No older than Kaatje was he when they met. 'Twas springtime. Beltane. She was to be crowned Queen of the May." She took another sip of ale. "Sixteen years old that very day—the first of May."

"My natal day is also the first of May," Brighida said.

"Brighida wasn't the May Queen," I put in, "but she walked alongside Vivienne Penneck, Tinker's half-sister, in the May Day procession the day she turned ten."

Ffion drank the last drops from her cup, looked inside it, and set it aside.

Brighida filled it with mead, then filled her own cup to the brim and took a deep swallow. "Do you remember all the dancing that day, Megge?"

"I remember *not* dancing after Agnes Gough pinched Vivienne's arm and made her keep us out of the dance."

"She must have realized that Vivienne and I were," Brighida leaned toward Ffion, eyes wide, and whispered the word, "related."

Why is she saying this? I wondered. *How much mead has she drunk?*

Nodding now, eyebrows raised, she reached for her cup. I slid it away.

"How old are you now?" Ffion asked.

"She's sixteen," I said and motioned for Brighida to be silent.

"Six years ago. Tinker would have been in Aldestowe for . . . four years by then." Ffion nodded slowly, the ale and mead no longer seeming to dull her eyes. She looked closely at Brighida. "'Twas about that time that Agnes began to repeat what Tinker had always said. That it was Claris's fault that his father had been cuckolded. But Agnes went further."

I watched Brighida's cheeks go pale.

"Just what did she say?" she asked slowly.

"She said that your mother was . . ." Ffion winced. "I cannot say the word."

"What did she call her?" Brighida leaned forward, her eyes dull but nonetheless steady on Ffion's.

"You needn't say more about this," I said to Ffion. I pushed back my chair and reached for Brighida's arm.

She shook me off and breathed the words, "A whore."

"Aye." Ffion let the word hang for a moment. "'Twas a terrible thing to say. And she lost what few friends she had, I'll tell you, for saying it. For don't we all hold the women of Bury Down in the highest regard."

She sat back and looked at both of us, her face tight with indignation. "But not long after that, Tinker seemed to go mad. He yoked himself to Michael, and the three of them all swore vengeance against Claris: Michael and Tinker with their campaigns against your family, and Agnes at her cauldron, stirring the pot."

Tinker, Michael, and Agnes Gough. *An unholy threesome,* I thought.

"I've long wondered how Tinker and Michael had come together against us," I said. "We knew that Tinker had blamed Claris for what he called 'her part' in cuckolding his father."

Ffion shook her hand. "I never believed it. What part could she have played?"

I wanted to tell her the truth. She knew so much already; perhaps she knew even more. But this was not for me to reveal.

I looked to Brighida. She nodded.

"You see, Ffion," I began, "as a young woman, Claris had been in love with Michael Gough and he with her, or so she believed. At the same time, Michael's sister, Jenifer, loved a young carpenter called Gregory Carver, and it seemed he loved her too." I waited until Ffion nodded understanding. "But Claris's grandmother, Gytha, explained to Claris that Michael did not love her. He wanted to wed her for . . . for her power. He only wanted the power of Bury Down. So, Gytha forbade Claris's union with Michael and quickly negotiated with Gregory's father a marriage agreement between Claris and Gregory.

Brighida interrupted. "My mother and Gregory were quickly wed; but by that time, Jenifer was already carrying Gregory's child."

"Ah." Ffion sat back and nodded. "She needed a husband, so she married the carter."

"Making Mister Penneck," Brighida concluded, "in his son's eyes, at least, a cuckold."

So silent that I had forgotten he was there, Alf pushed himself off the door jamb he had been leaning on. Keeping his gaze on me and struggling, it seemed, to make sense of this, he pulled out a stool and sat next to me at the table. Ffion filled his cup.

He looked at her. "Does everyone in Aldestowe know of this?"

"Oh, not this," Ffion said. "Even I never knew that Michael had ever loved—anyone. But from Aldestowe to Tintagel, and likely beyond, people all along the coast have heard Tinker rage against Claris, Jenifer, and his father, *The Cuckold*. For years."

"And no one warned us?" I stood and stared at her. "Having heard him rage against my aunt, no one warned us? Not even when Jenifer and her daughters were burned at the stake, or when my mother was burned alive in her hut?"

Ffion put up her hands as if to fend off an attack.

"We live in a secluded place, lady. We knew naught of those terrible deaths until, as Kaatje told you, the earl's men came searching for Michael." She jerked her head toward Martyn. "'Twas Martyn and Hugh who told us. We all knew of Claris, the kind, wise seer of Bury Down, so we had never believed Tinker's tales. And by the time Martyn and Hugh and the others came looking for them, Tinker, Michael, and a handful of other men from Aldestowe were gone. We've seen naught of them . . . until today."

She lowered her hands and regarded me with an expression of pity mingled with awe. "We all know of the women of Bury Down. Why, don't we all, out on the cliffs, know the tale of Murga, who summoned our own huntress, Anwen, to Bury Down to protect her apprentice and preserve her writings?"

I sat back down. "That was nearly a thousand years ago, Ffion."

"Aye, lady, but the blink of an eye to one such as me. To many of us out there." She pulled her chair closer to mine. "Anwen returned to the cliffs with Murga's writings and tried to put an end to a terrible thing—the Sisterhood. Do you know of it?"

Brighida and I nodded, then sat very still and listened.

"She said we'd never bring back the great healer—the goddess they called the Lady of the Cliffs—by killing young virgins. She said that the goddess would return only when *she* deemed the time had come." She leaned forward and looked from Brighida to me. "Ah, but it's an ancient place and doesn't change with time. The old ways are ever with us." She looked at Martyn and then at Alf. "It's the nearness of the sea, I suppose, that keeps the old ways alive. The north winds bring the new—new people, new notions—but the pounding surf pulses through us, and the sea breeze whispers of all that was." Her voice, now dreamy, faded away.

"And did she, Ffion?" I asked. "Did Anwen put an end to the Sisterhood?"

"No." Ffion shook her head sadly. "That's why that May Day I was telling you about—the feast of Beltane, when Kaatje turned sixteen—was so hard for me. It's why I took such pains to raise her spirits. To bring some color into that pale, pale face. It's why I wept silent tears for that beautiful May Queen."

"Why, Ffion?" I leaned closer.

"You see, on Beltane, the eldest virgin Sister is crowned Queen. Six months later, at Samhain, she gives herself up to bring back the goddess."

"What does that mean?" Alf looked from Ffion to me and Brighida. "She 'gives herself up'?"

"She gives up her life." Ffion looked at each of us in turn. "And that year, Kaatje was the eldest virgin."

We all went silent for a time.

"But Tinker Penneck changed that." A wry smile brought a dimple to her cheek. "I saw it the moment their eyes met. Kaatje was standing at the head of the procession of six young girls, and Tinker stood at Agnes's side. Agnes whispered something to him and then pointed to her daughter," she paused, watching us now, "the May Queen."

"Hold, Ffion." I leaned forward, mouth agape. "Kaatje is Agnes Gough's daughter?"

"Michael's sister?" A shadow crossed Brighida's face as she frowned and murmured to herself.

"She was more my daughter than ever she was hers," Ffion muttered.

"But if Agnes was her mother—"

"Agnes gave birth to Kaatje," Ffion said. "That—only that—made her Kaatje's mother. And though I did my best to comfort the child, to give her what her mother could not, she felt the snub. She suffered from the neglect. But I don't suppose you could find it in yourselves to pity her, for none of you would know what it is to be estranged from your own mother."

That dagger pierced my breastbone. I thought of the years I had spent at Morwen's side rather than at my own mother's.

"But Kaatje knew. By the time she was crowned Queen of the May, why, she scarcely knew her mother. And her brother, Michael? A stranger. A grown man he was when she was born. At sixteen, she didn't know him. And today? She'd see him hang."

"You said that Agnes pointed Kaatje out to Tinker," Martyn prompted. "At the May Day fair."

"Aye. Wasn't I watching them both that day. Kaatje noticed her mother pointing at her, and she quickly looked away. When she did, her gaze landed squarely on Tinker. The two of them locked eyes and—it was there for all to see—they fell under the spell of Beltane. By the next morning, Kaatje was no longer a virgin." Ffion slapped the table and picked up her cup. "The priestess held her Samhain rite six months later, but without Kaatje. For in the eyes of the Sisterhood, Kaatje, by that time large with Tinker's child, was well and truly wed."

CHAPTER 34

hen everyone began to talk at once, I looked through the hearth into the workroom, where Amice slept on Martyn's pallet, her arms flung out at her sides, her chest rising and falling in deep slumber.

"She brings to mind you as a child," Brighida whispered. "Those golden-brown eyes, that mussed hair.

I nodded. And Ffion, with that wry smile and that single dimple, brought to mind Morwen. And there it was again—that needle-prick. Tenderness, longing, and grief in one quick stab.

Ffion covered a yawn with her hand.

"Megge," Brighida motioned with her head toward the door. "Can you help me fetch some water?"

Alf scrambled to his feet. "I'll—"

Brighida and I both shook our heads.

"No, Alf," Brighida said softly. "Thank you. But Megge and I will go."

I dropped the bucket into the well and let it fill. Cranking it up, I whispered, "Do you mind that I asked Ffion to come live with us?"

"Mind?" Brighida reached out to steady the full bucket, and I loosed it from the rope. "She's one of us," she said tapping her breastbone. "She belongs here. Just as Amice does. Surely you know it's so. After all, you invited her to live with us. And a good thing! Think of all she's told us."

"Kaatje . . ." I couldn't stop shaking my head in wonderment. "One of the Sisters."

Brighida put up a finger. "I didn't notice a scar on her cheek."

I closed my eyes and tried to bring to mind her face. "She wore that veil."

"That's right," Brighida said nodding. "It covered the side of her face."

"And the scar likely has faded. Look how fine Amice's is. But can you believe she's Agnes Gough's daughter? And Michael's sister? And that she said nothing of this to us?"

"Yes," Brighida said, "But I think I understand. And I don't fault her for it. After all, she's here to bring him—and her *husband*—to justice."

"What was it Ffion said? 'Wherever we saw Michael, we could count on seeing Tinker as well.' We've spoken only of Tinker tonight. I didn't think of it when she said that, but if Tinker's here, surely Michael is too."

We looked at each other. "The books," we said in unison.

Brighida looked toward the cottage.

"We'll take them down to the lodge tonight," she whispered. "But where will Ffion sleep?"

"In the workroom with Amice. She'll want to sleep with her. Martyn can sleep either in the cookroom or out in the barn with Alf."

"We'll have to get the books out of the cottage without her seeing. We mustn't let her think we don't trust her."

The door opened, and Brighida went silent. Alf came outside followed by Ffion.

"Brighida's tried to show me Cassiopeia," he said, "but I can never see it."

Ffion pointed into a clear sky dotted with stars. "There. Can you see her?"

He looked into the sky, his hands cupped around his eyes. "There?" He pointed at a line of stars.

Ffion laughed. "Nay, Alf, that's Ursa Major. Look *there*." She pointed.

Brighida and I moved quickly into the cookroom. I took down the books, hid them beneath my cloak, and eased toward the door. Brighida watched Ffion and Alf through the window.

"Oh, Alf!" Ffion was laughing now. "Can't you see her? Look. There is Polaris, the North Star . . ."

"Go," Brighida mouthed and waved me toward the door.

I slipped outside and ran down the hill toward the lodge, the books pressed to my chest, my cloak wrapped tightly around me.

"Where's Megge bound for?" I heard Ffion ask Alf.

I kept moving as if I hadn't heard.

"The lodge," Brighida called to her. "Then the springhouse to get food for tomorrow. Cheese and . . . and turnips, I suppose. From the springhouse."

Keep talking, Brighida, I prayed.

"Look there," she said. "There's Cassiopeia, Alf. And Ffion, isn't that Virgo?"

I leaned on the lodge door while listening to Ffion's response, so like Morwen's might have been. "Oh, aye! Will you look at that! Why, the sky's so clear—"

From inside the lodge someone pulled the door open. A hand grabbed my arm and yanked me inside.

CHAPTER 35

Sprawled on the floor, I dared not breathe.

The light from the stars reached only far enough inside to reveal *The Book of Seasons* tented on the ground, *The Book of Time* open beside it, its pages catching the meager light, its symbols exposed to the cloaked figure striding toward it.

As I reached for the book, a boot came down on my wrist and a gloved hand scooped it up. The boot then came away, and a man with blazing red hair, the same man, it appeared, who had helped Michael burn my mother alive, bent down and pulled me to my feet. He clamped a callused hand over my mouth and pulled my head back against his chest. I bit down—hard—but that thick skin was like leather. Seeming to have felt nothing, he wrapped his other arm around my waist and pulled me tight to a hard belly. Hot breath huffed down the back of my neck.

Michael Gough came before me in his long, hooded cloak, both books now gripped in his gloved hands. I turned away from the pungent yet sickeningly sweet, somehow rotten, smell of him.

"Let her go." The stench of his breath made me gag. His voice dripped disgust. "She's no worthy opponent."

The arm gripping me squeezed even harder, and the hand over my mouth pressed so tightly I had to struggle to breathe. I thought I'd faint.

"I said let her go."

The muscled arm came away and the man stepped back. Sprawled once more on the ground, I fought to catch my breath. While I lay gasping, the blacksmith and his man slipped out the door, each holding one of my books, the shorter man's bright red thatch of hair catching the light of the newly risen moon.

"The lady chose well," a voice growled into my ear. "A girl with no will."

The voice had come from all around me as if from the walls themselves. I was on my feet in an instant but saw no one.

"A shepherd girl lacking the will to reclaim her destiny. Lacking the courage to wield the power she once possessed. Power she renounced. *Half* the power she held when the world was new."

"Power I *once* possessed? I'll show you power, Spirit."

Show me the blacksmith.

My dreamer's eye revealed Michael Gough and his squat, red-headed thug fleeing across the pasture.

Martyn, I thought, and saw him seated at the table fast asleep, his head resting on his folded arms.

See him. I cast Martyn the image of what I now saw: Michael's man running toward the sheep pen, followed at some distance by Michael, who tottered from foot to foot, his heavy cloak flapping behind him, *The Book of Seasons* clutched beneath his arm.

I ran toward the pen while watching in my mind's eye as Martyn woke and reached for his dagger. He ran out of the cottage, through the pasture, and across the field.

As I neared the pen, I saw Mister Gynneys standing in the shadow of the barn, moonlight glinting off the head of Hugh's great hammer, which he held high and at the ready.

The light failed me as a cloud moved over the moon, so I watched with my dreamer's eye as Michael's man rounded the corner of the barn. Mister Gynneys swung that hammer in a great, easy arc, striking him just beneath the breastbone, and then dove to save *The Book of Time,* which had flown out of the man's hands. He fell just short of it and lay stretched out on the ground, his fingers not quite touching it, as Michael took one long step and brought a boot down on his head.

With *The Book of Seasons* held tightly under one arm, the blacksmith wrestled *The Book of Time* into his other arm and splashed across the creek. He disappeared into the night. A whinny came from somewhere deep in the woods, and a moment later, I caught a glimpse of a long, black cloak billowing over the back of a horse galloping into the copse.

I could almost hear Claris's voice as she had once wept, *He's got the books.*

"Make no mistake, Blacksmith," I said. "I will have those books."

Mister Gynneys took sharp breaths through his nose and let out the air in a whoosh through pursed lips. Michael's man groaned and reached for the knife at his belt. Before I could find my voice to call out, Martyn had put his foot to the man's back and his dagger to his throat. With his other hand he took the knife from the man's sheath and slipped it into his own. "Where's he gone? Tell me. Where's Gough headed?"

The man only groaned.

"The woods, Martyn!" I pointed to the copse. "He's on horseback."

Martyn ran back to the cottage where his horse was tethered and, moments later, rode past us on his mare. Though he crossed the pasture at a gallop and swiftly crossed the stream, he entering the copse far behind the blacksmith. *How will he keep up with him?* I wondered. *Let alone follow his trail in the dark of night?*

Michael's man groaned again and spat.

Alf snatched a coil of rope from a fence post and tied the man's hands behind his back. Then he tied his ankles together, bent the man's knees, then tied his ankles to his wrists so he resembled an archer's bow.

"How did you know to come, Alf?" I asked as I helped his father sit up.

"I had a waking dream. I saw these two running toward the pen with your books."

"I too had a dream though I was full awake." Mister Gynneys rubbed his neck. "Murga chose well, I'd say." He slowly got to his feet and leaned over the trussed man who lay struggling to breathe, his breastbone likely shattered from that blow.

"You've learned." Mister Gynneys laid a hand on my shoulder. "'Twas you who sent us that dream."

"I couldn't fight him alone. I couldn't even stop him."

"Do you think you were meant to fight the likes of that blacksmith—and this lout—yourself?" He barked a laugh and shook his head. "Our Morwen always said you had not a notion of what lay inside you. If you believe what you did tonight was a show of weakness and not of power, then I see you still don't."

But I was beginning to. I was also beginning to see Mister Gynneys for what he truly was. A Companion.

Michael's man writhed. He tried to speak, but the words were lost in the rasp and hack of a harsh cough.

"Quiet, man," Mister Gynneys said. "Save your breath. I'll hear naught from you tonight."

CHAPTER 36

I looked toward the cottage expecting to see Brighida and Ffion running toward the pen to see what had happened, but the door was closed.

"My father and I will keep watch here until dawn," Alf said. "Then we'll put him in Hugh's cart, and I'll take him to Lostwithiel."

The bound man grunted and with each breath cried out in pain.

"You can't leave him all night with his legs bent up behind him like that. Surely his ribs are broken. He can't breathe."

"We can and we will," Mister Gynneys said. "He's just had the wind knocked out of him. I may tighten the ropes. He's strong as a bull, and he'll soon have figured out how to get out of them."

"When you left the cottage," Alf said, "Brighida said you'd gone to fetch cheese."

"I'll get you some. And some ale. No doubt you'll be setting out early." I ran to the cottage for the lantern but stopped outside the door when I heard Ffion's voice, as low and melodic as a bard's.

"And there she was. All alone. A child wandering the cliffs at dusk. Naught but a mite. I called out, and she turned, but she said not a word. Simply hied herself off to the woods. And was gone."

I gently opened the door and went inside. Ffion stood in the doorway to the workroom weaving her tale for a spellbound Brighida.

Ffion shook her head and turned her sorrowful gaze upon the sleeping Amice.

I came to myself, stunned to realize that I too had fallen under her spell, and called into the workroom, "Did you not hear the commotion down at the pen?"

"Commotion?" Brighida shook her head.

"Michael Gough." I kept my eyes tight on hers.

"He was here?"

"He and that man of his were lying in wait for me. In the lodge."

Ffion's hand flew to her mouth to stifle her gasp.

"He pulled the door open, clutched my wrist, and pulled me inside. And they—"

"Are you hurt, lady?" Ffion touched my arm.

I shook my head.

"Michael got away. He fled on a horse tethered in the copse. The other man tried to run, but Mister Gynneys stopped him with Hugh's hammer." I pulled my cloak tight around me, wishing with all my might that I didn't have to tell Brighida about the books.

"Martyn's gone after Michael," I said. "Alf and his father have Michael's man tied hand to foot. They're waiting until dawn to carry him to Lostwithiel." I looked from Brighida to Ffion. "How is it you heard nothing?"

"We were talking," Brighida said. "The door and window were closed."

"Aye," Ffion said. "It was getting cool. And the child was sleeping."

Even with the door closed, I heard crickets chirp and frogs belch. I heard Mister Gynneys and Alf talking out by the cart. Voices carried in the still night air.

But hadn't I too just fallen under Ffion's spell? I hadn't heard another sound as her storyteller's cadences drew me in and made me forget the terrible thing that had just happened.

"Brighida," I said and twitched my head toward the door. "Alf's asked for some cheese and ale. Would you come with me to the springhouse?"

Brighida lit a candle at the hearth and settled it into Morwen's lantern. When we got outside, she asked, "What's happened?"

I drew a deep breath. "Michael took the books."

"Both books?"

"Both. Martyn's gone after him, but I fear his mount is too slow to overtake Michael's."

"He's got the books . . ."

I looked down and waited for the sobs, the rebuke. Something. When a moment had passed without even a sigh, I looked back up at her.

Her grey eyes were dry and calm, her gaze far from me, far from the cottage, far from Bury Down.

"So," she said slowly. "It's begun."

PART THREE

CHAPTER 37

"What's begun, Brighida?"

I had to run to keep up with her. She wrenched open the springhouse door and went inside, calling over her shoulder, "Did he say anything to you?"

"Only that I was no worthy opponent. But something happened after he left." As I dropped cheese balls and vegetables into Brighida's doubled apron, I tried to recall the unstill spirit's words. I picked up a jug of ale and closed the door behind us as we set out for the slope.

"What happened?" Brighida finally demanded.

"The unstill spirit spoke. It said that a lady had chosen well. And that I had only half my power."

"Half your power . . ." She stopped and turned to me. "Did it tell you who this *lady* was?"

"No, and I don't know. I thought you might."

She said nothing for a moment, then swept an appraising glance over me from crown to foot. "The blacksmith didn't hurt you?"

"He didn't see me as a threat."

She smiled. "He didn't know."

So grateful was I for her kind words when she might have chided me, I laughed. "Did he believe I would suddenly become a giant? His equal in brawn? That I would overcome him? Morwen always said he did not understand the power of the books."

"Nor, apparently, did he understand yours."

"Nor did I until now." Something quietly settled in my breast. A knowing. I *would* carry out my charge.

As Brighida and I made our way in silence to the slope, Alf trotted across the pasture toward us. I handed him the jug.

"Take this for tonight and for your journey in the morning."

He took the cheese and vegetables from Brighida's apron.

"Please thank your father for what he did tonight," Brighida said. "And, Alf? Thank you for saving all our lives."

Alf touched his forehead in farewell. But rather than turn to go, he allowed his gaze to linger on my cousin, his expression confident. "Gough will pay, Brighida. The earl will see to it."

No, Alf, I thought. *I will see to it.*

Brighida linked her arm through mine. As we started down the hill to the cottage to look in on Amice and Ffion, I turned and called to Alf, "See that your prisoner gets some ale. Or some spring water. Something to drink."

"Ale, Megge?" Brighida gripped my arm. "For the man who helped the blacksmith steal our books and murder our mothers?"

"You've said it yourself many times, Brighida," I said as I laid a hand on the cottage door. "We don't kill." I opened it and looked into the workroom. Ffion and Amice were sleeping quietly before the hearth.

I closed the door. As we walked to the lodge, I let my voice soften. "The blow Mister Gynneys delivered may well have been a mortal one. This man may die, just as others have died at the hands of those charged with protecting the women of Bury Down. If he dies of his injury or on the gallows, so be it. But he'll not die of thirst at my hand."

"But the books . . ." Brighida's voice was beginning to tremble. She pulled open the door, swept the light around the lodge, and set down the lantern. Drawing back the blankets, she lay on her pallet and closed her eyes.

"They will never serve Michael Gough." Exhausted now, I blew out the candle and lay down beside her to borrow her warmth. "Both Mother and Morwen have assured us that the books will never serve him." I studied her face. "And with the help of the Guardian and the Mentors, I am going to get them back."

She nodded, then turned over and soon stilled.

I recalled the unstill spirit's words—*half the power*—and tried to remember the rest. *A shepherd girl . . . lacking the courage to wield the power she once possessed . . . half the power she held when the world was new.*

"Morwen," I whispered, "the blacksmith's got the books. I am ready to fulfill my charge. Lead me to the unstill spirit."

I fell into restless sleep. In my dreams, an angry sea rose up to pummel blackened cliffs. It drew away as if pulled by some great hand. At the foot of the cliff, the last of the sea emptied from a cave at whose mouth stood a small, brown-haired girl wearing a tattered tunic and carrying a lantern. She faced me for a moment and then opened her other hand to reveal her mulberry colored, egg-sized stones.

She turned from me, dropped the stones into the sand, and walked into the cave's mouth. The light from her lantern illuminated black walls and a sandy floor strewn with purple stones. Deeper into the cave she walked until her light fell upon a pool of water in a thick stone bowl—swirls of pink, white, purple, and green—atop of a pillar so eroded from the wash of the sea that it appeared a pedestal carved by a mason's hand. A crystalline drop fell from a long, jagged needle pointing down from the cave's ceiling and landed with a plink in the center of the pool.

Rising on her toes, the little girl cupped her hand, dipped it into that clear water, and held it out to me.

"Amice," I called, waking myself but still seeing that cupped hand, that palmful of crystalline water.

I shook Brighida. How could I explain? I knew that cave. That font. The very font I'd sipped from in that dream of myself—as a man—inside that cave.

And that girl. That silent girl. *Amice.*

Brighida murmured, "What is it, Megge?"

I sat up. With my brow in my hands, I breathed deeply and slowly until my heart had stopped tripping.

Something stirred outside the lodge. I got to my feet as Brighida lit her lantern and held it high. I opened the door.

Amice walked in and held out her hand. I took it and let her lead me outside, where Ffion stood.

"Ffion," I began, studying the woman's face. "What's happened?"

"I was having a lovely dream of home," she said, her voice soft. "The cliffs, the sea, the lady's font . . ."

"The *lady's* font?"

"Aye. A lovely thing." She looked down at Amice. "But then Amice woke me. She pulled me from our pallet and led me here."

I knelt beside the child. "What is it, Amice?"

Her eyes bore into mine as she lifted her hand and rubbed circles on her brow. With the other she touched the scar on her cheek.

"Lady . . ." Ffion said, looking at her.

Brighida, now fully awake, was at my side. "Megge, that look on your face—what are you thinking?"

I wasn't thinking. Voices were colliding.

. . . a lovely dream of home. The cliffs, the sea, the lady's font.

You know them, don't you . . . these cliffs of Kernow.

Return. Reclaim.

At Samhain, she gives herself up to bring back the goddess.

The sun was coming up, its golden light reminding me that it was late-October. In but a few days it would be Samhain.

And Amice had just touched that scar.

I could no longer ignore the calls to return to a place I knew only in dreams.

"We're going to the cliffs."

CHAPTER 38

Hugh and Martyn arrived dusty and exhausted at the cottage door late the next morning as I was making ready to depart with Ffion and Amice.

"What happened, Martyn? Why are you back?" I dipped two cloths into the bucket of clean water and handed them to him and Hugh.

As the men wiped their faces, Brighida set two bowls of pottage on the table. "Sit. Eat. Tell us what's happened."

"I crossed paths with Martyn on my way back from Lostwithiel," Hugh said as he dropped into a chair. "I had left Tinker in the gaol and was coming back for Martyn and some more men. Martyn told me what happened here last night."

"I lost sight of Gough on that monstrous steed of his," Martyn said, handing me the cloth and nodding his thanks. "There was no keeping up with him on my mare. On our way home, Hugh and I met Alf on his way to the gaol with Michael's man."

Hugh added, "We'll return to Lostwithiel on the morrow and learn what Neville's gotten out of Tinker."

"Neville?" Brighida asked. "That nice, young stonemason's apprentice? *Neville* stayed behind to question him?"

"Aye," Hugh said with admiration. "When we got to the gaol and the guards saw how Neville had Tinker quaking in that cart, they left him to it. Even the earl was impressed and bade Neville stay and question Tinker."

"Why does Tinker so fear him?" I asked.

"It seems Neville once found Tinker forcing himself on Neville's sister. The beating Tinker got that day gave him good reason to remember Neville. That was years back, but it won't take Neville long to get that coward to tell him where Gough is. Then we'll go after him with all haste."

"You said you were taking more men. Who will you take?" Brighida's voice revealed her worry.

Martyn hesitated. "The harvest's in, so the earl can spare our father. He'll come here to help Gynneys with the sheep."

"And you'll take Alf," Brighida said.

"Aye. He's young, and he's got a good eye," Hugh said. "He can scale a hill faster than anyone. We might need him for that out on the cliffs. And we'll take Neville. He's got the strength of three men. Once he gets Tinker to confess, he'll have earned the chance to serve the earl. I'll have a word with his father. Kaatje, Britlen, and my mother will stay here with you."

"Are you going to tell the men about *our* journey?" Ffion asked me.

"Your journey?" Martyn asked.

"Megge's taking me home."

Hugh looked from Ffion to me. "Just the two of you?"

"And Amice," I said.

"To Aldestowe?" Hugh asked.

"To my settlement, not far from there," Ffion said. "You know it, Hugh."

"Aye." He crossed his arms over his chest. "But three females crossing the country alone?"

Ffion spoke quietly. "You forget who you're speaking of, Hugh. This is the Lady of Bury Down."

"And how do you intend to make this journey of yours?" Hugh asked me.

"By river." I showed him the bulging purse Brighida had given me, the one her mother had been carrying the night she was killed. "This will more than pay for our passage. Have you time to carry us in the cart to the landing on the Fowey?"

"Yes, but you still haven't said why you're going." Confusion and worry colored his tone. "Why are you making such a long, dangerous journey now?"

"Work to do," I said.

"Are you certain Tinker will stand trial?" I asked Hugh as he handed me up to the driver's plank. I took off the woolsack that held our clothing and food and set it at my feet beside my walking stick.

"Aye, there'll be a trial. And he'll hang. But it'll take time to convict Gough once we get him." Hugh slung himself up and snapped the reins. The cart carrying the four of us started up the road that would take us to the riverbank along the village green.

"Since some of Gough's crimes involve the church, the earl will have to send for the bishop, and they must both reach the same verdict before they can hang him. A rare thing it'll be: a civil trial for a blacksmith posing as an abbot and executing innocents for heresy. It'll take months. And it remains to be seen if he'll be found guilty of any of it."

"Whyever wouldn't he be? He killed my mother and aunt. I'll testify to that, as will Brighida."

Hugh held up a hand. "I've talked to the sheriff, and there's a problem. It seems no one in the village has seen Gough's face in years. Not even the monks he spoke to when he came to the village posing as the Blackfriar abbot. And do you recall? When he came for your mother and Claris, he kept his head covered."

"Find him, Hugh," I said. "I'll attest to his murdering my mother. I was there when they set fire to her healer's hut. I was this close to him." I held up my thumb and forefinger, nearly touching. "I know it was him. I smelled him. Just like I smelled him last night. The same smell." I gagged recalling it. "Only worse now."

"Aye." He kept his gaze on the road. "But the earl will want to know, did you *see* him? Did you see his face?"

"Did I see his face?" I tried to recall that day, two years earlier, when he had grabbed me, tied me to a fencepost, and set my feet alight. Had I seen it then? Had I seen it when he dragged me into the lodge and took the books?

I shook my head. "But I know his smell, Hugh. And his voice. It's rougher now, and quieter, but I know it. What does it matter if I didn't see his face?"

Ffion spoke from the back of the cart. "They'll say it could've been another."

"You've got Tinker," I said, "and the man who attacked me last night. If only to save themselves, they'll swear it was Michael who set them on us. That it was Michael who committed the crimes. And you said it yourself: Tinker's a coward. He'll tell you where to find him."

Hugh put his arm around my shoulders and squeezed. "Never mind, Megge. The earl will get to the bottom of it. Rest yourself."

Rest myself? It had been days since I had rested.

Still fretting, I leaned on him and watched the fields go by to the rhythmic creak of the cart traveling slowly over stony, rutted paths.

"Megge." Hugh touched my shoulder. "Your boat."

I swam up from a dream of a black-garbed giant whose voice thundered from within a wide, heavy cowl, *Where are the demon's books?* And the taunting voice of the unstill spirit. *Half the power she held when the world was new.*

I sat up, my neck stiff, my mouth dry. "Where?"

He pointed to a boat lolling at the river's edge. "You'll sail the

Fowey nearly to Bodmin. Another, smaller boat will carry you down the River Camel to the estuary at Aldestowe."

I felt in my pocket for Claris's purse, hefted it.

"You've enough," he said. "It'll be a two or three days' journey, I'd say, the days getting so short now." He lifted Amice from the back of the cart, then helped Ffion out.

Ffion took my arm as I jumped down from the driver's bench and gathered my sack and stick.

"We'll sail upriver to Bodmin Moor," she said. "From there, it's a good long walk to the boat launch on the River Camel. It arises on the moors and flows awhile before it can carry a good-sized boat. But you're young and strong. If I can walk it, you'll have no trouble. Come now, let's be on our way. We haven't much time."

"Take care of this little one out there." Hugh reached over and pulled up Amice's hood. "The wind's picking up, child. Don't take ill."

I took him aside. I had to ask. "Do you truly believe Tinker will hang?"

"Oh, he'll hang." He lifted his chin toward Amice, his face hard. "I'd kill him myself for that alone."

"Amice?" The child chewed on the tender end of a river rush. "What did he do to her?"

"You don't know?"

I shook my head.

"She's the reason Britlen's here. It's what she saw Tinker do to Amice—what she'll testify to before the earl—that'll be the end of Tinker Penneck." He lowered his voice. "She's never told her mother, so Kaatje knows only that she saw *something*. But Britlen told me what she saw."

"What?" *Must I shake him?* "What did she see?"

"She saw Tinker cut Amice's tongue."

"Cut out her tongue—" I turned and stared at the child. Why had I never looked in her mouth when I realized she did not speak? Surely Mother would have.

"I don't know if he cut it *out*. Britlen saw him put a blade to Amice's tongue and then saw blood gush out of her mouth."

"How did she survive? How did he stop the bleeding?"

"With a hot poker. Then, when he realized that Britlen had seen what he had done, he took that poker and blinded her. He warned her that if she ever told her mother what she had seen, he would cut out her tongue and then blind Kaatje. Then he left her in that cave."

"To drown."

Hugh's hands came together as if he were strangling someone. "'Twas all I could do not to kill him myself. He's lucky he's in gaol. God help him if he escapes." He spoke now as if to himself. "I almost hope he does."

Still reeling from what he had told me, I let Hugh walk me to the boat. Ffion put an arm around Amice just as the child took a bite of hard bread. She chewed and swallowed it with what I thought must have been but a stump of tongue. Again I wondered how I had never noticed.

Britlen had said that Tinker had blinded her two summers ago, when she was eight. *Two years,* I thought. *Amice has endured this for two years.*

As I watched Amice work on that bread, I recalled how Michael Gough, as the imposter abbot, had forced a rope between his sister Jenifer's teeth to silence her when she was about to reveal his identity, then he had pulled back the corners of her lips into a ghastly, gurgling grimace and tied the rope behind her neck.

Had Tinker done the same to little Amice before he cut her? I looked away; but in my mind's eye, I could see him do it. Could see him grab hold of the child. Could see Amice, strangling on that rope, gagging and pleading, her tongue pulled out and held in Tinker's pinching grip. Could see the blade clutched in his other hand. The flash of silver against pink. The flailing child, the fountain of blood.

The arc of a silver blade being tossed away and the tip of a red-hot poker, drawn glowing from a firepit, pressed to soft flesh. I could hear the screams, could smell the stench of burning meat.

Then I saw Britlen, the golden girl, hidden in the cave's shadows, her hand over her mouth, her eyes black with horror, and I groaned when I heard her gasp.

I saw Tinker stiffen, look around for the source of that sound, and then take that poker into the shadows.

He held her down, Kaatje had said, *prised open each eye, and touched a hot poker it.*

The suffering. The horror those girls must have endured.

But Kaatje said she had found Britlen alone. Where had Tinker taken Amice? And where had Michael Gough been while Tinker mutilated her? Had he watched? Had he told Tinker to do it? Or had Tinker done it of his own accord?

And where has Amice been for the past two years?

"Come, lady." Ffion took my elbow. "They'll not wait."

"Come, Amice." I held out my hand. Wiping her hand on her dress, she looked at me calmly for a moment and then took my hand in her small one.

"Hurry, lady!" Ffion pointed to the men loosing the boat from its moorings. "It's about to leave us."

Amice and I picked up our skirts and ran. I paid our fare to a young man who reminded me of Martyn—tall and muscled, with brown hair made golden by the sun. As he took my hand to help me board, his eyes met mine and he smiled. I pulled my hand from his and looked about for Ffion and Amice.

"Over here." Ffion pointed to a bench large enough for the three of us and near enough to the bow that I could watch with delight as Amice pointed to the gulls screaming above us and the great, green river widening before us.

CHAPTER 39

The sun was rising on the second day of our journey when the boat drew up to a landing nearly hidden in mist and tall reeds.

"This is Bodmin Moor, lady," Ffion said. "It's a good long sleep you've had. Are you ready for a bit of a walk?"

We sat on the riverbank and broke our fast with bread and ale, then walked for miles until we reached a rickety landing on the bank of the River Camel. I handed a stick-thin boatman the coins for our fare, and he helped us aboard. As soon as we had taken our seats, I leaned on Ffion's soft shoulder and once more fell into dreamless sleep.

"We're nearly there, lady." She prodded my arm.

I lifted my head from her shoulder and looked around.

She pointed toward a wide beach at the foot of a cliff. "It's well after midday. In a few hours, the tide'll turn and this will be naught but sea. It's called The Sorrows Cove. It's protected by this cliff, that wall out there," she pointed to a wall of blackened rock that protruded far into the water, "and by the treacherous ridge of rock that gave it it's name." She drew a line with her finger over the narrow opening between cove and sea. "They call it Sorrow Shoal, for it's been the death of more than a few whose ships have run aground on it unawares."

"*Sorrow Shoal.* I've heard the tale of it sung by my dearest friend, Morwen. 'On its ruinous rocks they ran aground, and their widows wept, their tears to fill the cove they call *The Sorrows.*'"

Nodding her head and smiling, Ffion said, "A tale sung at the hearth by my own father! And, aye, this is the very place. Though the mothers here call this cove *The Sorrows* for a far different reason."

She pointed now to a stony patch of earth in the distance, fields cut to stubble. "And there is my settlement. Bare, now that the harvest's in."

We stepped out of the boat and onto a narrow path that led away from the riverbank and up to the top of the cliff. From there, it meandered between long, narrow fields and a hill that squatted near the bluff. As we neared the hill, Amice, who until now had seemed tired, became alert. She took my hand and pulled, as if to hurry me as we passed an ancient stone church separated from the road by a field overgrown with grasses and gorse. Its tower, topped by a crooked spire, boasted an enormous carved door but neither orchards nor gardens.

"Does no one tend this church, Ffion?"

"Look around you, lady," she said with a laugh. "This is not like your village. Why, it's hardly a settlement. A few families left now, nothing more. A field or two. Long forgotten is this chapel. And so perilous, no one dares draw near."

"Perilous?"

"It's haunted, they say. Screams and whines some are hearing of late. 'Tisn't but the wind blowing 'round the tower and through the spire, but no one dares go near this time of year."

"Samhain," I said.

"Three days hence, lady."

Amice tightened her grip on my hand, and I began to feel a clawing at my breastbone as my gaze climbed the hill that squatted between road and sea. I saw with my dreamer's eye the sea beyond, its white froth dashing into and out of small, black holes at its base.

With a deep breath, I pulled back from that vision just as a clutch of women dressed like Ffion neared us carrying bundles. They ushered before them girls wearing tunics that looked like the one Amice had been wearing when first she came to us.

As they passed, they nodded to Ffion but did not speak. They left the path and walked as far from it as they could, hugging the base of that beehive hill until they were well beyond the ancient chapel.

"Ffion, why did they not speak?"

"They were in haste to be gone. They're taking their daughters to stay with family across the river."

"Why?"

"The feast of Samhain."

"Didn't you say the goddess rites ended years ago?"

"There's fear here that they've resumed. Or something like them." She looked down at Amice and spoke quietly. "Haven't you noticed the mark on this child's cheek? I daresay those women did."

Her step quickened as we neared a row of widely spaced huts along the edge of a newly harvested field. It looked like the row of huts I had seen in my vision of Amice.

"Barley," Ffion said. The adjacent field lay fallow.

"There." She pointed to the hut at the far end of the row. "My man and I lived there from the day we were wed. Of course, he had lived there all his life." Her voice and countenance went wistful. "But he and his family are all gone. It's just me now."

"But you've Kaatje and Britlen."

"No longer, lady. You heard Kaatje's voice when she spoke of Hugh. Surely you saw how fiercely he protected her. They'll be wed before Michaelmas." She sniffed and then waved a hand as if to dismiss her sentiment. "We've had happy years here. When Kaatje came to me with the bairn, I welcomed them with joy. Why, hadn't Britlen saved Kaatje's life!"

I nodded but thought it was actually Tinker—perhaps even Agnes Gough—who had saved Kaatje from the goddess rite.

"But soon they'll be Hugh's," she said with a wistful sigh, "and a good thing for them all."

"They'll be nearby," I said, "So you'll have an even bigger family." I looked down at Amice, who was kicking a stone ahead of her and paying us no mind. "With them and with us, helping us raise Amice."

Ffion turned to me, her face once more bright. "Oh, and I've skills other than raising bairn."

"Of course you do," I said in haste. "You healed Britlen."

"Oh, aye, but that was just salves and poultices. I'm no healer. But I do spin and weave. All the women do out here. You saw our cloth in the village. After all, a body has more to do than one kind of work." She shrugged. "Did your mother keep to her healing? Nay, like the rest of us, she had other work. She tended sheep. And wasn't she a weaver as well?"

"You know about my mother?"

"Oh, aye. I told you I do. Don't we all out here? She and your aunt grew the herbs that healed more than a few women who made the journey to visit the seers at Bury Down grove. And though your Claris read the stars, made infusions, and healed in the grove, she also spun." She looked at me slyly, that dimple showing at the corner of her mouth. "Why, even my sister Morwen, a bard, also sheared sheep and made mead."

"Your *sister* Morwen?" I stopped walking and frowned. "*My* Morwen?"

She only smiled.

"Why did you not tell me sooner?"

"It seemed meant for a quiet moment."

Was I about to weep? To shout? To laugh? I touched her shoulder. Then I closed my eyes, put both hands on her shoulders, and ran them down her short, meaty arms to her little hands. Morwen's arms. Morwen's hands. "Morwen's sister."

She smiled. That same wry smile.

I had no need to ask if she was telling the truth. "Did you know each other?"

Without realizing that we had walked so far, I now noticed that we had crossed the wide field and arrived at a small hut of thatch and shingle.

"No, lady," she said, her hand on the door. "I was born long after she and Father left the family. But that's a story to tell over a cup of mead after a hearty meal."

She pushed open the door and held it for me. I leaned my stick on the hut and went in.

Even with the door open, it was dark inside, the shutters over the single window closed. I squinted. Near the door was a table set with three bowls, three cups, and a cloth-wrapped bundle. Three low stools sat beside it. A fire smoldered in a pit beneath an opening in the center of the roof. A kettle of soup hung over it, suspended by a chain from a tall iron tripod.

Ffion opened the shutters. As I set my woolsack on the floor, I noticed a small loom at the far side of the hut. Hanging from it was a length of light-green cloth just like the fabric Amice's tunic had been made of.

"We all make the same cloth here," Ffion said when she saw me touch the fabric. "But not the same clothes. Whoever was making Amice's tunic will no doubt know it when she sees it. I'll take it around the settlement tomorrow." She picked up the bellows and blew life into the peat. "This'll keep us warm tonight."

She dipped a long ladle into the kettle, stirred, and without turning, pointed toward the table.

"There's mead. Get the jug from under the table."

I hesitated. "Who prepared this supper for us?"

"My friends."

"Those women and girls we passed?"

"No, lady. The elder women who stayed behind."

"How did they know we had arrived?"

She shrugged. "They saw the boat, I suppose. Or heard it was coming. I told you, there are few enough of us here. We see to one another. Go on now. The cups are on the table. Pour us a bit of mead."

While I reached under the table and pulled out the jug, Amice blew dust out of the cups. I filled them with the golden liquid.

Ffion filled three bowls. "'Tisn't quite hot yet, but it'll be filling."

"Tell me about Morwen," I prompted.

She placed the bowls on the table and pulled Amice onto her lap. I waited for her to go on with her story, but instead she unwrapped the bundle on the table and handed me a thick plank of hard bread.

"Eat first. Then we'll talk." She let a crust of bread soften in her soup and then ate heartily.

Though I ate two bowls, I barely tasted them for thinking about Morwen.

When she had finished her meal, Ffion took a long drink of mead, refilled her cup and mine, and picked up the jug. She twitched her head toward three pallets lying on the floor along the wall. We arranged them so one lay flat on the floor and another leaned against the wall, then we sank into them. Amice nestled between us and fell asleep against me.

"My mother, father, and eldest sister—that would be your Morwen—" Ffion began, "left Wales when Morwen was but four years old. My father, a bard, had joined a band of strummers, harpists, and other bards crossing Wales on their way to England to carve out a living. My mother was with child—my elder sister, Hilde, now long at her rest—when they set out. Upon reaching Kernow, she could go no farther.

"My father pleaded, but Mother refused to take another step. Other families stopped as well. But Father? 'Your father was a wanderer,' my mother always said. And Morwen? 'Another with the wanderer's itch,' she said. 'Another bard.'

"Morwen never would have let Father continue his journey without her. Not for Mother, not for anything."

"So your mother let them go."

Ffion shrugged. "Aye. She let them both go. After Hilde was born, she took the babe and made her way with some others down the coast. Some settled with kin in Tintagel or Bude, but most settled here, near Aldestowe, where they made their living on the wharf.

"Mother learned much later that Father had fallen ill with fever somewhere near Lostwithiel. His companions had carried him to a nearby priory, and while he was being seen to by the monks, they went on their way.

"Time passed, and some of the travelers, discouraged by the welcome they'd failed to receive in the south of England, set about to rejoin their families. As they passed through Lostwithiel on their way to the Camel, they learned that Father had survived his illness though it had taken his sense from him. They also learned, much to their sorrow, that when he had been taken in by the monks and could neither think nor speak, his winsome little girl had gotten separated from him. It was believed that she had wandered off to look for him and gotten lost. Though the monks had searched for her, she'd never been found.

"My father, his mind a waste from fever, wanted only his wife and the daughter he'd yet to lay eyes on, so the travelers brought him here, where they eventually found my mother and Hilde."

"Your mother hadn't taken another husband?"

Ffion sat back and took a swallow of mead. "I believe she thought herself well shed of husbands. She was a weaver, a hard worker able to make her own way, so she didn't need one. But when she saw him looking so frail, she took him back and cared for him for the rest of his days, weaving cloth while he sang tales of a great round castle on a wide, green river."

"Then he could once more speak. He still had his tales."

"Oh, he could speak. 'Twas he who named me Ffion. He named me for a flower, the foxglove, for he said it had saved his life. And he could still tell his stories—what bard ever forgets his tales? But he was forever addled." She touched a finger to her temple. "I was a child of my parents' old age." She winked. "For apparently, Father wasn't entirely feeble."

I squinted at her. Clearly, she was much younger than Morwen; but how old, I wondered, was she?

"I'm older than I look." She picked up a lock of her black hair. "Myrtle berry." She winked again. "For I'm also vain."

Morwen's sister, I thought.

Her face went tender. "Morwen comes to me in dreams. 'For what are dreams,' she says—"

"But moments in spirit."

"Aye." Her gaze was far away now. "'The day Kaatje told me she was to travel to your village—not long after I first saw Amice— Morwen came to me. 'Go,' she told me. 'And bring back Megge, the Lady of Bury Down.'" She shrugged. "'Twasn't a thing I could say no to."

CHAPTER 40

"Megge." Ffion's voice startled me awake. "It's morning, lady."

Though she shook my shoulder, I tried to hold onto the dream I was having as it frayed at the edges . . . at least a dozen squat, muscular men were hewing granite boulders from the summit of a round, grassy hill and heaving stone upon stone into a massive cairn. Six young women wearing white gowns with crimson sashes surrounded the growing cairn, singing and weeping—

"Come, lady, break your fast. Amice and I ate long ago."

"Ffion," I said, about to ask her about that hill. Those rocks. That cairn. Those gowned women. But a sudden scratching beneath my breastbone silenced me. This, the clawing told me, was for me to learn.

I pulled back the blankets, got up from the pallet, and went to the table. Ffion set before me a wedge of cheese, a loaf of bread, and a jug of ale. Three sacks of grains and roots of all sizes and shapes were open beside the table, a kettle of water awaiting them.

She poured me a cup of ale. "A good long time you've slept."

"Where did all this food come from?"

"I told you. I've friends, haven't I? They know I've guests. And look here, lady. One of them brought me this." She shook out a folded tunic.

"Amice's!" But this one had sleeves and a finished neckline.

"Mistress Trevenna saw Amice yesterday as we passed her hut, and she brought this for her. 'A gift for the bairn,' she said. She told me she'd been making one just like it for her granddaughter months ago, but it was stolen before she could finish it."

"Does she know who might have taken it?"

"I asked her that very question and told her about poor little Amice wearing that sleeveless tunic. She said she knew the bairn hadn't taken it, but wondered who had taken the bairn."

"'Who had taken the bairn'? Why would she have assumed Amice and been taken? Have little girls been taken from their homes?"

"Not from their homes. But there are orphans aplenty in the bigger towns. And poor children begging at the side of the road. 'Twouldn't be hard to take one. And Amice wouldn't have been the first little girl to go missing."

"Why would anyone take a child?"

Her eyebrow arched and that dimple disappeared. "Not many mothers are willing to give up their girls to the goddess these days."

It's how the Sisterhood stayed alive, Brighida had said. *Always taking in new girls.*

Amice must have seen me shiver, for she ran to my pallet, tore off the blanket, and brought it to me.

"Thank you, Amice," I said and wrapped it around my shoulders.

As I took a sip of my ale, a breeze blew in through the window, and ashes flew up from the firepit. I squeezed my eyes shut. In the darkness I smelled not smoke but flowers, for in the vision that had come over me, I was standing on the summit of the hill I had seen in that morning's vivid dream.

Those crimson-sashed, weeping women have formed a circle around a pallet upon which lies a white-gowned woman, her hands crossed over her breasts, her black hair caught up in a score of looping braids, her smooth skin marred only by a single spot—a small, dark stain—beneath her left eye.

The men lift the pallet and carry it to a tall wooden frame surrounding an enormous fire pit. As they set the pallet on the frame, the women begin to chant. One steps forward carrying a flaming torch. As she approaches the corpse, the chanting grows louder, then higher in pitch, until the women are wailing. She lowers the torch to the kindling and bows her head as the dead woman's gown flares and her body is consumed by flames.

"I have to go, Ffion." I pulled off the blanket, stumbled out the door, and picked up my stick.

Which way? I looked across the harvested barley field. The fallow field. And there. In the distance was that hill. I started out at a trot.

"Where are you going?" Ffion called out the door. "You don't know this place!"

But I did. Behind my breastbone, something had begun to claw. *That pyre. That cairn.*

That hill. I ran toward it.

It was farther away and the slope much steeper than it had appeared the day before. Thankful to have my stick to lean on, I began to climb.

I stopped halfway up the hill to catch my breath. The summit was still far above me, the wind rising just as it did on my herder's hill. I leaned forward, hands on thighs. When I straightened, I saw Amice climbing the hill behind me carrying a small sack. Her cheeks were pink, but her breath came easily. She thrust the sack at me.

"Amice." I smiled. "You kind girl! You brought me food to break my fast."

Opening it, I found not bread but stones. Smooth stones the size and shape of eggs, nearly all the purple-gray of a thunderhead.

Stones just like the ones she had handed me in the dream I had had in the lodge, the vision that had called us all here.

Without a word, I slipped one in my pocket, gave the others back to her, and began once more to climb. Amice trotted alongside me, and when we reached the breezy summit, she pointed to a granite rock deeply embedded in the ground. In my mind's eye I saw those men, those rocks, that cairn, those women, that corpse.

Amice cupped one hand and moved it in a half-circle as if drawing an arch over the rock. Extending the forefinger of her other hand, she pointed into the top of that imaginary arch and then down at the ground.

"There's something beneath that stone?"

She nodded and with both hands drew in the air what looked like another arch, this one much larger. And my dreamer's eye saw it. The cave.

I held out the stone she had given me. "Amice, did this come from a cave?"

She nodded solemnly.

"Is it just beneath us?"

She nodded.

I turned in a circle. To the south was the bank of the River Camel, where we had disembarked. To the west, the sea. To the north, the rocky wedge that formed one wall of this great, wide cove.

To the east was that abandoned church with its stone tower and its crooked spire, the church the village women so feared that they had taken their daughters and fled three days before Samhain.

Show me why. I opened my dreamer's eye and, in a living vision such as only Morwen could send, saw the tall, heavy door of the church tower open and a woman emerge dressed in a hooded white robe.

Slowly she glides around the base of the hill and then down a path that leads into dense, high rushes, where she disappears from view.

One by one, six girls, whose unbound hair falls to the crimson sashes of their light-green gowns, emerge from the church. They process along the path the hooded woman had taken and then descend a steep, stony path to a beach. One by one they enter the cave beneath me.

At the center of the cave, the woman—*a priestess*, I think as I watch—awaits them beside a small fire pit, her hair and face hidden beneath her cowl.

The first of the girls—*a Sister*—holds out a taper as she approaches the woman in white.

The priestess lights the candle from her own flame, and the girl returns to the other Sisters.

The cave fills with golden light as each Sister comes forward and lights her taper from the priestess's. When the fifth girl's candle has been lit, the priestess blows out her own and walks to the rear of the cave.

Candlelight reveals six unsmiling faces. The tallest Sister holds no candle. She stands apart from the others and looks all about the cave as if searching for a route of escape. Her breath comes fast and her lips move though she makes no sound. Then her eyes fasten on something in the depths of the cave, and her lips still.

The priestess walks toward the mouth of the cave and stops beside the basin of white, pink, purple, and green stone. She raises her arms, and one long, wheat-colored curl escapes from the hood and falls over her shoulder.

She lowers her arms and beckons the smallest of the six girls, the first to have lit her candle. The girl comes forward and stands facing her. With her candle held in hands clasped at her sash, she bows her head. The flame illuminates a solemn countenance—a smooth brow, closed eyes—and four fine, raised marks on her left cheek: a straight line with three short lines descending from it.

The priestess gestures toward the font. The girl approaches

and waits.

When the priestess nods, the Sister dips her left hand into the basin, fills her cupped palm, and sips. A smile touches her lips as she straightens and looks into the priestess's hood.

The next four Sisters, each appearing slightly older than the last, do the same. Each wears the same knowing smile after sipping the water. As each looks up, the candlelight reveals the same fine scar on the left cheek. Each Sister returns to her seat somehow changed, resolved.

The sixth girl, the one who stands apart from the others, the frightened Sister with no candle, approaches with halting steps, her hands at her sides as she wipes her palms on the skirt of her gown.

She kneels before the font, her slim shoulders square, her hands clenched, her eyes on the priestess. The five Sisters come forward and form a half-circle behind her.

The trembling Sister stretches her arms over the font, her hands palms-up.

With a nod, the priestess summons from the shadows a child in a short tunic belted at the waist with a saffron sash. She carries in her outstretched hands a polished stone rod, its tip a silver blade.

The priestess takes it, dips the blade in the water, and sweeps it across the kneeling girl's wrists. One high scream, and the girl begins to sway. The other girls move in to steady their kneeling Sister as the crystalline water goes red.

I stepped back, unable to awaken from this vision, and stumbled over the block of granite embedded in the ground.

Morwen! I silently called as I struggled to get back up and open my eyes to dispel the image. *That girl knew she was about to die. She knew, and still she approached the font and held out her wrists.*

Something touched my hand. I pulled away, my breath coming in gulps, my heart pounding.

It touched me again.

Finally able to open my eyes, I saw Amice's fearful expression.

I slowed my breathing but did not dare look down the hill toward the cliff.

"Amice." I wrapped one arm around her waist and drew her to me. "All's well, Amice. All's well, child," I crooned. "I had a dream, is all."

But that had been no dream.

I looked down at the protruding rock I had tripped over. *Granite,* I thought, *like the stones the men in my vision had heaped into a great cairn.* With my mind's eye I looked beneath it and saw once more the font in the cave just beneath my feet.

"*. . . I was having a lovely dream of home when Amice woke me,*" Ffion had said that night at the lodge. "*The cliffs, the sea, the lady's font . . .*

This, I now knew, was what I had been called here to see: the font I had drunk from in my life as a man, when it was but a shallow depression in a hip-high pillar of stone. How many sacrifices had that font seen?

My heart slowed to hard thuds as I recalled the faces of those girls. *Sisters.* Someone had etched that goddess mark on their cheeks just as someone had carved it into Amice's. But when had the goddess rite I had just seen taken place? Yesterday? A year ago? A hundred, perhaps a thousand, years ago?

It mattered not, for someone was still playing the priestess, and Amice bore her mark.

I took Amice's chin gently between my thumb and forefinger and studied that scar. She turned her head and looked away. I followed her gaze toward the sea and was once more inside the cave.

The girl with the bloody wrists lies on her back at the base of the font, her head cradled in the lap of the solemn Sister. Two sit next to her, one on each of her sides. Two stand at either side of the font.

Apart from them, at the rear of the cave, the priestess nods. All the girls rise and step back into the line they had formed before their Sister went to her death, the girl who had stood next to the sacrificed Sister trembling in the dead girl's place. Now they are but five.

The little girl with the saffron sash comes forward with a silver pitcher, dips it into the font, and fills it with bloody water. The priestess takes it from her and leaves the cave.

The five Sisters stand frozen in place, naked hope on their faces.

Drop after drop of water falls into the font as they await the return of the goddess.

But it is the priestess who returns, still but a priestess for she has not been transformed into the goddess. She points to the yellow-sashed girl.

The child goes to her, one tentative step after another. She stops before the towering woman and stiffens, her eyes darting all around the cave, her breath coming fast.

The priestess's hand strikes like a viper. And with a glint of silver and a flash of red, the girl is marked.

The solemn Sister comes forward and removes the girl's sash. She drapes it over her arm and replaces it with the dead girl's crimson one, then leads the young girl to stand beside her in the row of Sisters.

Across time, the child catches my gaze and holds it as the eldest Sister leans down and presses a cloth to her bleeding cheek.

That child is doomed.

The image faded, and the church and the cliffs and the sea rushed back.

Amice caught my gaze and held it. I was looking into the eyes of the doomed girl.

I swept her into my arms. "They'll not hurt you, Amice. You're ours now, not theirs. Morwen, I am certain, guided you to me, though I know not how—through dreams, perhaps—and you brought me here to see this. I will put an end to it."

I was holding her so tightly now that she struggled to get free. I loosened my grasp but took her arms and held her away from me.

"Amice," I said and opened my mouth wide. "Show me."

She drew back for a moment and then opened her mouth slightly.

"Wider." I looked closely. "I won't hurt you. Put out your tongue so I can see it."

She closed her eyes and put out her tongue. Her jaw trembled and her tongue darted in and out. It had not been severed. The end was blunt, the tip having been cut off, but much of the tongue was still there.

Still, I thought, she's never tried to speak.

But suppose someone had ordered me never to speak? Suppose they had held me down, taken out a blade, and cut off the end of my tongue? Burned it to stop its bleeding. Even if I could speak, would I ever risk another word?

She closed her mouth and pulled away from me, her eyes wide. They darted back and forth over my face as if trying to read my thoughts.

"I'll never ask you to speak, Amice, though you may one day choose to do so. You are a brave child, but I'll never make you speak."

We descended the hill. As we passed the church, I wondered when that ceremony had taken place. Britlen had seen Tinker cut Amice's tongue two years earlier, perhaps in that very cave. But the goddess mark was still pink—fairly fresh—so her tongue had been cut long before the priestess had marked her cheek.

Could Tinker have cut it *for* the priestess?

Amice had been the youngest, but all the girls had been silent. Had Tinker silenced them all in this way? Could he have been part of this . . . this coven? A man? In the Sisterhood?

Or had Amice simply been an orphan Tinker had taken from some village and mutilated for his own pleasure and then given—or sold—to the priestess when the mothers of the settlement stopped sending their daughters to their deaths?

CHAPTER 41

The ether was still the next morning as I picked up my stick and walked with Ffion and Amice along the foot of the hill.

"Where are we going, lady?"

"There's a field just beyond the hill, along the sea bluff," I said. *Where the priestess and the Sisters had walked*, I thought.

"I believe I know the patch," Ffion said, "and you don't want to walk through it, I can tell you."

"Why not?"

"Stinging nettles." She raised a hand above her head. "They're this high this time of year."

As we neared the path I had seen in my vision the day before, I pointed. "There. Are those nettles?"

She shook her head. "No, they're beyond this field, though there may be some strewn about in there. I'll point them out if I see any. If we don't go too far, we'll be safe."

By following the same path the Sisters had taken in my vision, we soon reached the twisting, rocky path to the beach, and I began to notice scatterings of rocks the same purple-grey of the ones Amice carried in her sack. As we neared an outcropping, I noticed the ground was strewn with them.

Excitement bubbled in my chest as we neared the wall of stone that jutted from the bluff onto the beach and out into the sea. We were approaching the cave. I could feel it.

And then I saw it. An opening in the wall with rocks spilling out onto the sand. *This is it.*

Leaving Ffion behind, I hurried toward it. Would the font be inside? Would I find the chamber in which my twin had drowned?

The cave's damp breath smelled of rotting sea plants and decaying fish. The morning sun was not yet overhead, so the cave was fully in shadow. With my arms thrust out before me, I stepped with care toward the place where, in my dreams and visions, the font had stood.

When the toe of my boot struck stone rising from the cave's floor, I dropped my arms and touched the cool, smooth, rounded edge of the font. An image of that Sister bleeding into it came to me unbidden. I drew back.

"What is it, Megge?" Ffion's shoes crunched in the stones as she neared.

"An image, is all. An image from a dream I had."

"Of the goddess?"

My breath caught.

"The Lady of the Cliffs." Ffion bent and picked up a smooth black stone. "A great, tall woman. A beauty, so the legend goes, with hair as black as this stone. Braids that coiled over her neck, down her shoulders and back. A faint mark over the apple of her cheek." She brushed a finger under her left eye.

The woman on the pyre.

"I've seen her," I breathed. "In a dream. Gowned in white."

"The Deathbringer, the ancients called her. But here on the cliffs, we knew her only as a healer."

"She clips the string of life," I said, hearing Mister Gynneys's voice.

"She renounced that duty." Ffion pointed to the sand at our feet. "Right here in this cave, where she'd hidden herself from the gods. Having ended so many lives, she'd vowed never to take another.

She came here, to the cliffs of Kernow, to live as a healer, for we had none. But her other duty found her." Ffion looked at me. "We're all so many things, aren't we? She was created a deathbringer, but she saw in herself a healer who might bring cures and comfort rather than doom. But the gods beckoned, and when she failed to respond, they tormented her.

"So, one day, she came to this cave, where for so long she had healed. Surrounded by her novices, she vowed to return to the living world a healer, a protector of life, and she sacrificed the goddess." Faye pointed upward. "At the top of the hill her remains were burned, the ashes scattered over a granite cairn that's now but one stubborn rock." She bowed her head for a moment and then looked up at me.

Unable to speak, I merely nodded, but Ffion's eyes remained on mine. "She revealed herself to you."

"I've had two dreams," I said. "In the first, a woman with long, looping black braids—a corpse gowned in white—was burned upon a pyre at the summit of this hill with six young women surrounding it, weeping." I looked at her, watched for her response, but there was none. "In the second, it was a different woman I saw."

"Tell me."

"This one wore a robe with a cowl that covered her face, her hair. But I saw a lock of it slip from the hood and fall past her shoulder. A long curl the color of wheat."

"That wasn't the goddess."

"Then who—"

"Have I told you," Ffion asked, "about the ancient goddess rite?"

I could still hear her voice as she told us about Kaatje's coronation. *On the feast of Beltane—May Day—the eldest virgin Sister is crowned Queen. Six months later, at Samhain, she gives herself up to bring back the goddess.*

"You told me about the Sisters and their priestess, but not about the rite; only that Kaatje had been spared it."

"In that rite, a woman who calls herself a priestess—one of our seers, conjurors, women-who-would-heal—takes the life of the eldest virgin Sister in the same way the goddess took her own." She slashed her right hand over her left wrist. "A very young girl then fills a pitcher with the bloody water from this very font, and the priestess drinks it."

"Drinks it?" In my vision, Amice had filled that pitcher with bloody water, but the priestess had not drunk it. She had taken it away.

"Aye, she drinks it." Ffion's mouth twisted into a grimace. "And if the Lady of the Cliffs does not return to life in the body of the priestess, then the child who had given the priestess the pitcher is marked, taken into the Sisterhood, and for the next five Samhain festivals, trained to perform her part in the rite."

"Why does no one stop them? Why do mothers let their girls go? Surely they realize those *Sisters* are dying."

"Being *sacrificed*, they would say," Ffion said. "A sacrifice for what they believe is a greater good. Do you know how many true healers there are?"

Your mother and aunt are gone now, and the village needs a healer. I shook my head.

"Few. Even in your village there is now but one. Your cousin, Brighida. There are none in places like these cliffs. People need a healer, someone to teach others to heal. When the lady died, there was no one else. Out here on these cliffs, the Sisterhood came to be much like the Church is in your village. A part of life. A hope of better things. And as your villagers rely on—and obey, and sometimes fear—the priests, we in our settlement have always feared and obeyed the priestesses."

"And the Church does not stop them?"

"Some places are beyond the Church's rule. I don't believe the Church even knows of the Sisterhood. You see how secluded we are. Why, the priestesses always made their home in the chapel now haunted by all those lost girls. It's a dark part of the story of this place, and I thought it had ended when Kaatje . . . did what she did." She chuckled. "Three other Sisters soon did the same, and after four Samhain festivals with no eldest virgin and no rites, we heard no more of it. It's been years. I had thought the thing done."

We both looked down at Amice.

"But someone's now carrying out that rite in secret," Ffion said. "With girls from . . . I know not where. Where's this child from? Not from my settlement. Surely she was taken."

When we arrived back at Ffion's hut, she hung the kettle over the peat. After we had eaten, she led a sleepy Amice to her pallet and covered her with a soft blanket. We sat on our pallets, each with a cup of mead, and spoke quietly.

"Women who play the priestess have always believed they would receive from the goddess the power to heal. But 'tisn't true. Morwen told me."

I waited. "What else did she tell you?"

"That there's power here on the cliffs, but it's power no one would want: the power over death, which the goddess went to her own death to be free of. The other half, the healing half she died to preserve, lives on, but not here. Not on the cliffs. It lives at Bury Down."

"At Bury Down? What did Morwen mean?"

"I wouldn't know." She sipped from her cup. "But that's what she said when she told me to bring you here. Go on, now. Drink."

I looked into my cup but could not drink. I could think only about the unstill spirit, who had spoken of *half* my power. *Half the power* I had possessed when the world was new. Power I was too fearful to wield.

My breath came fast and short as I pondered those words and that goddess ritual. Before I could calm myself, a vision came to me of a hooded woman standing before a hip-high pillar of white stone, murmuring over still water puddled in a shallow depression at its top, as six girls looked on.

And then I saw only that stone pillar, that water, and those six girls. Girls, I realized, who were gazing up at *me*.

What must I see this time? I silently demanded of Morwen as I recalled with horror the former life, as Murga, that Morwen had made me relive at my vowtaking. *That I was once that priestess? Must I now watch myself take the life of one of those girls and then drink her blood?*

A tremor began somewhere in my backbone and rattled its way up my neck and then down to my bowels. I could do naught but watch as each girl stepped forward and dipped a hand into the water.

I am about to kill one of those girls, I thought.

Two hands presented themselves over the rim of the font.

I will not look away. This is what Morwen brought me here to witness. If I did this thing, I will own my foul deeds.

But those were not a girl's hands. And the right hand held a blade.

"Into the ether I exile the deathbringer," I, the woman in the vision, called out, "that the healer might return, forevermore the Lady of the Cliffs."

Heat flashed over my left wrist and blood spurted, but I held that hand over the tiny pool of still water. As the water went red, my breath went shallow and my backbone seemed to melt as I swayed until I could no longer hold myself erect. Falling backward, I was received into the waiting hands of my novices.

"Lady!" Someone patted my face.

Pain coursed from the back of my head to my eyebrows, throbbing and then settling into a deep ache. Opening my eyes, I saw only Ffion.

"Lie still, lady, you hit your head when you fell." Kneeling at my side, she dipped water from the bucket and wiped my face.

I turned my hands over to examine them. Dirty and calloused, they were not the slender hands of the goddess but the work-scarred hands of a herder. My wrists . . . no gash . . . no blood.

As I slowly returned to the waking world, I began to understand what the unstill spirit had implied when it told me that the life we had shared when I lived as Murga had not been my first.

My spirit, I now knew, had been birthed at the dawn of time, and my first mortal life had ended the day I stretched my arms out over my font to rid myself of a terrible burden: the power no woman of Bury Down would ever wield, the power to bring death.

And so, in this life, as Megge of Bury Down—as in my life as Murga, Seer of Bury Down—I held only half the power I possessed when the world was new.

Here, too, the unstill spirit had spoken the truth.

CHAPTER 42

"It's late, lady," Ffion said as she helped me to my pallet. "Are you quite all right? Your poor head . . ."

"I'm fine, Ffion, thank you."

It was very late, but I had work to do before the morrow. As Ffion prepared to go to her pallet, I asked "Have you a knife?"

She went to the table and picked up a short knife with a wooden handle. "Will this do?"

"Aye, thank you." I pulled my pallet nearer to the hearth and set to work.

For most of the night, in the glow of the peat embers, I whittled my stick. When it had a tapered end the length of my hand, I whittled the point until it was nearly as sharp as a needle. Even if I lacked the power to kill—and I was not certain I did—I would protect myself as I put an end to the rites that were about to take place in that cave.

At dawn, Ffion stirred. I woke and helped her cook fresh eggs.

"Do you know what day this is, lady?"

"Samhain." I began to eat but tasted nothing, my mind still on the hard truth I had learned the day before.

Amice soon woke and came to the table, but she only pushed her eggs around on her plate until they got cold.

Ffion leaned over her. "Aren't you hungry, lass?"

How could she be hungry on this of all days, I wondered. No doubt she would hide in this hut until the day had passed.

The moment I finished my meal, Amice got up from the table, came to me, and took my hands. I put an arm around her to comfort her, to make her feel safe. But instead of leaning against me, as I had expected her to do, she tugged at my hands and pulled me to my feet. Still gripping my hands, she led me outside and handed me my stick, then ran across the fields and down the path skirting the base of the hill. When we reached the bluff, she stopped, held up a hand, and cocked her head, eyes closed, and listened.

I too strained to listen but heard only the sea. I moved to the edge of the bluff, just above the cave, and looked over. The tide was out. Low waves shushed onto the beach far from the cliff.

And then sunlight glanced off a thatch of red hair and a bright red beard as a squat young man appeared in the distance and strode toward the cave with purpose. When he reached its mouth, he called inside, "The priestess is ready."

Amice sucked in a breath. I clutched my stick as if it were a spear.

From inside the cave a deep, ragged voice ordered, "Leave me."

I knew that voice.

This was no Samhain rite.

"Hide there, Amice." I pointed with my stick to a patch of dense brush. She remained rooted to the spot.

"Go." I nodded toward the bushes. "Hide yourself."

She parted the branches and slipped between them. When she was fully hidden, I picked my way down the stony trail, careful not to let pebbles fall into the water, then crawled and slid down to the beach and hid myself in tall grasses. The young man was no longer outside the cave.

His voice echoed from its depths. "The priestess sent me, Michael."

I slipped inside the cave's mouth and stood in shadow, my back pressed to the wall, my fist gripping my stick.

"She knows where you hide," he went on, "and says you have what she needs. I'm to bring it to her. And to find her a girl."

"Hugh," I silently called while casting him an image of the cove, the cliff, the cave. *"See this place. In the cove they call* The Sorrows. *Gough is here."*

"She demands the books and the whore's blood. Give them to me. I'll take them to her."

He still has the books! And they're here somewhere! Relieved, nearly gleeful, I strained to see in the dimly lit cave but could not see even the blacksmith. And other than his feeble voice, there was no sound from the heart of the cave. No footsteps, no movement.

"Books. Blood. Rites," he muttered. "And for what?" He coughed until something in his chest rattled, then spat.

"But the priestess—"

"Will not take another life." Though the words were but breath, his will was clear. "All the *Sisters* have escaped. And it's Samhain, you fool. Look around. There's not a virgin in sight. They've all fled. They're in hiding. Go back to the tower. Tell her it's over."

"Without bringing her what she demanded? She'll—"

"Go." The word set off a flurry of coughing.

In his haste to be gone, the young man fled the cave, passing me without seeing me.

Moving swiftly, quietly, I followed the sound of that hacking cough and found Michael Gough lying on the cave floor wrapped in his hooded black cloak. Still coughing, seeming not to have noticed me, he tried to raise himself on an elbow.

I pressed the point of my stick to his throat and forced him back.

"The books, Blacksmith."

"Women of Bury Down do not kill," the faltering voice mocked from within that hood. "So I've naught to fear from the powerful *Megge.*"

Though I could not see his mouth, I heard the sneer.

"Women of Bury Down heal," he rasped. His breath stank worse than ever. "They bring life. They search the night sky and find in the stars solace for the suffering. But they hoard their magic, hide it amid symbols and scratches." The rasping words came hard now, and I had to strain to catch the accusations hidden in that gritty tirade.

He began to raise a gloved hand. I pressed the point of my stick deeper into his neck.

"The *books*."

"You've finally the might to stay me, herding girl. But have you the courage to look upon me?"

I willed myself not to retch as he slowly removed a glove to reveal a wasted hand covered with knots, scabs, and oozing sores. Some of the fingers were missing their nails. Some were missing altogether.

"My hood." He shook his head as if to free himself from it.

Still pressing my stick to his windpipe, I pushed back his hood with the toe of my boot. His eyes were closed. The face he had for so long hidden was misshapen, the brow covered with nodules and weeping craters, the flesh sagging at the jaw. His nose was flat, indeed it was sunken at the bridge, the nostrils as grey and lumpy as old truffles.

I tried not to imagine what was hidden beneath that cloak.

He opened his eyes, and I met not the fearsome violet eyes of my childhood nightmares, but the rheumy, squinting, blinking ones of a diseased man. A husk.

"A lazar," he said. "A dead man who yet lives. A corpse that wants naught but the grave. I await only the afternoon tide." He tilted his head to offer his throat. "Or have you brought me a swifter death, Megge of Bury Down?"

"Do you think I pity you, Blacksmith? That I'd hasten your passing?" I pressed harder on his throat. "The books."

His countenance changed, and he spoke not as my enemy but as a supplicant. "They were meant—" He choked on his words. Cursing, he turned away, coughed, spat.

"To cure you." I lowered my voice and let up on my stick. "Where are they, Michael?"

Ignoring my demand, he closed his eyes and spoke as if recounting a dream. "The skin patches—scaly, numb—came upon me soon after . . . after *your aunt* . . . married that carpenter." He spat. "Then came lumps. Festering sores. And this . . . this smell of decay.

"The priestess believed the seers' books would give her the power to heal me. She told me you owed me those books and ordered me to get them for her." He coughed, then licked blood from his lip. "I defied her at first. But this," he lifted his face for me to look upon, "became torment. I began to go mad. I'd have done anything to be cured."

"Still you seek my pity?" I wanted to pierce his windpipe. "After you burned my mother alive and slit my aunt's—" Something came to me. "What did you say?"

He shook his head as if confused.

"When did you fall ill?"

"Years ago. I hardly noticed at first."

"After Claris had wed Gregory Carver?

"Aye. After she cast me aside for that *carpenter.*"

"When did the priestess demand that you steal our books?"

"When her potions and salves no longer helped."

"But you had wanted *The Book of Time* long before that. Gytha told Claris that you wanted her only for her book. It was for that reason that she forbade Claris to marry you."

He shook his head. "I knew naught of those sorcerers' books back then."

"Why did you kill my aunt? My cousin said you were seeking revenge."

"Revenge?" His ravaged face contorted into an expression of confusion. "No. 'Twasn't for revenge. I had gone to the priory for a cure." His voice was so quiet I had to lean closer to hear. "The brother told me that the lepra had come upon me from fornicating and that a cure could come only from righting that wrong. From making amends. The priestess agreed with him; she told me that only Claris's blood—and her death—and the death of her spawn could cure me."

Her spawn.

"But you spared Brighida. Why?"

He shook his head. "I could not harm my daughter."

Daughter.

That's it, I thought. *That's what he had called Brighida that night.* And that, I suddenly knew, had been Claris's burden.

That word, *daughter*, explained the anger and betrayal I had seen on Brighida's face as she poured Claris's infusion into her grave and then cast the vial into its depths.

Claris had told Brighida, when Brighida was but a girl, that she resembled Vivienne Penneck because Gregory Carver had fathered both girls. She had implied the same the night before I took my vow, when she confessed to Brighida and me her onetime love of Michael Gough.

And the very next night, Michael Gough had called Brighida *daughter*. It had taken time for Brighida to realize that she resembled Vivienne not because they were related through Gregory Carver, but because they were related through the blacksmith. And when it did, she understood that her mother had lied to her.

"You heartless fool," I said. "You blind, foolish man. You took the life of a woman who had loved you. She gave herself to you. She bore your daughter, and then she bore the burden of that secret all her life. And after you took that life, you poisoned her daughter's memory of her." I shook my head in disgust. "Claris and my mother would have helped you had you come to them instead of going to some . . . *priestess*. Instead, you took their lives—" The tip of my stick trembled at his throat. It took all my will to keep from running him through.

"Claris's blood," I demanded. "Why does the priestess want it?"

"She means to blend it," he began, his words coming now in short bursts punctuated by wheezes and gasps, "with a virgin's. And with water from this font. While speaking an incantation. One she believes she'll find in your books." He cleared his throat. "Already she has the water. She lacks only the blood and the books." He barked out a laugh. "And a virgin." He coughed into his hand, then looked at what he had brought up and wiped it on his cloak.

"The blood. Give it to me."

He reached into a pocket and withdrew a small clay vial.

"Take it." He held it out with fingers bone-white at the tips. "The tide'll soon be in. That'll be my cure."

I took the vial from him and slipped it into my pocket. "The books, Blacksmith. Now."

"Scratches and symbols. Moons and stars," he scoffed. "Take them."

He tried to sit up, but the cough that came over him became a racking spasm that drew his knees into his chest, pulling up his cloak and revealing what he had hidden beneath his scarred, scabbed legs.

I tossed aside my stick, picked up my books, and clasped them tight to my chest.

The clatter of boots upon rocks and the clink of metal upon metal came from outside the cave, and a huge man appeared at its mouth. Though he was in shadow, the sun at his back, I knew that form in an instant.

"Hugh," I shouted. "In here."

"Megge!" He strode into the cave carrying ropes and chains, Martyn and Alf close behind him. "It was you—" He stared at me for a moment and then looked down.

"Michael Gough?" he shouted at the blacksmith, who now lay curled in a ball wheezing.

"Aye."

Martyn and Alf grabbed the blacksmith under the arms and hoisted him to his feet.

"We won't need these." Hugh tossed the chains to Alf and bound Gough's hands with the rope. Then he looked at me steadily but said nothing. After a long moment, he looked away.

"The crew are waiting on the ship," he said. "There are rowboats for us on the beach. We'll talk once we're all safely aboard." He exhaled hard and waved his hand as if to blow away the blacksmith's putrid smell, then pulled up Michael's hood. Keeping the lazar at arm's length, he led him away.

"Careful, Hugh," I said. "He's suffering."

"Not enough to suit me." Hugh said. "And the earl won't thank me for bringing a lazar into Lostwithiel."

He led his prisoner out to the long, stony beach, where two rowboats sat side-by-side in the shallows. As he and Neville settled the blacksmith in one of the boats and began to row out to the ship, Martyn touched my elbow and motioned with his head toward the other.

"Come, Megge. We've got what we came for." He looked around. "Where's Amice?"

"Amice!" I had left her alone on that hill.

"*. . . you have what she needs. I'm to bring it to her. And to find her a girl.*"

I ran with all my might up the cliff, my books still clasped to my chest. My boots skidded over slimy rocks and sent stones tumbling down the path behind me.

"Go for Ffion, Martyn!" I called over my shoulder. "She's in her hut."

"I'm here, lady," Ffion shouted. With my woolsack slung over her torso, she waved from the hill.

It wasn't Michael who had wanted my books, I chided myself as I struggled up the steep path trying not to drop them while grasping weeds and cutting my hands on thorn bushes. *Why had I not seen?*

This *priestess*—some conjuror, some woman who wanted to be a goddess—had used Michael's suffering to induce him to steal them from us. And because he had so suffered from the ravages of that terrible disease, he would have done anything to get them for her, even if it meant murdering us. When Brother James had given him another way, she had twisted his words and sealed Claris's fate. No wonder the good brother had been so stricken with guilt.

I had been wrong. We all had. Michael Gough had been desperate not for our power but for a cure. And the war he had waged on us had not been at the goading of the unstill spirit but at the urging of this unholy priestess. It was she, not the blacksmith, who served as the vessel for the unstill spirit. A woman. A stranger. And none of us had guessed.

CHAPTER 43

"A mice!" I shouted when I reached the top of the cliff.

No response.

I ran as fast as I could to the tuft of bushes where she had hidden and pulled the branches aside. She was gone.

A high, wavering whine came from the direction of the church. Dread surged through me.

Lightning shimmered over my arms and legs as I ran to the tower.

The monstrous tower door, taller by half than Hugh and thicker than both my fists, groaned as I pulled it open. The tower was lit only by narrow shafts of light that filtered through damp air and fell in stripes on a stone floor slick with moss.

A slap. A growl. "Silence, Sister. You'll be *silent*."

Huddled on that floor over a small body was not the tall, slender priestess I had expected to see, but an old woman in a dusty black dress. Her wide, thick back hid the girl's head and chest, but I recognized the thrashing legs and the small bare feet that protruded from beneath the woman's bulk.

"Lie still, Sister," she snarled. "You thought you could flee? Thought I wouldn't find you?"

"Amice!" I dropped my books. The sound of them striking the stone floor echoed through the tower as I hurled myself into the woman's side. That boulder of flesh did not budge. Her hand pressed to Amice's mouth, she turned her head slowly, and her silvery eyes met mine.

"Megge of Bury Down," she sneered.

"Get off her!" I thrust my shoulder into Agnes Gough's chest and pushed her hand off Amice's face. A wad of bloody cloth dropped to the ground as a scream emerged from Amice, carried on a gush of blood.

Her tongue! She's cut it out.

I looked into Amice's gaping mouth. Her front teeth were missing and blood was streaming from where they had been, but her tongue was intact. Staunching the flow of blood with the wad of bloody cloth Agnes had dropped, I looked through the doorway on the other side of the tower and into the church, hoping to see someone there. Anyone. But it was empty.

Agnes spat at me as she struggled to her feet. Then she stopped. "The books."

She scooped them into her arms and made haste from me, her footsteps echoing as she hobbled into the church and down the center aisle toward the door.

"Whore!" she screamed.

Though she was limping, she had made it halfway to the door. I couldn't let her leave. Surely she would hide herself away somewhere on these cliffs, and we would never find her or the books. I looked back down at Amice's pallid face. She had stopped wailing but was still sobbing.

I leaned over her. "Hush now, hush. Be still, Amice. All is well."

I patted her hand to calm her and noticed beneath it a crimson puddle that grew as I watched. I turned it over. Blood pumped from her wrist. I took the cloth Agnes had used to gag her and pressed it hard to her wrist as I began to call on the Mentors for help. "*Scientia nupta sapientia potestas est. Scientia nupta sapientia potestas est.*"

Agnes stopped and turned. Her eyes glittered in a shaft of sunlight.

"That's it," she rasped. "Those words." She held the books out in front of her and spoke over them, but her voice trailed off into silence after "See entya . . ."

She hadn't gleaned the words.

Amice's face was ghostly white, so much blood had she lost. *A virgin's blood.* No doubt Agnes had a vial of it. I looked up. She was nearly at the door. She would be gone before I could move.

I had just picked up Amice's wrist to examine it when the door Agnes was stumbling toward was wrenched open. A man stood in shadow, the sun at his back. I knew that form as well as I knew Hugh's.

"Martyn," I shouted, "She's got the books!"

Another shadow appeared in the doorway, slipped past Martyn, and trotted down the aisle.

Without slowing, Alf shot out an arm and grabbed the tottering Agnes Gough around her thick middle, lifted her off her feet, and carried her toward me as if she were but a ewe trying to evade the shearer.

He spoke as if nothing were amiss as he neared with the struggling, spitting Agnes Gough. "You ran so swiftly up the bluff, we lost sight of you. Then we heard the screams coming from the tower."

"He'll die," Agnes shrieked when Alf set her on her feet, still holding her tightly about the waist. Martyn took the books from her and laid them on a pew.

"That whore aunt of yours, that fornicator. She cursed my son. *Cursed him.* He'll die. Take me to him. He has what I need to prepare the cure." She flailed, then swung an arm as if to strike Alf.

"Quiet, Agnes." Martyn took off his belt, brought Agnes's hands together, and bound her wrists.

I reached inside my pocket for the vial Michael had given me and held it out. "It's too late. Michael's on his way to the earl's gaol." I pointed with my chin to the pew. "Martyn, will you bring me my books, please?"

He picked them up with care and laid them on the floor beside me.

"*Witches* of Bury Down," Agnes spat. "Whores. Sorceresses. Fornicators. You cursed my son."

Amice began to cry.

"Take her away, please, Martyn." I pulled Amice closer.

As Martyn led Agnes away, Alf knelt beside us and whispered to Amice, "In the springtime, we'll have a dozen lambs for you to guard with me. Little lambs. They'll be mine and yours and Megge's. What do you think you'll name them?"

I leaned forward and looked at her mouth. There was little bleeding, and it would soon stop. I held tight to the dressing on her wrist.

"Amice," I began, pointing to Agnes. "Do you know who she is?"

Eyes gone wide, she cringed. Then nodded.

"You've seen her before?"

She nodded.

"Did she keep you in this place? This tower?"

Another nod, her eyes never leaving mine.

I brushed my finger over the goddess mark on her cheek. "And she gave you this mark."

She shook her head.

"No?" I pulled away and studied her face. "She didn't give you this mark?"

Her lips went tight.

"Then who did?" Remembering my promise never to force her to talk, I softened my tone. "You needn't speak, Amice, but can you show me what she looked like? I promise no one will ever hurt you again."

She looked from me to Alf. When he nodded, she raised her free hand to the top of her head. Fingers fluttering, she lowered it to her shoulders.

"Someone with long, curling hair?"

Lips tightly puckered, she nodded.

"That's not Agnes," Alf said.

And it certainly wasn't Michael.

Though Agnes had craved the goddess's power and had held Amice and the other girls—*how many girls?*—captive in this tower, someone else had played the priestess in those rites.

But why would she have allowed another woman to play her part? And then I recalled her hobbling gait and that steep bluff. Never could Agnes have descended that path to the cave. And the woman who had led that rite had not drunk the blood. She had carried it away.

To the tower, I thought.

I called upon my vision of the priestess in the cave. That tall, slender form. That long, pale-gold curl.

And then I saw Amice run screaming from Brighida the night we had found her.

"Amice, was it someone who looked like Brighida?"

She sucked in her breath and nodded.

I scoured my memory for someone whose face and hair resembled Brighida's. And then such a face finally emerged.

"Alf," I said. "Have you ever seen Tinker's hair? I've only ever seen him wearing a hat."

"Tinker's hair?" He looked surprised. "Oh, aye, I've seen it. Once."

"What does it look like?"

He leaned back, his mouth agape in that crooked smile. "It's beautiful." He laughed. "It is! Or, rather, it was when I saw it. Long. Almost as pretty as Brighida's. But he plaits it." Alf mimed winding a braid around his head. "Hides it under that hat."

"What color, Alf? What color is it?"

"Nearly the same as hers. But even lighter."

"Amice, did the man who cut your tongue and hurt Britlen's eyes do this?" I touched her cheek.

A nod.

"And did he do this," I touched her wrist, "to you and the other girls?"

Another solemn nod.

I thought of Agnes Gough and Tinker Penneck, and then of Brighida's long, sharp knife.

A quick death . . .

Agnes had held Amice and the other girls captive in that cold stone tower while Tinker had led them to the cave and played the priestess. He had bled those girls and then taken that pitcher of virgin's blood mixed with sacred water to Agnes.

Had she used it in an effort to resurrect the goddess? I wondered. Or to concoct a remedy that never would have cured her son?

It mattered not what she had done with it, I thought as I looked down at the little girl she had tortured, a child with the canniness to escape and somehow find me, and the courage to bring me back to the very cave where those rites had played out.

"Amice," I asked, nearly overwhelmed with awe, "how did you ever hear of Bury Down?"

Shouts rose from outside the church. "Seers and healers of Bury Down!" Agnes shrieked, cursing us just as she always had. "*Thieves* and *whores* of Bury Down," she spat. "Be damned!"

Amice lifted her good hand and pointed toward the window.

"You heard Agnes speak of us. Of Bury Down."

She nodded, and I felt something hum inside me. "But how did you *find* us?"

She lifted her hand and rubbed circles between her eyebrows.

I thought of the other times she had done that. Once, when I had asked her how she had found me; and again, the night she had awakened both Ffion and me from our dreams of this place. A rush of understanding came over me. *A dream.* Amice had been guided on the long journey to Bury Down through dreams.

Morwen had told Ffion in a dream to bring me to this place. I now knew in my marrow that she had also sent the dreams that had guided Amice to me.

I needed air.

I moved Alf's hand to the cloth on Amice's wrist and pressed it hard to her skin. I went to the window and took a deep breath of cool air just as Agnes cast one last, frantic glance at the church as she took her first step down the path to the beach. Her face was twisted not in rage but in what I recognized as the desperation of a mother with a sick child, the very torment that had drawn the unstill spirit to her. Raw, strident emotions it had harnessed for its own ends. I shuddered as I imagined Agnes Gough holding my books and speaking the summoning incantation over them. Who knew what that might have wrought?

"Michael won't be the only one to hang," Alf snarled. "That mother of his. And Tinker."

I nodded. Those monsters had tortured Amice. Had forced her to flee into the unknown, searching for safety, guided only by a dream.

How many other girls had they tortured? How many had they sent to their deaths in that cave? How many other lives had Tinker ruined—or ended?

He had not wanted the books. He had helped Michael torture my family simply for the pleasure of inflicting pain and fear. Nor had he sought to return the goddess to the living world. He had played the priestess just for the pleasure of silencing and then taking the lives of all those girls. Their terror and pain had been his reward. One for which he would pay.

But would Agnes Gough, conjurer and harridan though she was, have asked Tinker to perform those rites had her son not been stricken with lepra and had the voice of the unstill spirit not been always at her ear?

Soon enough, I knew, whether through old age or the hangman's noose, death would come for Agnes. And when it did, it would unleash the unstill spirit. Untethered, the spirit would find another kindred: someone in the living world who craved the power of the goddess. And I would not know who that was until the killing resumed.

I walked back to Amice and lifted the edge of her bandage. Her wrist was no longer bleeding. I tied the cloth tightly around it and nodded to Alf. Gently picking her up, he started for the door.

"I've one more thing to do," I said.

"I'll take her down to the boat, Meg. We'll wait there for you. But make haste, the tide'll soon be in."

I picked up my books. It was time to finish this.

CHAPTER 44

I descended the path to the cave. Waves were now lapping near its mouth, so I had little time.

I stepped inside and felt my way along the wall to its farthest reaches and found the fissure my twin brother had passed through just before the sea claimed him.

Holding the fingers of one hand tight to the edge, I reached across the divide and felt for the other side. The opening was twice the width of my shoulders and higher than my fingertips could reach.

I stepped through. As I entered the chamber where my twin had drowned, a mist rolled in, a sea-scented fog that billowed into a dense, black cloud. And then, from the very depths of the chamber, a long, slow push of breath dispersed it.

"'Twas a rash vow you made." My brother took a step toward me. His handsome face went bitter. "'And then, Blacksmith,'" he sneered, "'I will see to you.'" He shook his head. "You, a herder in this life." He spat. "A midwife's mewling daughter too fainthearted to wrest a babe from a womb. The niece of a whore. The cousin of a blacksmith's spawn. You would 'see to' me? The spirit that has honed the deathbringer's arts since the dawn of time? The very part of yourself you deny? The portion of your own spirit you tremble before?"

"A voice." I put aside the many times I had indeed trembled before it. "You're naught but a voice at my ear."

"And you are a murderer," came the coarse whisper I had heard as a girl whenever I had reached for my mother's book. "*My* murderer." The voice rose in volume and pitch. "Knowing that only one of us could carry the goddess's spirit and walk in the living world, you drank from the font and left me to die in that cave. And this *voice* you hear, Megge of Bury Down? It will soon call my next vessel to me. The vessel through which *I* shall speak the summoning incantation and unite those books in the presence of *my* font. I shall drink its sacred water and walk once more in the living world, bringing *my* skills to the cliffs, the caves, and the grove you call Bury Down. Yes, herding girl, *I* shall unite our spirits. And then I shall crush yours beneath my heel."

And there they were. The consequences of my failing to unite the books.

"Speeches from a totem." I waved an arm in dismissal. "In the living world, Spirit, you and your threats are naught but smoke and fog. Be gone."

My brother's image vanished and the fog dispersed. I slipped through the crevice and back into the larger chamber.

But my twin was more than smoke and fog, I knew. His spirit held half the power of the goddess Atropos. Mine the other half.

And hard times were coming.

That silken voice spoke into my dreamer's ear. "Will you, Megge of Bury Down, now fulfill your charge? Will you unite the seers' books, thereby binding deathbringer to healer, and reclaim our power—the power of the goddess? Will you serve forevermore as Lady of Bury Down?"

In my mind's eye, I saw once more the fierce battle in which Amareth's husband had been slain and the war fires that even now were charring forests and pastures and grain fields to the north. I heard Murga's warning: *a famine such as the world has never known.*

I had vowed to protect our people when those times came.

"Protecting life is a sacred trust," Mother had taught while trying to awaken in me the spirit of the healer.

But protecting life required more than a healer. I had learned this the night the wolves attacked my flock, the night the *imposter abbot* arrested Mother and Claris, and that very afternoon, as Agnes Gough bled a virgin child she called *Sister.*

Mother had brought relief to the lazars. Though a healer, had she done so with remedies that eased pain? Or by quietly ending their lives? I recalled the row of lazars sitting in Brother James's infirmary with their bandages and crutches, their stink and their ooze, and I heard his wistful words. *How I—how* they—*miss her.*

I recalled Michael Gough's desperation for the pain to end. *The tide'll soon be in. That'll be my cure.*

I gave you dominion over death, the goddess's father—my father— had declared. And not to the deathbringer, but to the woman of Bury Down who bore the healing half of his daughter's spirit.

I ran my fingers over the great bowl that had bloomed out of a pillar of stone since the day I cast the deathbringer's charge into the sea and my own life into the fire. As Atropos I had been a tormented young goddess who hadn't understood that the healer within her could have bent the deathbringer's charge to her will.

I was no longer that young goddess.

But by binding the goddess's power to my own power to see and to summon the Mentors and companions who would serve, I would become the Lady of Bury Down, the protector the hard times would call for.

It was time to end an ancient tyranny.

Holding my books in one arm, I touched my finger to the water in the font and spoke the summoning incantation. "*Scientia nupta sapientia potestas est.* Knowledge wedded to wisdom is power.

"Come to me now, Brother," I called, "for as I wed the knowledge of *The Book of Seasons* to the wisdom of *The Book of Time,* and the power of Bury Down to the power of the goddess Atropos, I bind your spirit and reclaim dominion over death."

Can you slaughter that ram when its leg festers?

Have you brought me death, Megge of Bury Down?

Slow, unutterably painful, death . . . But your mother eased their way.

"And to the deathbringer's charge I bind the skill and compassion of the healer and the might—and the mercy—of the protector."

I dipped my hand into the cold, clear water, raised it to my lips, and drank.

CHAPTER 45

settling came over me. *Peace*, I thought. For the first time in my life, I felt at peace.

I touched my font not in farewell, but in promise. *There will once more be a healer here on these cliffs.*

"Meg!"

Careful not to drop my books in the water that now lapped at the cave floor, I walked out into the sunlight and then waded through shin-deep water toward Alf and Martyn, who beckoned me to a rowboat tethered to a rock by a long rope attached to the bow. Ffion sat on one of the seats with Amice on her lap and that woolsack between her feet.

Ffion looked in the direction of my gaze. "Your belongings, lady. And a few of mine. I've left the rest behind for the friends who have provided for us these past days. The manor lord will see to the hut. Amice and I will need new clothes, but if you'll allow the use of your spinning wheel and loom, Kaatje, Britlen, and I will make all the clothes any of us could ever need."

"Britlen?"

"A fine nettle spinner," she said as she moved over to make room for me. "Such clever, nimble hands. A fine apprentice she'd be for Brighida, I'm thinking. But let me warn you—once Brighida's taught her how to spin fleece, it'll be all she can do to keep the girl away from her wheel. And all we can do to weave all the beautiful thread she'll make."

Alf took my books so Martyn could help me into the boat. "What's that on your face?" he asked as I leaned forward to hand them over.

I brushed my hand over my face then looked at my finger. No blood, no dirt. "Where? What does it look like?"

"This spot?" Martyn leaned close and touched my left cheek. "It looks like . . . like a stain from a drop of mulberry juice."

"A stain?" I stepped into the boat and lowered myself onto the seat beside Ffion and Amice.

"Aye." Alf bent down and squinted at it. "A stain shaped like a tiny eye."

"Move away, please." Ffion brushed Alf away and turned my face to her. "Martyn told me you climbed up that bluff as swiftly as ever Alf could. No doubt you scratched yourself on a stinging nettle. Let me have a look."

When Alf and Martyn leaned nearer, intent on that mark, Ffion gave them a stern look I had only ever seen on Mother's face. "Go on now, you two. Haven't you something to do to this boat? Or are we to sit here on the beach all night?"

Alf laid my books in my lap and went around to the back of the boat with Martyn.

Ffion took my face in her hands and turned it from side to side.

"I was wrong," she said. "'Tisn't a nettle scratch." Her tone went low and reverent. "It's the true mark of the goddess Atropos, the Lady of the Cliffs."

I stroked my cheek just under my left eye.

"Anwen spoke the truth," Ffion said.

"Anwen?"

"Aye, when she taught that the Lady of the Cliffs—that *you*, lady—would return when you deemed the time had come."

I could never explain all I now knew: that though I shared the lady's spirit, I was, in this life, not the Lady of the Cliffs but Megge, now the Lady of Bury Down, as she had known me from the very first.

"Alf told me what happened in the tower, lady," Ffion said quietly. "*Agnes Gough*. Imagine." She shook her head slowly. "I never dreamed even she could do such a thing." She brought her hands to her face and covered her eyes. "Taking girls. Torturing and murdering them. In your name. For that son of hers."

"They called her a *priestess*, Ffion." I looked at her steadily. "Had she once been willing to sacrifice even Kaatje, her own daughter?"

"Oh, no, lady." Ffion shook her head fast and looked at me. "She wasn't the priestess in those days. There was another. It was a true Sisterhood back then, with novices and rites and festivals. It must be that once the Sisterhood died out after all those girls followed Kaatje's example, Agnes secretly stepped into the role of priestess. But she never had true novices, not to my knowledge or anyone else's in the settlement. We all simply believed the old church haunted. I'd wager now that she and Tinker have been *taking* girls and hiding them in that tower for some time."

We both looked down at Amice. She nodded solemnly.

I put my arm around her and spoke quietly. "One day, Amice, you may want to tell us. But though I hope you will, I shall never ask. And I shall never allow the Sisterhood to rise again. Never will there be another priestess." I looked now at Ffion. "Though there will be a healer here. You've my word."

"Meg, look," Alf shouted and pointed beyond the cove to the great ship standing at anchor. Hugh waved from the ship's bow.

"Tell me, Alf," I asked as I waved back. "Why did you journey by ship rather than horseback?"

"We were making ready to travel on horseback, but when Tinker told Neville we'd find Gough in one of the caves in *The Sorrows*, and that we'd have to approach by sea if we were to take him unawares, Earl Edmund gave us his own ship and crew."

"But this cove is dotted with caves. How did you know which to search in?"

"Do you recall my dream?" he asked. "The one in which I am standing aboard a ship awaiting the signal to make ready for battle?"

"Yes . . ."

"It happened just that way. As we neared the cove, Hugh stood at the bow searching the coast, muttering, "Where is he? Where is he?" All at once he seemed to be listening, straining to hear something over the rush of the waves. And then he nodded. He spoke to the captain while pointing to this very cave. And then he told Martyn, Neville, and me to make ready. He raised his arm, and the moment they dropped anchor, he ordered us to lower the rowboats."

Alf looked to the ship, where Hugh stood gazing toward the cliffs, then turned back to me. "I know what happened, Meg. You sent him a dream. You showed him the cave."

Neville joined Hugh at the bow, and both men waved to us. Amice stood on the seat and waved back, then brought her uninjured hand to her mouth and tried to whistle but blew out only air. Laughing, Alf put his fingers to his mouth and blew a high, wavering salute.

"Onward, then," he shouted, smiling at Amice, "not stopping until we reach Lostwithiel!"

There'll be a trial, Hugh had said. I remembered the note of resignation in his voice as he added, *But it'll take time.*

Time, I thought.

Months, he had said.

The blacksmith wouldn't live long enough to see the gallows, I knew. This man, who had never served another in his life, and who had murdered those who had—not at the urging of the unstill spirit, but to cure a disease which his victims themselves would have helped him endure—would never live to face punishment. Why, I thought, he would have died at his own hand this very day, when the tide had turned, had I not come upon him.

But now he's headed for the gaol. I tried to summon vindication by imagining the dank cell that awaited him. The chains that would bind him to a stone wall as he struggled to breathe through his last horrific weeks of life.

But vindication would not come. Letting him rot in a gaol cell would be . . .

A waste, I decided. It would be a waste to allow the blacksmith, who had deprived an entire village of their healers, to languish in the earl's gaol when he could be making recompense.

"We'll stop once, Alf," I said.

"Oh?" Martyn, poised to at the bow to loose the boat, straightened and looked at me. "Where?"

"The village. You can take Agnes on to Lostwithiel, where she can share a cell with Tinker for all I care. His crimes have earned him a swift trip to the gallows. Agnes may join him there, but there are . . . circumstances. Brighida and I shall counsel the earl before he decides her fate."

"And Michael?" Ffion asked.

"I'll see to the blacksmith," I said. "We'll take him to a house I've heard of just outside the village."

Alf sucked in his breath. "The lazar house."

Yes, I thought. The lazar house, where Michael Gough, who would never hang for his crimes, would make restitution. He would provide the village with a healer.

By working at Brother James's side to tend this man, and by seeking Mother's guidance from the ether, I would learn all I needed to know about this dread disease. From the blacksmith I would learn how it came on, how it worsened, and which remedies brought relief. From Brother James, how to tend a lazar's wounds. And from Mother, the secret draughts and incantations that would relieve pain—and the ones that would ease the lazars' way when the pain could no longer be stemmed and death was at hand.

Never could the blacksmith undo the sin of fornication. Nor would I—nor anyone—have desired such an end, for that *sin* had brought Brighida to this life. And never would he be cured. But for serving those he had wronged by restoring to the village a healer, the blacksmith would be spared the slow, unutterably painful death he otherwise faced.

He will not have gone to the gallows for his crimes, I thought, *but he will have made amends.*

Martyn studied my face for a long moment and then nodded.

"Alf," he shouted. "Let's be off!"

Alf waded around to the bow and helped Martyn shove the boat into hip-deep water. And then, as one, they climbed aboard, picked up the oars, and rowed us out to the earl's great ship and the journey that awaited us beyond The Sorrows Cove.

CHARACTERS
Listed by first name

Adaem: (*Ah-dehm´*): Captain of *The Navigator*. From Aldestowe.
    Husband of Gytha of Bury Down
    Father of Natalje
    Grandfather of Claris and "Mother"
    Great-grandfather of Megge and Brighida
Agnes Gough: (Agnes *Goff*): Conjurer
    Mother of Michael and Jenifer
    Grandmother of Harold, Vivienne, and Gwyneth Penneck
Aleydis: (*Ah-lee´-dis*): huntress. From Aldestowe.
    Daughter of Beatrix Couper. Sister of Arjen
    Aunt of Claris and "Mother"
    Great-aunt of Brighida and Megge
Alf: Shepherd and shearer
Amice: Orphan from the North Coast
Anwen: Huntress from Tintagel
    Scribe and protector of the writings of Murga
Arjen: Stonemason, builder, artist. From Aldestowe
    Former holder of *The Book of Seasons*
    Son of Beatrix Couper. Brother of Aleydis
    Husband of Natalje
    Father of Claris and "Mother"
    Grandfather of Megge and Brighida
Beatrix Couper: Midwife and conjurer
    Mother of Arjen and Aleydis
    Grandmother of Megge and Brighida
    Sister of Egbert Couper ("Roon")

Brighida: (*Bri-gee´-dah*): Apprentice seer
> Heir to *The Book of Time*
> Daughter of Claris, cousin of Megge
Britlen: Daughter of Kaatje and Tinker
Brother James: Benedictine monk
> Physician/surgeon trained by Megge's mother
Bryluen: (*Bree-loo´-en*)
> Apprentice to Murga
Gregory Carver: Master carpenter
> Husband of Claris
Claris: Seer of Bury Down, Holder of *The Book of Time*
> Mother of Brighida
> Twin sister of "Mother"
> Aunt of Megge
> Widow of Gregory Carver
Colluen: (*Cah-loo´-en*): Blacksmith
> Rejected apprentice to Murga, the Seer of Bury Down
Derwa: mother of Gytha
> A Mentor.
> Former holder of *The Book of Time*
> (Lowenna, in a former life)
Dora Tucker: Shopkeeper
> Wife of Gus
Edmund: Second Earl of Cornwall (reign: 1272-1300)
> Husband of Margaret de Clare, Countess of Cornwall
Egbert Couper ("Rudh"):
> Brother of Beatrix
> Uncle of Arjen and Aleydis
Elizabeth: Lady-in-waiting to Lady Margaret
Ffion: Former "Nursemaid" to Kaatje
> Sister of Morwen
Francis Penneck: Carter
> Husband of Jenifer Gough

Father of Tinker, Harold, and Gwyneth

George Gynneys: Herder, shearer
Father of Alf

Gregory Carver: Master carpenter
Deceased husband of Claris

Gus Tucker: Weaver, tucker, wool merchant
Husband of Dora
Gwyneth Penneck:
Daughter of Francis and Jenifer Penneck
Sister of Harold and Vivienne
Half-sister of Tinker

Gytha: former Seer of Bury Down
former holder of *The Book of Time*
Wife of Adaem
Mother of Natalje
Grandmother of Claris and "Mother"
Great-grandmother of Megge and Brighida

Harold Penneck: Assistant carter
Son of Francis and Jenifer Gough Penneck
Brother of Vivienne and Gwyneth
Half-brother of Tinker

Hugh Caerlin: Herder
Son of Lowenna
Brother of Martyn

Irene: Wife of Odo
Holder of *The Book of Time* in eleventh century
A Mentor
(Lowenna, in a former life)

Jago: Field hand
Patient of Brother James

Jenifer Gough Penneck:
Daughter of Agnes Gough, sister of Michael Gough
Second wife of Francis Penneck

Mother of Harold, Vivienne, and Gwyneth Penneck
Step-mother of Tinker Penneck
Kaatje: Wife of Tinker Penneck
Mother of Britlen
Daughter of Agnes Gough
Sister of Michael Gough
Mister Kendall: Surgeon at Restormel Castle
Lady of the Cliffs: Atropos
Goddess
Deathbringer-turned-healer
Lowenna Caerlin: Homemaker
Mother of Hugh and Martyn
Margaret, Countess of Cornwall: Wife of Edmund, Second
Earl of Cornwall
Martyn Caerlin: Weaver,
Son of Lowenna
Brother of Hugh
Megge: (*Meggie*): herder, shearer, apprentice weaver
Heir to *The Book of Seasons*
Daughter of "Mother"
Niece of Claris, Cousin of Brighida
Michael Gough: (Michael *Goff):* Blacksmith
Son of Agnes and Robert Gough
Brother of Jenifer Gough Penneck and Kaatje
Morwen: Bard and shearer
Companion of Megge
Guardian of the Books
"Mother": Healer of Bury Down, Holder of *The Book of Seasons*
Mother of Megge
Sister of Claris, aunt of Brighida
No first name. Called *Mistress, Mother, Sister, Aunt, Niece*
Widow of stone mason
Murga: First Seer of Bury Down

Natalje: (*Nă-tal´-ee*)

> Former holder of *The Book of Time*
>
> Wife of Arjen
>
> Mother of Claris and her unnamed twin sister ("Mother")
>
> Grandmother of Megge and Brighida

Nellie Trelawney: Shopkeeper, wife of the village potter

Neville Angwin: Stonemason's apprentice

Odo: Manor lord of Bury Down at the time of the Norman conquest

> Husband of Irene

Polly Pounfrect: Governess at Restormel Castle

Richard, First Earl of Cornwall (reign: 1257-1272)

> Son of John, King of England
>
> Father of Edmund, Second Earl of Cornwall

Robert Angwin: Stone mason

Robert Gough (*Goff*): Blacksmith

> Deceased husband of Agnes Gough
>
> Father of Michael Gough

Tinker Penneck:

> Son of Francis Penneck and Francis's first wife (deceased)
>
> Half-brother of Harold and Gwyneth Penneck
>
> Husband of Kaatje
>
> Father of Britlen

Vivienne Penneck:

> Daughter of Jenifer Penneck and Gregory Carver

Vitale Magor: artist (deceased). Former holder of *The Book of Seasons*

> Father of Arjen
>
> Husband of Beatrix Couper

ACKNOWLEDGMENTS

To beta readers Peg Di Pastina, Nancy Jeffries, and Connie Kondravy, my deepest thanks for taking the time to read a draft of this book and offer comments and impressions that made a difference.

Special thanks to Nancy Jeffries and Jacqui Doran, my accomplices on the 2018 site visit to Cornwall, for searching sea caves with me from Tintagel to Padstow. Along with historian Mary Jones, of Lostwithiel, they helped me find in Daymer Bay the very cave in which I had "seen" the young twins discover the lady's font and had "watched" the goddess rites play out as the earliest images of this story came to me. Church historian Carole Vivian, of Looe, once again supplied vital information about the church in medieval Cornwall.

I am deeply indebted to church warden Bill Nimmo for allowing me to tour the lovely St. Enodoc's church, the model for the ancient church in Ffion's settlement.

Sincere thanks to my editor, Vinnie Kinsella, for his insight and exceptional skills.

To Tamian Wood, cover artist and book designer, goes endless appreciation for her work, which so beautifully captures the essence of *The Bury Down Chronicles*.

My thanks to all of you,
Rebecca

About the Author

Rebecca Kightlinger holds an MFA in creative writing from the University of Southern Maine's Stonecoast MFA program. The full-time writer of the *Bury Down Chronicles* series, she studies medieval medicine, Anglo Saxon wortcraft, the arts and manuscripts of the mystical healers, and the history of Cornwall. She travels to Cornwall, England to carry out on-site research for each new book.

About the Editor

Vinnie Kinsella is an editor and book publishing specialist from the Pacific Northwest. His work with books began when he and his second-grade classmates wrote and illustrated a story about the adventures of an ice-cream-loving giraffe. Years later, he earned his master's degree in writing and publishing from Portland State University. He has since helped hundreds of authors and publishers release quality books into the world. For more information about Vinnie's work, visit vinniekinsella.com.

About the Poet

Award-winning feminist poet **Annie Finch** is known for mesmerizing performances and deep, holistic expertise in poetic craft. Annie's most recent books include *The Poetry Witch Little Book of Spells* and *A Poet's Craft: A Comprehensive Guide to Making and Sharing Your Poetry*. Based in Washington DC, she travels to perform her work and offers online classes for poets & seekers. She can be found on line at www.anniefinch.com.

About the Designer

Tamian Wood, born near Oxford England, is currently living and working in her cozy lake front office in North Florida. Using art, photography, typography and digital collage techniques, she creates book covers that sell, in a variety of genres. She works with several publishers and a growing number of indie authors. Her most famous client to date is Pope Francis, whose Encyclical Letter, won first place for cover design. She holds degrees in Computer Science and Graphic Design Technology, and is a proud member of Phi Theta Kappa National Honour Society. She can be reached at Tamian@BeyondDesignBooks.com, www.BeyondDesignBooks.com

About the Audiobook Narrator

Jan Cramer is a London born actress trained at The Central School of Speech and Drama and has worked in Theatre, TV, Film, and Radio. Now a very busy voice over artist and award winning Audiobook Narrator, Jan is proud to have narrated over 100 audiobooks. She has enjoyed every single one of them. Find her online at:

www.voiceannouncements.com

Excerpt from
THE SISTERS OF THE SORROWS COVE
Book three in the Goddess Trilogy

CORNWALL, ENGLAND
NOVEMBER, 1285

"Amice!" Alf called into the rising wind. He bent his back into another swell as he rowed us toward the waiting ship. "How do you like the sea?"

Amice looked to Ffion and then to me, still wrestling with the demons that had taken her voice.

Barely breathing, I awaited her response as we labored against the tide, leaving in our wake the rugged cliffs that haunted this silent child, the sacred cave that whispered of death and rebirth, and the standing stones atop Cairn Hill, where our past lay in ashes—lost to time, but no longer forgotten.

PART ONE

CHAPTER 1

SPRING, 1284

My mother struggled onto her side on her narrow pallet, bits of dust and straw escaping in puffs from a small hole in the seam. She drew a whistling breath through a nose so flat its wings lay on her cheeks like brittle bark on an aging tree.

Her thin voice rasped, "There should be dancing, my little Anna. The women should bring their best breads and pies, the alewives their finest caudles and mead." She drew a husky breath. "Everywhere else, May Day is a time of sunshine and music. Of rejoicing in the promise of new life. But here . . . it is something else. Something dark. Something wicked."

She inclined her head toward the poppyseed infusion that Eleanor, the healer, had taught me to make. Never would her numb, shortened fingers have been able to hold the cup, so I put it to her lips. She took a sip, sighed in relief, and lay back. Her voice went low.

"It's time you knew."

A shiver crawled up my spine.

"The fete's been outlawed, but it always returns. Always a horror. For always, a girl goes missing."

She coughed, and I handed her a square I had cut from soft, clean cloth. She spat yellow matter into it, took a breath, and continued, her voice strengthening.

"Now, mothers take their girls away—to Aldestowe or Bodmin—late in April, where you should have gone, days ago, to be safe." Anger hardened her voice. She seemed to draw strength from it. She pushed herself up on one elbow and looked toward the door of our tiny cottage. "I begged your father to take you away. But he said you are all we have and that he needs you here to tend me. That my fears are for naught. That he would protect you should those demons come for you."

Her voice sharp with spite, she spat, "Those *Sisters*. That coven of demons. Long ago, they claimed May Day as their own. Like heathens, they called it Beltane. And every May Day morn, amid flowers and feasts, they would crown a girl Queen of the May. Six months later, on Samhain morn—" her eyes went wide and filled with tears.

I could not take my eyes off hers. "What, Mother? What happens to the girl on Samhain morn?"

"No one knows for certain. I can only tell you this: the Sisters call out to the Lady of the Cliffs to summon the healer back from the dead—and after the rite, the girl who had just been crowned Queen of the May is never seen again. The men issued decrees meant to end those fetes, and even now, they believe the Sisterhood's done. But though they have banned those blasphemous rites, I and every mother I know believe that the Sisters still hold them—in shadow.

"I, especially, fear their rites, for I know—here—" she raised a gnarled hand to her brow and lowered it slowly to her breast, as if drawing knowledge from her consciousness, from her very spirit, into her heart, "that you shall one day face them. So, Anna, there is something *you* must know."